Caterpillar Days
Christian Barnes

Fox Cub Press

Copyright © 2024 by Christian Barnes

The right of Christian Barnes to be identified as the author of this work has been asserted in accordance with the Copyright Design and Patents Act 1988

No part of this publication may be reproduced, distributed, or transmitted in any form or by any means, including photocopying, recording, or other electronic or mechanical methods, without the prior written permission of the publisher.

For permission requests, please contact sales@foxcubpress.com

The story, all names, characters, and incidents portrayed in this production are fictitious.

No identification with actual persons (living or deceased), places, buildings, and products is intended or should be inferred.

Cover created by www.getcovers.com

"The two most important days in your life are the day you are born
and the day you find out why."
Mark Twain

I dedicate this book to my wife, without whom
none of this would have been possible.
Christian Barnes

Chapter 1

Present-day - Hackney, East London

No one was on the street, and with the weather, who could blame them? The street lamps hadn't turned on, but the combined illumination of the setting sun and the rising moon did nothing to dispel the gloom of Carrie's mood.

She jogged between the shop awnings, playing hide and seek with the sheets of rain. She had coaxed her blond bob under the waterlogged baseball cap. The leather jacket was definitely a mistake. What the hell was she doing here? Fat gobbets of water splattered and danced on the pavement, drenching her feet, and her jeans clung to her legs.

As a chill wind blew into her face, a shiver went through her whole body, and she took shelter in a shop doorway. Almost nine, a few minutes until her meeting. She fished her mobile from her pocket, almost dropping it as her hands were so cold. She glanced up and down the street. Still no one. Carrie dialled a number from memory. Stamping her feet to dispel the cold only squished the warm water from her socks. She waited for her call to go through.

"Allo?"

"Is that you, Jessie?" asked Carrie.

"Course, who else? Is it done?"

"If it was, you shouldn't be answering your phone without waiting for the ring code."

"Oh yeah, sorry I forgot," said Jessie, "I'll 'member next time."

"We spoke about this? It's dangerous. If they twig anything, Rats will be on your case and mine. Rats don't fuck around. I want us all to walk away from this and you to have a life away from the Smoke."

"Yeah, I want that too, Carrie. But if Darren hears you calling him Rats, it'll be your arse in a sling."

"OK, Jessie, remember I'll ring three times and cut off; I'll do the same again, and when I ring the third time, you pick up. Remember. Even if it's my number, unless I do the code ring, don't answer."

"Yeah, I understand. Take it easy. You're a good person, Carrie; from the first time we met, I knowed it."

Carrie ended the call, and with a sense of foreboding, continued towards her meeting with Darren, the Rat.

She slowed as she approached the alley, which ran down the side of the fish and chip shop. Passing the entrance, she casually glanced down to the next street. Save for piles of rubbish and the ubiquitous cardboard boxes; the alley was clear to the streetlight shining at the far end. The side door of the chip shop was open, and the faint light from the kitchen shaved the darkness a little.

She rocked back and forth on her feet, looking into a women's boutique. In reality, she looked for anyone paying her attention in the reflection of the glass. At least the rain had eased. Satisfied, she retraced her steps and turned into the alley.

A figure approached from the opposite end. As she stepped over puddles and dogshit, she passed the open side door of the chip shop and caught the orgasmic waft of hot chips and vinegar. Right now she would love to be tucking into a chip butty and a mug of tea. Heaven.

The darkness grew deeper, and there was no escape from the drizzling rain. Carrie couldn't rid herself of the feeling the meeting wouldn't go to plan. Mainly because Darren planned it, and for all his possible hidden strengths, Darren wasn't a planner. He was more of a 'by the seat of his pants kinda guy'. Whatever that meant?

As the figure came closer, she called out, "Is that you, Darren?"

"Yeah, let's get outta the rain." Darren strode a little further and ducked into a doorway.

Carrie inched towards the door. It opened into a lit small rubbish storage area for another shop. It smelt like rotten vegetables and piss. Standing, leaning against one of the large metal bins, was Darren. Early thirties, greasy, mousey hair pulled back in a ponytail to reveal a rat-like face, an impression not helped by one protruding upper front tooth where two had been. He was skeletal thin. His designer Barbour jacket and jeans hung on him like they hung from a hook, not a human frame. But he wore his trademark white £500 trainers, which now looked like soggy market knockoffs.

"Looking good, Carrie." His eyes gave her the once over; it didn't take a psychology degree to know what he was thinking. "Did you bring it?" he asked.

Carrie looked around and glanced over her shoulder into the alley. A bead of sweat ran down her back. She needed to portray confidence. Darren was street through and through, like a hyena he would sense fear. A quick peek into the alley again and all business now, she turned to face Darren.

She said, "Did you?"

Darren nodded and tapped the bin he was leaning against.

"Let me see it."

Darren shook his head. "Nah, that's not how this works. You show me yours, then I'll show you mine."

The times Carrie had met Darren, he was always bobbing or bouncing, but tonight he was actually twitching. He was on something. Great. Darren, stone-cold sober, was a fuck-up, but twitchy Darren, hyped up on some shit, propelled the likelihood of this going according to plan to whatever the direct opposite of that was.

Carrie said, "Mine is nearby; I'll get it. Just wanted to make sure the meet was OK."

"Fuck that, Carrie!" he seethed.

He had something in his right hand—a gun. It looked like a 22 automatic. Probably. It looked old, but if it didn't blow up in Darren's face if he pulled the trigger, she could get hurt. Big time.

"That wasn't the deal!" Darren screamed. "You bring me the money, we make the exchange, and we're both happy. Now I'm not happy. Where's the fucking money?"

"What the fuck, Darren? Why the shooter? We're not in Chicago."

"For my protection and to make sure things go my way. Where's the money?"

Darren twitched so much he was almost twerking. This deal was going to rat-shit fast.

"OK, OK, calm down. We're all friends here. I've stashed the money close by, two minutes tops, and we can do the deal." She used both her hands in a calming gesture. "We can both walk away, and both win. Don't fuck this up."

Darren levered himself off the bin and moved towards her.

"Darren, for fuck's sake. You know me. I'm not a threat to you. Stop waving that thing around. You're making me nervous."

Darren was up in her face now, raging.

"But I don't know you, not really. You could be trying to rip me off."

A new version of Darren appeared. A hungry Darren, a quick trip away from loony toon Darren.

Carrie faked a smile. "If that were the case, I would be holding the gun, not you."

Darren appeared to take note of that and took a step back. Then, with a leer on his face and eyes fixed on her crotch, he moved towards her and said, "You're right. Maybe I should make sure you're not carrying."

Carrie shoved him back a few paces. "Get out of my face!"

Darren came right back at her, holding her by either side of her jacket. He had finally lost it.

In the same instant, faint blue light trickled into the storage area, accompanied by shouts and running feet.

Darren screamed, "Fucking move, bitch!" Like a squirrel caught in headlights or, in this case, flashing blue lights, he turned feral before her eyes.

Fixated only on escape, he pushed Carrie back and twisted her out of his way, still holding the gun in his right hand. A deafening explosion within the small storage area echoed off the metal bins and reverberated into the alley. The running feet stopped for a second, and Darren ran out of the doorway and back the way he came. Carrie fell into the alley, landing on her back, looking up at the sky, hyperventilating air and rain in equal measure before the darkness took her.

She woke with a start. It took time to realise she hadn't been running 'round the swing park. The same old nightmare.

Opening one eye, she realised it didn't give her enough perspective, so she slowly opened the other. Wow, her head was banging. Everything ached. Gingerly, turning her head to the right, she saw tubes going into both arms hooked up to drips and tubes coming out of her chest, going below the bed, probably a drain. OK, hospital. So, not dead then.

Turning her head to the left, a young, uniformed police constable sat on a chair reading a book. She tried to speak, but her mouth seemed full of cat litter. She coughed.

The constable looked up from his book.

She mouthed, "Water."

The constable stood and poured a little water into a plastic beaker. He tried to hold it to her mouth, but spilled most of it onto her chest.

Enough went in for her to croak, "What time is it? What day?"

The constable checked his watch and said, "Five-thirty in the afternoon, Friday. You've been here for two days."

"What happened?"

The constable looked over his shoulder to the open door. "Maybe I better get the Inspector. I'm meant to call him when you wake up."

"Ok, but first tell me what happened," she rasped.

The constable looked at her. "From what I understand, you got shot in the chest. It was all a bit dodgy when they first brought you in."

An overweight man in his late forties wearing a grey suit that looked like he had been sleeping in it entered the room as the constable was talking.

"That's enough, constable. Go grab a drink, and on your way back, I'll have a white coffee, two sugars and some digestives."

The constable turned. "Yes, sir, sorry, sir."

As the constable left the room, Detective Inspector Bob Fisher said, "Well, Christine, that was a right royal cluster fuck, wasn't it? How are you feeling?"

Christine breathed, "Like hammered shit, if I'm honest. Could I have a little more water?"

Bob Fisher poured water into the plastic beaker and held it to her lips. This time, more of it found its way into her mouth and down her parched throat.

"Thanks, what happened?"

Bob Fisher lowered himself with some difficulty into the chair recently vacated by the constable.

"There'll be a formal debrief when you're up and about, but basically, Darren the Rat brought a gun to the party and freaked out when you told him you didn't have the money. The team heard you mention a shooter and then confirm a gun and went into protect our asset mode."

Christine grimaced in pain as she tried to sit further up in the bed, but waved away Bob Fisher's movement to assist. "Yeah, remind me again, who was the asset? 'Cos, I got shot."

"Well, according to Darren, he had hold of you. He saw the blue lights and heard the cavalry running down the alley. As he pushed you out of the way to escape into the alley, he accidentally pulled the trigger. We found him standing at a crowded bus stop two streets away with his hands up."

Christine smiled with gritted teeth, "He must have thought, having shot a member of London's finest, something dire would have happened to him in a dark, secluded place."

Bob Fisher shook his head and said, "The things criminals believe! But he hadn't put it together at that stage."

Christine asked, "But he has now?"

"Well, yes, and he had help from the Met's media team."

"What does that mean?"

"The initial info we had was you died on scene. The paramedics gave you cardiac massage. Part of your recovery is going to be mending the ribs they broke. Somebody told the media team you had no relatives to inform, and they released your picture. During the media frenzy in the immediate aftermath of the operation, it came out the officer was Detective Sergeant Christine Woolfe, and you were working undercover for Specialist Crime and Operations."

"For fuck's sake, Bob. So, my face is all over the media. Fantastic. No more undercover work for me."

They sat in silence until Christine finally uttered, "I thought it was a 22. Surely, it didn't get through the vest?"

"No, by a fluke; when he pulled the trigger, the end of the barrel had worked its way under your left armpit. The back of the vest caught the bullet after it collapsed your lung."

She shook her head in disbelief. "As you said, Bob, a cluster fuck. So, I guess while I'm lying here contemplating my navel, I should apply for a new job?"

"Wow, most coppers would be worried about getting shot and dying, the collapsed lung, the broken ribs, maybe collecting an ill-health pension, but Christine is worrying about getting back to the job."

"You know me, Bob. I'll worry about all that stuff when I need to."

"Yes, I do. You're a very scary woman, Christine. If you don't mind me mentioning it, you need to get a life. Don't worry, we'll find you a home. When you've recovered. You were very lucky, you know. We wouldn't be having this conversation at all if he'd had a nine mill."

"I don't feel very lucky right now." She winced again as jolts of pain radiated around her chest. "Just tell me we got the half kilo of coke?"

"Nope, it was a scam for money all along. Darren cooked it up with his cousin Jamie, an informant for the drug squad. The plan was to rip you off for the money and sell you some cut crap, then sell you out to the drug squad as a quantity dealer. Win, Win. Of course, we didn't know about the family connection beforehand. Darren and Jamie will have a secure address for a few years."

Christine looked away to a corner of the room. "What about Jessie? Did you speak to her?"

Bob Fisher shook his head. "She's vanished. Jamie called her for a meet after the Op went south. I've interviewed him about her involvement and whereabouts. But no."

"Bob, we should have protected her. Taken her off the street. I told her not to answer the phone."

Bob Fisher held Christine's wrist, avoiding the cannula. "You can't save everyone, Christine. You know that. Some people just get themselves involved in shit."

"But we let her down big time."

"It was my decision. I'll take the rap if there is any."

"It's not about taking the rap, Bob."

"I know. Look, I can see you're exhausted. I'll swing by tomorrow. The doctors say you'll be here for a week or two."

"Thanks for the update, Bob. On your way out, tell the nurse I need more painkillers."

"Will do. See you tomorrow."

He struggled out of the chair and walked out the door.

With effort, she moved further up the bed and reached for her mobile. The battery was running low. She had missed no calls, and the only messages she had received were from her colleagues, now former colleagues, wishing her a speedy recovery. Fucking media arseholes! She was going to miss that job.

A short while later, the young constable returned from the cafe. "Has the inspector gone?"

"A few minutes ago."

"Good," the constable said, "He's been kipping in the relatives' room and 'spelling' me and the other officers here for the last day and a half. Do you want the coffee and biscuits?"

"Nah, you have it. I had something plentiful and opioid from the nurse."

Christine snuggled down in the bed, which the painkillers made less painful, and closed her eyes.

"S'later," she said.

Chapter 2

Christine discharged herself from the hospital after two and a half weeks. Bob Fisher offered her a stint at one of the police rehabilitation places scattered around the country. She declined. She wanted to look for a new job.

A couple of years before Christine's mother died, her mother had bought a new-build flat in Balham, South London. Christine moved in a few months after the funeral. Her mother had not bothered to make a will. As the only surviving next of kin, everything her mother left came to her. It included a shockingly large credit card debt, a bank loan, and an existing mortgage on the flat. She paid off the debt with most of her savings and applied for a new mortgage. The process had not been easy as she hadn't been in the police long and didn't have the required amount of monthly wage slips. But, once the rules of intestacy kicked in, her mother's equity in the flat became hers, which swung it as far as the mortgage company was concerned.

The flat was on the second floor of a four-storey, purpose-built block. It had one bedroom, a kitchen-diner-lounge, there wasn't enough space for three separate rooms, and a combined shower room and toilet. The main window looked out onto another similar block. Still, it had an allocated parking space outside the main entrance door. As rare as rocking horse shit in London. It was also within walking distance of Balham tube and a quick journey to Scotland Yard, where she was based. Or where she used to be based.

Bob Fisher called her a week after she came home from the hospital for the debrief. It had gone as she expected, with everyone trying to distance themselves from the fuck-up. The drug squad claimed no way they could have known Darren was a cousin of Jamie, their informant. The protection team claimed they responded rapidly but didn't want to mess up the op by acting too hastily. Basically, Christine thought, everyone was upstairs collecting fares when all the action was happening downstairs.

Drug squad officers questioned Jamie again about Jessie's whereabouts. He claimed she had not turned up for the meet after he had contacted her. No one believed him, but not believing is not evidence. You learn that fast in the police. Jessie may have skipped London and was living a good life, but no one believed that either.

Christine sat in her living room, looking at the bare walls and her 40-inch HD TV, standing on two unopened packing boxes left over from her move. She kept her mum's double bed and the sofa and took everything else to charity shops or the dump. She'd been there ten years and hadn't put up a picture. But it suited her. She could do whatever she wanted, bring anyone back here - although not much of that had happened over the years. Unsociable hours and often working away from London, as she had done a lot during her undercover days, were not conducive to lasting relationships. In any case, lasting relationships were not her thing. Her longest lasted three months. Andrew, a bank cashier at the local branch of NatWest, had told her he could not get through to her. Told her she shut her emotions off like a switch. Told her she needed help. She told him to sling his hook.

Christine picked up her mobile and keyed in Bob Fisher's number. He answered after it rang twice.

"Christine, everything alright?"

"Yeah, A-OK here. Watching daytime TV and contemplating whether to poke sharp sticks into my eyes. Any news on the job front?"

There was a long silence at the other end of the call. "Christine, are you sure you want to come back so soon?"

"Yes, Bob. I need to get back on the horse. Be useful. Catch bad guys."

"Ok, the crime squad local to you at Tooting is looking for a DS, and I've got you the gig if you want it. You can start Monday week."

"I'll take it. Can't I start this coming Monday? I'm starting to hum along with the Good Morning show music."

"No, Christine, you can't. Monday week. Take the time to rest and recover. Report to Chief Superintendent Charlotte Mackensie at 10 am. She's good people Christine. She runs a tight ship."

"Thanks, Bob, I'm sorry it ended this way."

"Not as sorry as I am, Christine."

Chapter 3

The home Bob Fisher had found for Christine after five months of home recuperation was with the South West London Crime Squad. Despite not being fully fit, Christine relentlessly badgered Bob Fisher to find her somewhere. And now here she was, Detective Sergeant Christine 'Gopher' Woolfe. Christine ran the team, doing the admin and taking it easy. She would 'gopher' banal meetings and 'gopher' witness statements, but drew the line at 'gopher' coffees. Rank had its perks, after all. Still, things were looking up, and it was far better than the daytime TV alternative.

The area was knee deep in a placate the angry natives' job at present. A small group of young rapscallions had been ripping the arse out of the crime squad's policing area, sometimes breaking into three or four posh drums a night. The Guardian-reading, golf-playing and taxpaying homeowners were none too pleased. Christine believed one homeowner played golf with the local MP or maybe the Commissioner, which explained the urgent summons she had got a couple of days ago from Charlotte Mackensie. She was a uniform supervisor through and through, but she welcomed Christine with open arms when she first arrived. Rumour had it she had been a decent enough thief-taker during her short time on the streets before ambition and luck had started her on the path to greatness. Now, approaching the end of her career, Mackensie wanted nothing more than a peaceful life and not to get shat on. As Bob said, she ran a tight ship. She projected efficiency in her crisp uniform jacket and skirt. She talked Oxbridge, but sometimes her Peckham roots glimmered in her choice of words.

"Christine," she said as Christine walked into her office, "I want your team to take this on. I'm getting dumped on from on high, and as you know, it only rolls one way. The intelligence team thinks they have identified one of the gang members, Dennis Armstrong. In an ideal world, short-term surveillance should identify the rest of the gang and wrap this up."

She handed Christine the file and fixed her gaze on the pile of documents on her desk, making it obvious the meeting was over.

"Yes, Ma'am," said Christine and left her office.

Grabbing a mug of coffee, Christine sat at her desk and started to read through the thin file. Dennis 'Spider' Armstong, 25, white, medium build, 1.7m tall, with an address in Morden, South London. She perused his Crimint record. Wow, form as long as both of her arms and twice as stupid. In the past, his preferred method of earning an income was street muggings. But he had a problem. Because he's stupid; some years before, he'd had a spider's web tattooed over the left side of his face. He found even the 'oldies', his victims of choice, could not fail to notice the tattoo. He kept getting nicked. Then, in a flash of genius, he had splashed out some of his hard-stolen cash and had it removed. No one mentioned the tattoo now—they just described a big red scar shaped like a spider's web. Night-time burglaries were his thing now.

Fed up being office-bound, Christine allocated herself to the surveillance team for the following night. Back into action, doing good for King and Country.

Chapter 4

Why did she volunteer for this? Midnight, falling snow, icy roads and...

Christine turned to Bob Jackson, her partner for the night, "What the fuck is up with this car, Bob?"

With a sheepish glance, Bob tried again to coax something greater than frozen air out of the heater.

"Sorry, Chris. The pool guy 'as stitched us up good 'n proper, my bad," he said in his strong South London accent.

Christine asked why it was his fault, and he explained, "Recently I had cause to detain a youth trying to 'ave it away on 'is toes with me briefcase 'n car stereo."

When Christine inquired how that resulted in a decidedly sketchy pool car with no heater in the middle of a snowstorm, Bob informed her, "The youth is the pool guy's nephew."

Christine tried to decide if getting angry would warm her up. She decided not, so she shook her head and called Bob a tosser.

She picked up the radio and checked in with the team. She had strategically placed three other cars and a poor sod in the back of a van with sight of Armstrong's front door.

"DS Woolfe to eyeball, any change?"

The poor sod replied, "Certain bits of me have a lot less feeling than when I woke up this morning, but apart from that—negative."

Christine shivered. But she could move around. If he moved, he might give the game away. She almost felt sorry for him... almost.

Christine keyed the mike, "Do what you can to stop the important bits falling off. We'll call it a night if nothing stirs by three."

Maybe the gunshot had affected her hearing, but she thought the burst of static coming from the speaker sounded like a string of naughty words.

Nothing happened for an hour, and Christine's resolve started to wane. Poor timekeeping and the sheer bone idleness of the criminal classes does more to keep them out of jail than anything else. Bastions of law and order get paid for a living and paid extra for overtime. It meant as a supervisory officer; she ran a budget and needed to keep an eye on the clock. The London taxpayers are not too keen on paying coppers to sit around doing sweet FA, waiting for the great unwashed to climb out of bed and nick something.

Bob had been steadily increasing the level of whinge for at least 40 minutes, and Christine seriously considered leaving the car before she did him some severe damage. Luckily, Spider picked that exact moment to surface.

"Contact, contact, contact—target out, out, out." Christine acknowledged and waited for further info. "Target to Zulu 1 and off, off, off towards Lodge Road. Loss of eyeball."

Christine knew Spider had left his home, got into his car, driven off towards Lodge Road, and was now out of sight of the popsicle in the van.

A textbook surveillance ensued, with cars swapping the eyeball at regular intervals. Spider was heading towards the good part of town. Come to mama!

After ten minutes, the eyeball told them, "Stop, stop, stop. Target out and on foot and left, left, left into... wait... Swallow Heath Lane."

Christine planned to give him enough rope to dangle himself, but not so much as to leave her open to criticism. Of course; best-laid plans... the team had a loss. Actually, it was down to PC Chambers. The same PC Chambers who will buy the team breakfast later.

Leon Chambers, 30, fit, built and the only Black officer on the team. He was soft-spoken and hadn't raised his voice to anyone. But, as a six foot three rugby player, who would chance annoying him?

When a loss happens, the team scrambles to determine where the target has gone based on 'time, pace and distance'. Considering the speed at which he was moving, how far would the target have gone in the time?

Christine, not one to blow her own trumpet, found the house. Not precisely a Sherlock moment. With snow falling, she traced the shallow footprints in the slush on the pavement from his car to a wall. She pulled herself up to look over the wall and saw an open window round the back of the place. The house was large, secluded by mature trees. Christine saw the alarm bell box, but no alarm was sounding. Disabled or not turned on in the first place?

Christine arranged for the team to surround the house, telling them they would wait for Spider to walk into their web.

He ran. Straight out of the front door, almost catching them out. They expected sneaky. He gave them full-on brazen. PC Chambers reduced his fine to a round of coffees with a superb rugby tackle halfway down the drive. Immediately, Spider gave them his best 'Shaggy' impression by repeating over and over, "It wasn't me."

Christine countered, "It is you and you're nicked."

Meanwhile, Bob, who had missed out on all the fun, wandered into the house and a few minutes later wandered out again, looking like he had seen a naked, murdered woman slowly cooking on her bed—which, as it turned out...

Sometimes, Christine would have preferred to be a lowly nobody with no responsibility whatsoever. Instead, because she had sat and passed the sergeant's exam a few years before, she took on the role of head nanny at a nursery. Seven officers stared at her childlike with blank looks on their faces. Bob relayed to all what he had found in the house, accompanied by the same 'Shaggy' backing track, until Christine ordered Spider to be taken to the station.

She detailed two officers to search the ground floor while she followed Bob up the stairs. They were careful to disturb as little as possible at the scene and en route. Cooked humans do smell like roast pork, but the smell assaulting her nasal cavities halfway up the stairs resembled roadkill, warmed by the summer sun. Bob had done well to make it as far as the bedroom the first time, and he wasn't chomping at the bit for a return visit.

The room was huge, at least compared to Christine's flat, as was the bed. The naked woman was lying on her back, eyes open. Christine recalled in the past, people used to place pennies on the eyes of dead bodies to keep their eyes closed. The woman looked well and truly dead. In books, when the author says the victim looked like they were asleep? Bollocks, dead is dead, pale and cold; they don't call it a deathly pallor for nothing.

She had what looked like expanding yellow foam, the sort plumbers use, filling and protruding from her nostrils and mouth. Two fingers of her left hand were in her mouth, encased in the foam. She had foam smeared on her right hand. As the killer squirted the foam, she must have known she was dead. She had died trying to clear her airway. Not a nice way to go.

Christine noticed a few drops of blood on the bedsheets near her left ear and dried blood in the left ear canal. Had the killer injected something?

Nothing appeared out of place or rummaged, and the timing was off, so she was right in her assumption Spider was not their guy. She told Bob to return to the front door and start an MI log sheet. Good for the continuity of evidence. It would also stop 'looky loo's' passing by and screwing up the crime scene. Not members of the public, cops. Curiosity was part of cop DNA.

Alone in the room, Christine took a few to calm down and gather. There was a silence in death. After the trauma and cacophony of the event, there's always silence. Silence for the deceased, but also for those around. A little bubble of peace before the inevitable jolt back into reality. The victims had lost their voice, but she and her colleagues sought to restore it long enough so the victim could accuse their killer. She often thought Samantha called to her. That's why she became a copper in the first place. She couldn't blame anyone else for what was her fault. Put up or shut up.

Now she had to get her act into gear. The first thing was to arrange forensic and the local CID down to the scene. Christine hoped she would remain on the murder investigation. But, it didn't do to step on local toes until your boots were official. She used her mobile rather than put the details over the air, then rang her boss, who said he was calling the Major Incident Team.

Detective Chief Inspector Steve Balcombe from MIT called ten minutes later and was surprisingly pleasant, considering her discovery had woken him at 3.17 am. Christine explained the situation and asked how she should proceed. The DCI told her to keep a lid on things until he rang back.

In the meantime, she looked carefully around the bedroom. The victim was Sarah Jessica Davies. She was 34, the same age as Christine, but born two months earlier in June. Her driving licence and a company ID swipe card were on the dressing table. She worked for a soft drinks distributor based in South West London. It didn't specifically spell out what she did for the Company, but from what she'd seen of the house and the clothes in the section of the open wardrobe, Christine guessed some kind of middle to high-level executive. She had done well for herself. Except now she was dead.

Bob called up the stairs. The local CID had arrived, and a young, fresh-faced DC joined Christine in a green Parka, a 'Mott the Hoople' T-shirt, jeans and trainers.

He held out his hand. "DC James Menday, night duty CID."

He must have caught her looking at his attire as he added, "Yeah, sorry, we had a drug raid planned for 5 am. Cancelled it on the way over, as we'll be busy."

Christine took off her latex glove and shook his hand. "DS Woolfe, Christine, Crime Squad. Are the SOCOs on their way?"

DC Menday stepped closer towards the bed and wrinkled his nose at the smell. "They should be. After you notified them, Control called the team."

He squatted down for a better look at the head. "Damn, that looks nasty."

Christine's mobile rang. The DCI. "Hello, sir, night duty CID has arrived, a DC Menday and forensics are close behind... Ok, that's great, see you shortly." She hung up.

"James, that was DCI Balcombe. He's on his way; be here in about 40 minutes. In the meantime, this is now officially an MIT case. You are the local liaison. He's cleared it with your boss, and I, for my sins, am the exhibits officer."

Stoked as she was to be the exhibits officer, her problem lay with the responsibilities of the role. The XO had to be present at the postmortem, especially since she had been the first officer on the scene. Despite having encountered her fair share of dead bodies throughout the years, she never grew accustomed to it. The mere thought of witnessing a dissection mere feet away filled her with dread.

Chapter 5

The SOCOs arrived twenty minutes later. They asked Christine and DC Menday to leave while they did their thing. Christine noticed a few lights coming on in houses nearby and called the local station to ask for uniforms to police the crowd she knew would gather sooner rather than later. Christine busied herself securing the crime scene. DC Menday found some crime scene tape in the boot of his car and closed off the entrance to the drive.

Once the uniforms arrived, Christine ordered one to man the front drive. She directed the other three to secure tape across the road, ten houses on either side of the murder scene. She also explained who they should let through and who to re-direct elsewhere. It's more complicated in a residential street as the residents need to go about their business. Yet, she needed to keep non-residents, reporters, and the general rent-a-crowd far enough away so they couldn't interfere.

DCI Balcombe arrived, and Christine brought him up to speed. Once they had suited up with white paper coveralls, masks, gloves, and bootees, she led him into the house. She called up the stairs, and a scene of crime officer gave them permission to walk up and into the bedroom.

To 'give Jack his jacket', the DCI took the murder scene in his stride. He didn't even comment on the smell, which seemed worse now, even though the techs had switched off the heated blanket.

The SOCO lead came over and introduced himself as Simon. Christine hadn't met him before, but from how he had directed his team since arriving, she sensed he was her kind of SOCO. He was red-faced, although it may have been the paper suit hood pulled tight around it. Clean-shaven, at least around the mask. He looked about thirty and had done well to head up a SOCO team at a murder scene.

He said, "We're waiting on the doctor to pronounce death officially, so we haven't touched the body yet, but she's clearly dead. Her eyes have glazed, and signs of blood pooling," referring to corneal opacity and livor mortis, Christine surmised. "I believe from what I can see, a small round screwdriver or, more likely, an awl caused the wound to her ear. Nasty."

Christine said, "What's an awl?"

The DCI answered, "It's a small, pointed tool mainly used to make holes in leather." Both Simon and Christine looked at him.

"What?" he said. "It's a hobby of mine. My father taught me." The DCI made a gesture to tell Simon to move on.

Simon told them, in his opinion, from what he had seen, someone had likely been in bed with her or on the bed with her, and his team hadn't found the awl so far. He also thought it unlikely they would get much in the way of forensic trace evidence. They all smelt the bleach.

Bob called out, "The FME's here. Shall I send her up?"

Christine went to the bedroom door and said, "I'll come and collect her in a minute. Give her a suit, Bob, will you?"

Simon said what Christine had already guessed: "The electric blanket's going to mess up the time of death. You might narrow it down, like when she was last seen at work or anywhere else."

Christine walked downstairs and introduced herself to the doctor. "Hi doctor, I'm DS Christine Woolfe."

The doctor raised her hand in greeting. "Dr Janice Brown."

"DCI Balcombe is upstairs with the scene of crime techs. When I take you up, can you follow me and walk where I walk? SOCO has laid out a path. The smell's bad, but we think only one wound is on the body. Although she has stuff blocking her airway."

"Thanks. I know Steve Balcombe. I attended another murder for him about eight or nine months ago."

As they entered the bedroom, the DCI confirmed with Simon, Christine was the XO, and he would call the pathologist and the Coroner once their offices opened.

Christine said, "Sir, this is Dr Brown."

The DCI turned and looked at her. "Janice, right?"

Dr Brown nodded.

"Ok, Simon here will take you over to the body."

Simon did so, and Dr Brown looked at the wound. When she touched the skin, she remarked, "I don't think she's been dead long, Chief Inspector; she's still warm to the touch."

The DCI replied deadpan, "Yes, that may be the case. Still to be determined, though."

Dr Brown nodded and said, "For your records, I can confirm the woman is deceased at 5.20 am."

The DCI and Christine returned to the front door with Dr Brown.

As she left, the DCI turned to Christine and, in a low voice, said, "I think we should keep the awl, the foam and the electric blanket to ourselves. Pass the information to the team and SOCOs."

Christine nodded, "I've been wondering, where did he get the stuff he used for the murder and clean up? The bleach he could have found in the house, but that's not guaranteed. The foam and the awl he must have brought with him as they're specific things, and I doubt he'd say to the victim 'before we shag; do you mind if I have a look in your garden shed?'"

The DCI smiled tightly, "No, that's a good point, make a note of it. We're just starting. Answers will come. I'm off. I'll brief the Chief Super and see you back at the office once you finish here. Keep what you need of your team here, but send the rest home, as we'll need them back here first thing to start door-to-door. I'll let control know we'll need some early turn uniforms to police the cordons until we finish."

Christine watched the DCI leave, turned, and trudged wearily back upstairs.

Chapter 6

Christine drove to the MIT office at 11.30 am, absolutely shattered. She had sent Bob home around 6.30 am, so she was driving the pool car, and the heater still didn't work. After a missed turn, she found the entry to the car park and parked in a visitor's bay.

Christine carried several non-forensic exhibits in clear plastic exhibit bags as she approached the reception desk. She fumbled with her coat pocket before putting the bags on the floor to show her warrant card to the security guy sitting behind a screen.

"Hi, I'm here to see DCI Balcombe, MIT. I'm DS Woolfe."

The guard looked at the card and checked a logbook. "OK," he said, "take the lift to the second floor. I'll call, and someone will meet you."

Christine picked up the exhibit bags, walked over and pressed the up button—the guard, true to his word, was talking on the telephone. The lift came; Christine stepped inside and ascended to the second floor.

The lift door opened, and a woman waited for her. Christine guessed she was in her early thirties. She had rich brown shoulder length curly hair, but the roots gave the game away, showing her original colour was pure mouse. She was slightly too plump for her frame and dressed in last season's finest, but she had applied her make-up well. Christine replayed her thoughts. Yep, I'm a bitch!

The woman held out her hand towards Christine. "DS Woolfe?" Her voice rose at the end of the question. "I'm DC Lucy Worthington, MIT, come through to the incident room. Can I help with the exhibit bags?"

"Thanks, I'm Christine." She smiled at Lucy, handing over two large bags.

Lucy led Christine down the corridor and into the incident room.

The incident room was nothing special—an office with tables, chairs and computers. Three HOLMES 2 terminals, the contrived acronym for the Home Office Large Major Enquiry System, sat on a separate table.

Two large whiteboards were located outside DCI Balcombe's small office at the far end of the room, displaying a picture of the victim and the briefest of timelines. The painted walls were light green, as seen in government buildings the length and breadth of the United Kingdom.

DCI Balcombe was on the phone, but he gave Christine an acknowledging wave of his free hand.

Lucy said, "Let's find you a desk to call your own, and I'll give you a hand to take those bags to the storeroom downstairs."

Christine looked around the incident room. Four male detectives sat at desks, fixated on their computer screens. However, they had looked up when she and Lucy entered.

She sighed, "Any coffee going? It's been a long night."

"We have an industrial strength brew for such occasions," Lucy said. "How do you take it?"

"Black, as it comes. Nothing fancy."

Christine arranged the exhibit bags on her desk. She had filled two exhibit record books, but Simon's team had taken most of the items to the forensic science lab for examination.

DCI Balcombe left his office and said, "OK, everyone." The detectives turned to face him. "I'd like to introduce DS Christine Woolfe. She'll be joining us for the duration of this case." Christine smiled around the room. "I've appointed her as the exhibits officer, as she was on scene this morning. Let everyone know we'll have daily briefings at 8 am and 5 pm. I expect everyone to attend unless there's a good reason not to. The pathologist has scheduled the PM to start at three this afternoon. So you'll have an excuse to miss the afternoon briefing, Christine. You'll get to meet everybody in the morning."

Grabbing some statements off a desk, he returned to his office.

Lucy placed a large mug of steaming coffee in front of Christine. "Here, get this down you. If you don't mind me saying, you look knackered."

"Looks aren't deceiving. Give me a hand to get the bags to the store wherever it is."

Lucy smiled and said, "The store's in the basement three floors below, strategically placed to be a right royal pain in the arse."

Slurping coffee, Christine said, "Give me a quick rundown on the guys here now."

Lucy looked around the room. "Well, the guy with the dark wavy hair and the pin-stripe suit is DC Dave Wilde, been here about six months. Came from the Drug Squad. PC Dave Pritchard sat behind the two huge monitors is our tech guy. We call him Pritch so we don't have two Daves. Rumour has it he used to be a white-hat hacker for fun in his teens, tracking down scammers. The guy on the phone is DC Kumar Singh. Came to us about five months ago from the robbery squad."

Christine said, "OK, Dave, from drugs, Pritch, the tech guy, Kumar, ex-Sweeney, which leaves…"

"DS Pete Rabbet. E T not I T. Been here since the dawn of time. The Boss relies on him a lot. With DI Andy Kerr on secondment, Pete will probably step up as deputy SIO and office manager."

"And what about Lucy? What's your story?"

"Oh, I came here over a year ago from CASO to help with a paedophile case and ended up staying."

Christine said, "CASO, child abuse and sexual offences, right? It's got a good rep. OK, show me where the store is so I can get the exhibits logged in, and I can grab a shower and change clothes before the PM."

Chapter 7

Christine showered and changed into some spare clothes she kept in her gym locker. She was well and truly cream-crackered.

She was no gym bunny, but thought about going once or twice a month. Having a gym membership made her feel fitter.

Christine drove around the hospital car park looking for a parking space and was fifteen minutes late for the three o'clock deadline. She hoped she had missed the cut.

The pathologist was finishing his external summation when Christine bowled through the door full of apologies she didn't mean. Simon, the SOCO, told her the electric bone saw had broken down, and they had tried to find a replacement without success.

Simon's job was to take the exhibits from the pathologist, bag and tag them, and hand them to Christine for entry into the exhibit record. He brought a photographer, John, to record the gruesome details.

Christine introduced herself to the pathologist who, in an antipodean accent, said, "Call me 'Doc'"

They had placed a desk and chair a few feet from the autopsy table for her to use, and she settled herself down, arranging the blank exhibit books and her pens.

An attractive, blond-haired woman about twenty-five wearing scrubs, who she assumed was the pathologist's assistant, came into the autopsy room with a bone handsaw. Christine noticed the pathologist had already used a scalpel to slice through the skin around the upper part of Sarah's skull. The assistant climbed onto the table and started to saw around the top of the skull. Sarah's head was rocking from side to side with each stroke of the saw, and the young woman was trying to support the head with her knee. After about 10 minutes, the assistant got off the table and, smiling, said to the pathologist, "All yours, doc."

The pathologist, or 'call me Doc,' looked fiftyish, thin in his scrubs and almost entirely bald. He told Christine he was on an exchange program from New Zealand, and it appeared he wanted to show the techniques used in the colonies were every bit as good as those in the mother country. He used a piece of wire and stuck it into the wound in the ear to gauge the depth. Four and a half inches or almost 12 cm. So, most likely not an awl. Christine had researched on her phone, and the pointy bit of an awl was half the length.

The Doc said, "I've been thinking your killer may have Paraphilia."

Christine said, "What's that? Is it contagious, or will it help us catch him?"

The Doc smiled. The type of smile you give to a child who has put one block on top of another for the first time without wanting to knock it down before adding another block.

He said, "Maybe. Paraphilia is obtaining intense sexual pleasure from atypical objects or situations. Sexual interest in anything other than 'normal' sexual intercourse with a consenting human partner, or probably not in this case." As he said normal, he made the bunny ears sign with his gloved fingers.

Simon said, "Are you talking about the insertion of the tool into the ear?"

"It's called Piquerism," Doc said, "deriving sexual pleasure from penetrating skin with sharp objects. Although, mainly, you find Piquerists take their sexual pleasure only from that act. Yet, here, we have evidence of penile penetration and piquerism. It's a little confusing."

Christine said, "I'll be sure to discuss it with the bastard when we catch him."

The Doc popped off the top of the skull and removed the brain. With a stainless-steel dish at the ready, the assistant weighed it. The pathologist spent some time examining the entry wound; now the brain was free of the skull. John took pictures, the Doc dictated notes, the assistant assisted, and Christine felt very queasy.

The Doc extracted most of the foam from her throat by a cut resembling a capital H on its side. Two transverse cuts above and below the foam and a single cut to join them at the centres. He laid the skin flaps back and delicately sliced the foam from where it had stuck to the inside of the throat and windpipe. He carefully cut away the foam from inside the mouth. When he pulled it out, Christine could see the internal shape of the throat and windpipe in the foam. It had expanded about eight inches down her trachea. He cut the foam from around the two fingers of her left hand. Simon bagged and tagged the foam and handed it to Christine to make a record.

After about two hours, they took a break. For the life of her, Christine could not understand why anyone would want to work around dead people all the time. John leaned in for a close-up shot of various bits of body. The assistant, who introduced herself as Chloe. What was she doing here?

Christine noticed Simon eyeing Chloe. As they drank tea, he had to go there.

He said, "What's a nice girl like you doing in a place like this?"

Before Christine could interject and point out how inappropriate that was, Chloe replied, "Oh, I've always been around death." They all stared at her as she continued, "My last job was working in an animal research lab, killing the animals after the experiments were complete."

Christine asked, "Did you not feel sad injecting the animals?"

"Oh no," she said, "it would be too expensive. I snapped their necks. You can easily hold their necks between your fingers and jerk with mice. With larger animals such as monkeys and dogs, you need to use a short piece of broom handle." She smiled and continued, "I want to train as an embalmer."

Christine, Simon and the Doc continued to stare.

"I've learned not to tell people I meet what I do. One friend didn't want me to babysit her child after she found out. I haven't got a boyfriend," she said, looking directly at Simon.

Simon busied himself with his exhibits, and the pathologist cleared his throat and said, "OK..., back to work."

The Doc made the Y incision. Chloe appeared to take a grim delight in using the bone croppers as she cut through the ribs on either side of the breastbone. The Doc removed the breastbone to the dish Chloe had ready. He then removed lots of bits dripping blood and slime, weighed and placed them in metal dishes. Christine kept her eyes down, looking at the XO log and writing as Simon called out the details.

Rather than take scrapings from under the victim's fingernails, the Doc used pliers to take the whole nail, all ten of them. Sitting three feet from such acts made Christine think she would rather be anywhere else but there.

An hour and a half and fifty-two exhibits later, it was finally over. But it made no difference. They had nothing. Even without the lab results, Christine could tell they were in a forensically screwed situation. The smell of bleach still lingered on everything.

Chapter 8

Lucy didn't want to arrive early; in her mind, it would show desperation, but she also didn't want to keep Sebastian waiting alone in the restaurant. Their date, the first, if you discounted the shared coffee in Starbucks, would be great. No reason it wouldn't be unless she messed it up.

Her last date, too long ago, hadn't gone so well. The guy turned out to be a bit of a shit. Getting leery after a few pints and trying to force a kiss and more on the street outside the wine bar. On the cab ride home, she decided never to swipe right again.

Trouble was, where did she go to meet someone? The gym? Most of the guys were there either to work out big time with their mates lifting heavy weights or there to check the women out and comment on the fitness of their bods or the tightness of their butts. At work? Yes, there were some guys who were in shape, but she wasn't interested in their overly macho attitude. And the quiet ones, well, they did nothing for her.

She decided she was a bit messed up. Still, hoping Sebastian would be different, she pushed open the restaurant door ten minutes later than the table booking.

Lucy glanced around the dining room, and anxiety kicked in. She couldn't see him. Maybe she was still too early, or he wasn't coming. No, think positive; he probably got held up at work, running late. Sebastian wasn't the type of guy to let her down without at least a text. On reflex, she checked her phone for the umpteenth time, but nothing. Then he was by her side, smiling that smile of his. He kissed her cheek and led her to the bar area.

"Our table's not ready yet; it should only be a few minutes. I'm having a glass of wine; what can I get you?"

"Whatever you're having, thanks."

Lucy was aware how much her breathing had increased, and she took some deep breaths while Sebastian ordered. She checked him out. Brown Oxford's, chinos, crisp white shirt and a dark blue suit jacket. She had a date with the best-looking guy in the place. She caught a woman seated at a table with her man glancing over and checking Sebastian out. Lucy liked it. Note to self: don't screw this up.

Sebastian handed her a glass of white wine.

She took a sip. "Thank you, I needed that. Busy day at work."

"The other day, you told me you were working on a major incident team. I can't imagine what it must be like. I get catching the suspect, but you must see and hear the details. I don't think I'd have the stomach for it."

Taking another sip of wine, "It's not something you ever want to get used to, but you learn to cope. Our new Detective Sergent, Christine, got shot on an undercover sting late last year and, shortly after her return to work, found our scene. We caught a murder today."

"Wow. Undercover sting and caught a murder?"

Lucy smiled, "Oh, sorry, police jargon. We call it catching a case. A sting operation is where a police officer acts as a criminal, such as a drug buyer, to arrest a drug dealer. Christine's op went sideways. They arrested the guy, but she got shot. Anyway, enough about morbid stuff. How are you?"

"You know, I'm not too bad, actually. Work's good, but my private life has taken a recent upturn." That smile again, "All in all, life is good."

The waiter came, bringing menus and led them to their table, asking if they wanted more drinks. Sebastian had finished his wine and ordered another. Lucy was pacing herself, so she declined. They spent a few minutes looking over the menu.

Lucy said, "I think I'll have the Melanzane alla Parmigiana," She hoped no one Italian was in earshot as she had mangled the language, "the veggie aubergine dish."

"And I'll have the chicken with blue cheese linguine."

When the waiter returned, Sebastian ordered in flawless Italian. Even the waiter looked impressed, and Lucy suspected the closest he had ever come to Italy was this restaurant where he worked.

"OK, English and Italian. Any more?"

Sebastian flushed. "I'm not fluent in anything. Well, English, but I can get by in Italian, French, some Spanish, and a smattering of Thai."

Lucy sat back. "And yet, who would have guessed a normal British bloke like you had hidden depths?"

"Lucy, you saying that has made me happy in ways you can't imagine?"

Lucy saw the sincerity in his eyes as he said it. This guy was more profound than the ordinary blokes she went with.

Their food arrived, and they both tucked in.

Making sure she had thoroughly chewed and swallowed before speaking, she said, "Tell me a little more about your travels; you mentioned time spent in Thailand. How long were you there?"

"About four years. When I was out there, I needed an operation, and there was a bit of recovery time."

"Are you fully recovered now?"

"I am, fighting fit," flexing his right arm, Lucy stared at the bulging bicep showing through his jacket.

He flushed again. "Sorry, don't know why I did that."

Lucy giggled, "Don't mind me; I love to see a man in top form."

"Anyway, I drifted back to the UK via Italy and France after Thailand. The Spanish I picked up long ago in school."

Lucy finished her wine. Sebastian called the waiter over.

"Another?"

"A small glass. School day tomorrow."

The waiter nodded and walked away to fetch her drink.

Sebastian asked, "School day?"

"Sorry, more police talk. Learning day. Especially in my job, every day's a school day."

Chocolate and hazelnut cheesecake for her and Tiramasu for Sebastian followed.

Coffee, and then they were saying goodbye outside the restaurant.

"I really enjoyed our date, and thank you for treating me. Next time, I'll pay."

She could have kicked herself; why had she said it? There may not be a next time. She wanted there to be, but there was something about him she couldn't read. Nothing off-putting; she liked him even more as they spent time together; he had a depth of character. Maybe a troubled past or a secret not yet revealed. She realised she was talking to herself like a Mills and Boon character. She smiled.

"I'll hold you to that," he said.

She smiled even more.

He hailed a passing black cab. They embraced, and Sebastian softly kissed her on her lips. She climbed into the taxi; Sebastian closed the door and watched as it drove away.

Wow, that couldn't have gone any better. Lucy still felt and tasted his lips on hers, and the feeling in her tummy wasn't anything to do with the aubergines.

She noticed the cab driver looking at her in the rear-view mirror. Lucy realised she had a broad smile plastered over her face.

Chapter 9

Christine was in early the following morning, typing up her notes from yesterday's PM. A man entered the incident room. He ducked his head as he came through the doorway. He looked at Christine with a quizzical stare, then recollection dawned.

"DS Christine Woolfe, I presume? DCI Balcombe mentioned you were joining us at the briefing last evening. DC Ray Finn." He extended his hand, and as Christine shook it, she felt his long fingers wrap around her hand.

"How'd the PM go? Not much fun, are they?"

"No, as you say, not much fun. We took a lot of exhibits, but I doubt we'll get anywhere. We'll have to solve this the old-fashioned way without the benefit of forensics."

"Yeah, the DCI said the scene, and the body was forensically compromised." Smiling, he said, "I hope you don't mind me asking, but are you fit and well? Last time I saw about you online, they were announcing your death in a SCD10 operation shooting?"

"As they say, reports of my death were greatly exaggerated. I'm fighting fit. Thanks for asking, though."

Before either could say anything else, DC Finn turned towards the door as it opened. "Hi, Lucy."

Lucy smiled at them both. "Morning Ray, I see you've met DS Woolfe. Pritch and Kumar are just behind. I saw them parking up." As she spoke, both officers walked in and introduced themselves to Christine. While they were getting to know each other, DCI Balcombe arrived.

"Ok, ladies and gents, let's get on with it. Dave and Pete send their apologies. Dave is back at the scene, and Pete's wife is sick, so he's had to do the school run, but he'll be in later. Ok, Pritch, where are we with the MO?"

Pritch grabbed his notebook off his desk and said, "So far, I've found three that fit the bill. All suffocated by plumber's foam and all with a punctured ear. Gillian Michaels in Leeds five years ago, Rachel Evans in Edinburgh three years ago, and Jennifer Simkins in Hove, near Brighton, nine months ago. The last case is still being investigated, but with a reduced team. Physically, nothing to link them, but the thought has just come to me. If they had lived, they would all be around the same age as our victim. I've printed basic details off the HOLMES2 system, including the case file numbers, so whoever's tasked with research can read all of it."

"Thanks, Pritch. Can you give me the names and numbers of the SIOs for each case? I can see you've all met our latest recruit, DS Woolfe. Christine, anything from the PM?"

"Not a lot, to be honest. It took a lot of work to clear the hardened foam from Sarah Davies' mouth and throat." She noticed the team, who had not been at the scene, grimace. "Simon from SOCO and I took fifty-two exhibits, but I doubt we'll get anything forensically."

"The Pathologist said something interesting, though. He said our killer may have Paraphilia and a particular type called Piquerism." Noticing the blank looks from all, she said, "Yeah, not a clue myself, but it's basically someone who prefers to stick sharp objects into people rather than their penis. He remarked on it particularly as there were signs of normal vaginal penetration in this case, which he said was unusual in Piquerists. Oh, one more thing, he measured the depth of the piercing, and it was 12 cm deep, so too long for an awl." Noticing further blank looks from all but the DCI, she added, "It's a sharp spike tool used in leather work, but they're shorter. It might be an ice pick; they're about that length." Smiling, she added, "And before anyone says anything about my knowledge of spiky tools, I looked it up on the internet."

The DCI said, "Thanks, Christine. Has the victim's father identified the body yet?"

"No, the mortuary team is going to make her presentable this morning, and I'll call him and take him down for the ID. We couldn't have made him see his daughter with all the foam."

"No, of course not. Thanks. Ok, uniforms are continuing door to door in the street this morning. Dave is down there coordinating things. SOCO should finish the scene later today. Christine, when you've done the ID, I want you back here working with Kumar and researching the previous victims. I need to be sure as we can be; it's the same killer. Speak to the SIO at Brighton and ask if they have picked up on the similarity of the crimes at Leeds and Edinburgh. Pritch, you're on Sarah Davies' research. Dig into her life, personal and work, boyfriends, social media, all that stuff. Dave can give you a hand when he returns unless the door-to-door throws anything up. Lucy, when Pete gets in, I want you to collate and review our statements so far. Pete will work out if anything further needs doing, and at the moment, Ray will be your guy to allocate actions to."

Christine was pleased she had things to do. The exhibit work was frantic at first but trailed off unless they arrested someone. She knew the mortuary team would call her when Sarah's body was fit for her father to view and identify, so she collected the printouts from Pritch on the alleged previous victims.

She started to read with the first identified victim, Gillian Michaels, who was twenty-nine and single. She lived alone in a rented flat. People described her as a loner, unemployed, and down on her luck. The investigation rapidly became frosty and relegated to cold case status after a couple of months. Each year, detectives dusted off the case and mothballed it again when nothing new surfaced. She made a note in the margin to acquire more details and statements from HOLMES2.

The second victim was Rachel Evans, 31, single. According to friends, she had recently taken out a mortgage on her two-bed house and was a bit of a home bird. Home-work-home was her routine. They found her lying on her back on the living room floor. Bleach forensically compromised the scene, as theirs had been, and Gillian's beforehand. The murder team had looked hard at a male colleague about whom 'water cooler' gossip had built a budding relationship between him and Rachel. The line of enquiry proved worthless in the end. Once again, they filed the case and occasionally dusted it off, for appearance's sake.

The most recent case to fit the MO was Jennifer Simkins, 34, estranged from her husband after allegations of domestic abuse and a trial pending. At the time of her death, she lived alone in the flat she owned with her husband in Hove, East Sussex. His bail conditions required him to find alternative accommodation. Fortunately for him, he had been pissed out of his head at a rugby club awards night, the proud recipient of a man of the match award and a much-needed cast-iron alibi for the time his wife was being murdered.

The only glimmer of a lead came when they discovered Jennifer frequented a fetish nightclub in nearby Brighton. The club's CCTV was not functioning because it wasn't connected, and neither the staff nor the clientele would admit to knowing anyone else by name or ever having seen Jennifer. Trained personnel had watched weeks' worth of CCTV footage from the surrounding area at the John Street police station. Jennifer was spotted going to the club twice, and she appeared to leave alone on both occasions. They could not find any footage of Jennifer on the night she died.

The murder had taken place nine months ago. The investigation was still in progress, but the team had downsized to two detectives, with the SIO occasionally monitoring the case.

Every case had fallen into a forensic black hole with no witnesses, evidence, or leads. The MO suggested a link between the cases. However, they couldn't ensure a conviction relying only on that, even if they apprehended someone for Sarah's murder.

DS Rabbet rushed into the incident room and stopped by the DCI's office. Christine could see the DCI was on a call, and the DS mouthed sorry to the boss before heading to his desk. She walked over to him and put out her hand, "Christine Woolfe, I saw you yesterday but had to rush off to the PM."

"Peter Rabbet, Pete," he said, shaking her hand. "Welcome to MIT and the team. They're a good bunch."

"The DCI said your wife was unwell? I hope she's feeling better."

"Just a case of a cold or flu. Left her snuggled in bed with magazines and a thermos of hot chocolate. I had to drop the kid at school. I heard you've been in the wars. Everything ok now?"

"Only hurts when I laugh," she said. "I heard you've been here a while?"

"Almost ten years. I've seen some changes. Not all of them for the better. But Steve Balcombe is by far the best boss I've worked with. We're in good hands. What came out at the briefing?"

Christine filled him in on everything said at the briefing and asked him for a login to the HOLMES2 system, which he gave her.

The phone rang on her desk. "DS Woolfe." She listened and said, "Ok, I'll be over as soon as I've spoken to her father."

She called to Pete, "That was the mortuary. Sarah's body's fit for viewing. Let the boss know I'm heading over once I call her father."

She rang Mr Davies and arranged for him to meet her at the hospital.

Chapter 10

Christine met Frank Davies inside the main hospital entrance. She was looking for an elderly man in a beige raincoat, as he had told her. But she would have picked him out by his military straight back and the look of anguish on his face. He looked like if he relaxed his back muscles, he'd be a pile of skin and bones on the floor.

"Mr Davies, I'm Detective Sergeant Christine Woolfe. Thank you for agreeing to this."

"If not me, who else is there? I'm the only one left now."

"It's not too far to walk if that's ok? Sarah may not look as you knew her."

"It's alright, Sergeant, I've seen dead bodies before. I was in the army in Northern Ireland. More recently, my wife. You know, today I'm pleased my wife died. She couldn't have coped with Sarah being killed."

They walked in silence until they arrived at the viewing room door. Christine went in first and asked Mr Davies to sit while she checked the arrangements. Less than two minutes later, she returned.

"Mr Davies, I'll knock on the glass. When the curtain is pulled back, Sarah will have a sheet covering her, with her face visible. Are you ready?"

He nodded. Christine knocked on the viewing window, and the mortuary assistant pulled the curtain back.

As he looked into the viewing room at his daughter's body, Christine could see the toll being here was having on him. He blanched before her eyes, and she noticed his right hand shake. She went to knock on the window again, but he stopped her with a hand on her shoulder.

"Can I have a few minutes alone?"

"Of course."

Christine waited outside the door. An altered Frank Davies came out a couple of minutes later. The muscles in his face looked as if cut from stone, and his skin was an alabaster shade.

"Tell me you'll catch the bastard who did this to my Sarah. Promise me that."

Taking his hand in hers, Christine said, "I can promise you this. We will do everything we can to catch the person responsible for Sarah's death. Mr Davies—"

"Frank, please."

"Frank, let's grab a tea or coffee and talk for a while. Would that be ok?"

Christine brought two lattes to the table and sat opposite him.

"Frank, for the record, can you identify the woman you saw in the viewing room as your daughter, Sarah Jessica Davies?"

"I can. What did he do to her?"

In a soft voice, she said, "He killed her. That's all you need to know. We can talk another time if you still want to know. For now, can I ask when you saw Sarah last?"

Frank appeared lost in thought. He took a sip of his coffee before replying. "About three weeks ago. Sarah's mother died almost two years ago from ovarian cancer. We had a falling out over her mother's cancer treatment. Sarah wanted the chemo to continue, but I knew my wife had had enough. She wasn't giving up. She just knew it was her time. What Sarah didn't know was the cancer had spread to her liver and brain. There really was no hope."

"I'm so sorry. It must have been terrible for all of you."

"You think you're doing the right thing? But, actually, there is no right thing to do. It's all a pile of shit... Sorry."

"Don't apologise."

"Sarah didn't speak to me for almost six months after her mother's funeral. We've probably only seen each other five or six times in the last year. I missed her."

Christine could see tears rolling down his cheeks. She offered a tissue, which he took with a thin smile.

"Look at me now. Alone and having to plan another funeral. All those missed opportunities." He straightened in his seat. "Grab life with both hands, Sergeant. It ends too soon."

"Do you know where your ex-son-in-law lives or works?"

"James? No, I don't. He wouldn't hurt her. Physically. Their break-up hurt her emotionally, though."

"We can arrange for a family liaison officer to come to your house and explain how we handle the investigation, as well as help make arrangements."

"No, Sergeant. It's just me now. I need to do this myself. For Sarah, her mother, and for me."

Christine said, "Is it ok if I call you in a couple of days? I'll need to take an identification statement and some family background."

"Of course." Frank said, "Anytime." Although he didn't look too happy about it.

They sat in silence and drank their coffees.

Chapter 11

Christine arrived back at the incident room at half eleven. Kumar was at his desk reading the printouts Pritch had given him.

She wandered over and asked, "What have we got?"

Kumar looked up from the printouts. "Not sure. All three seem to be a carbon copy of our murder. Ear pierced and plumber's foam for the kill."

Christine said, "Let's get together around a HOLMES terminal and read each case file. Maybe there was an escalation in the MO from the first kill to Sarah's? Maybe the pathologist is right about the Picquerism because he uses the sharp pointed tool, but why the foam?"

"It's a very nasty way to go. Maybe he gets some sick pleasure from watching them struggle to clear their airway and breathe. He knows it's impossible, and so must they."

"I agree, but it also keeps them quiet. Most victims would call out when they were being attacked. Using the foam renders that a moot point... Sorry, didn't intend for it to sound the way it did."

Christine booted up the HOLMES terminal. She keyed in the case file number for Gillian Michaels.

She said, "OK, Gillian Michaels, Leeds, five years ago. As far as we know, our killer's first victim."

The file appeared on the screen. Christine clicked on the investigation timeline.

Kumar said, "Wow, they estimated they didn't discover her until a week and a half after her death."

"Apparently, the smell alerted the other residents in the flats," said Christine.

"I've been to a few of those in my uniform days. One time, you know those old council flats with open balconies? I came up the stairs, and I could smell it as soon as I turned onto the balcony. The old boy had fallen over his electric fire. It had basically cut him in half. He died alone and had been there for a month. Inside the flat, the air was black with flies."

Christine said, "Thanks for the image now seared into my brain. But Gillian wasn't alone. Her killer was with her, and what does Locard's principle tell us?"

"Every contact leaves a trace."

"Give that man a gold star. Yes, it does, and we have the advantage over the initial murder team. We have three other scenes to compare. Even if forensically we're screwed, we still have how he chose his victims. Did he stalk them? I think he did. I mentioned it to the boss at the scene yesterday." God, was it only yesterday? "Plumber's foam and an ice pick are hard to conceal in casual or formal clothes. And it's not the type of thing easily found in the average residence."

"So, what are you saying? He had access to the property?"

"It makes sense. Maybe our killer is a handyman, a plumber? It would explain the foam. Any form of tradesman, or maybe he breaks in. He leaves no sign, so maybe he's good at it."

"And how did he know all four women lived alone, with no husbands, boyfriends, or kids?"

"Exactly. I'm sure the forensics team did a good job in the other three cases, and we'll review their findings, but I'm more interested in what the neighbours and friends have to say. Someone must have seen something, maybe not on the day of the murder, but in the days or weeks leading up to it. Something insignificant, but once your neighbour or friend gets killed?"

"It was the same on the robbery squad. The criminals would case the joint watching for staff movements and timings of deliveries, follow certain staff home or to the Pub and get talking to them. All part of the plan and before anything really criminal took place. So no one paid any attention."

"OK, let's read everything and work back from Sarah's case. We can bring in Lucy and Pete as they're going through the house-to-house forms and statements. If Pete thinks the idea has legs, we can bring it to the DCI."

With his years of experience, Pete thought the plan was valid, and together, they went to the DCI, who agreed. Pete would write actions to send someone back to the street and ask about any activity before the murder that seemed out of the ordinary or stuck in the mind for some reason. No matter how seemingly trivial.

Christine gave a long sigh. "There's nothing here. We've reviewed the case files, statements, and house to house. Each case was a mirror of the others. Forensically shit and zero suspects."

Kumar stared wistfully into his empty coffee cup and said, "What connects the victims? The murders are too far apart in time for it to be a spree."

"I agree, five years, three years, and nine months. Let's not forget Leeds, Edinburgh, and Hove. Random or what?"

"I think if we find the connection, we'll find the killer. None of the four victims we know about have a similar appearance. Gillian was a redhead, Rachel was a natural blonde, Jessica had dyed her hair jet black, and Sarah was a dyed blonde. Sarah was slim, Gillian and Rachel were on the heavy side, and Jessica was wasting away. Coffee?"

Christine said, "Is the Pope Catholic?"

Kumar grinned and said, "How would I know?"

He returned with two steaming mugs.

Christine said, "Let's dig into their lives more tomorrow. Maybe they all attended the same school or university or worked for the same company. Either our killer is targeting these particular women based on what he sees at a point in time; for example, he travels for his job. Or it's a geographical history; he knew them from back in the day and targets them based on what he knew."

The DCI halted their musings by bringing the team together for the afternoon briefing.

Dave Wilde reported the house-to-house teams had found nothing useful besides everyone who knew Sarah said she was a lovely woman. Forensic had finished at the scene. The house remained cordoned off, uniforms provided security within the cordon, but they had reopened the street.

The DCI said, "OK, we need to keep a presence there for now, and it ties in with Pete and Christine's suggestion maybe our suspect stalked Sarah before the murder. Ray, Pete will write an action for you to re-canvas the street, asking particularly about any suspicious activity seen or heard before the night of the murder."

Ray said, "Right, boss. I'll pop down there after the briefing; folks should be getting home from work."

"I'll help out tonight, Ray," Kumar said. "Me and Christine were talking about it. The timing of the murders and the geographical locations. All very random unless he travels for work or knew them from someplace in the past?"

Christine said, "We need to figure out where they met. How would he know she lived alone? Had she told him? How does it connect, if it does at all, to the other three murders we're linking as of now?"

The DCI said, "OK, all good points to which we need answers. Pritch, what have you got?"

"Not a lot. Sarah Davies was very private with her social media. She was on Facebook, WhatsApp and Twitter. When I crack the password on her laptop and phone, we should be able to access her accounts properly. If I can't do so, I'll contact the media companies to get access. But it could take a while."

Christine said, "Speaking to Frank Davies this morning, I asked him about his ex-son-in-law, James Much. He didn't think he would be capable of physically hurting Sarah, but he needs to be spoken to."

The DCI said, "Pete's already got an action. Pete, allocate it to Dave, will you?"

Pete nodded in response and carried on making his notes.

"OK, that's it for today. Briefing at 8 am."

Ray and Kumar headed out.

Dave Wilde came over to Christine, "Fancy a quick drink? I asked Pete before the briefing, but he had to get home to his missus. I'm going to ask Lucy and the Boss. Pritch is always up for a pub visit."

Despite feeling drained from the activities over the last two days, she thought she should agree in the spirit of team bonding. Besides, she was still buzzing, and maybe a few drinks would help her destress.

She said, "Give me time to sort my desk. Ready in five?"

Dave said, "That's great. I'll ask Lucy and catch the boss before he heads out. I'll let you know when we're ready."

Christine sorted and tidied the paperwork on her desk. Putting it all in the drawer under lock and key. She turned off the Holmes terminal and turned to see the DCI and Lucy walking out the door.

Dave approached her and said, "The boss and Lucy have other commitments tonight, but Pritch and I are ready when you are."

"Just finished. Where're we going?"

Dave grinned. "Pub 'round the corner. It's nothing fancy, but they serve a good pint and they have white and red wine."

"So the sort of place they give a mix of both, if you dare to ask for a Rosé?"

"Nah, they'll ask you to leave. Too poncy," said Pritch, who sidled up, "We going then?"

Chapter 12

As Dave said, the Dragon's Head was nothing fancy. In fact, it looked as if they had only recently swept the sawdust off the floor. Even though the clientele must have been used to detectives coming into their boozer, the six men in the Pub turned to look at them when they came in. Conversations only started again when Dave and Pritch were recognised.

Christine felt an anomaly. The barmaid and her were the only females, and she wasn't at all sure about the barmaid.

"Let me get these guys, being new to the team."

Dave and Pritch said thanks in unison. Dave wanted a pint of Guinness and Pritch a pint of John Smith's. Christine opted for a bottle of cider as she spied an open bottle of red sitting in its own dust patch and no sign of a bottle of white anywhere. Dave stayed to help her with the drinks while Pritch found a table far enough from the other customers so anything they said wouldn't be overheard.

Dave carried the two pints to the table. Christine asked for a glass to go with her bottle of cider, and the look she got from the barmaid would have shrivelled a plum to a prune.

Christine approached the table and said, "The barmaid's customer service personified, isn't she?"

Pritch said, "You're new in here. Keep coming in, and she'll be openly hostile. Everything she knows about customer care she learnt from Basil in the old Fawlty Towers show."

Christine grinned, "I'll remember. Cheers."

They each took a drink. Pritch drank half of his pint in one swig.

Dave said, "So Sarge—"

"Christine, please."

"Christine," and in a lower voice, "What do you reckon on this case? Are we hunting a serial killer?"

"It certainly looks like it. I'm no expert, although I've worked on murder squads before as a DC a few years back. I guess what I'm saying with what Pritch dug up from Holmes, the MO fits to a tee. Either we have a copycat, but that's very unlikely as the murders are spread out around the Country and wouldn't have made a big splash at the time to attract a copycat. But, if it is the same person, the time between kills is strange. From what I've read on the subject, unless they're prevented by some reason such as prison, once they kill, they escalate and don't stop."

Pritch said, "Yeah, I thought that too. It's weird. It's almost like he was looking for certain people."

"Yes, that's a good point. Kumar and I were discussing it earlier."

Dave shook his head and said, "He's figured out a really nasty method of killing. Damn. And what's with the ice pick? I looked it up on Google. I thought having something shoved in your ear would do for you. But I saw something called transorbital lobotomy, where they went in through the eye and pierced the back of the eyeball into the brain. Sometimes Google is really not your friend."

Christine grimaced. "We need to get this guy." She took another drink of cider. "Anyway, let's save this for the morning briefing. How are you both liking MIT?"

Pritch was draining his pint, so Dave answered, "I definitely like it. It's different from the drug squad, with less surveillance and more detective work. But it's not like on the TV. There's a lot of tedious paperwork, statement-taking and interviews. But I've worked on some big cases since I've been here. Did you hear about the people smuggling ring we shut down a few months ago?"

Christine shook her head.

"Pritch was instrumental with his online tracking of suspects. We rounded up all the traffickers on this side of the channel, including some in France. Politics got in the way there, as you can imagine. They're all banged up now, no bail, and the case should come to trial later in the year."

Christine said, "And what about you, Pritch? Lucy told me you used to be a 'white-hat hacker' in your teens."

Pritch blushed a little. "Well, let's just say I did some of that and some other stuff. You have to understand the dark side to operate in the light. To answer your original question, I'm loving it. I get to help take some bad guys off the street or the web. Never thought I'd be able to use my computer skills in the way I am when I was patrolling the West End during my probation. Another round?"

Christine said, "OK, one more for me. It's been a long couple of days. I need my bed."

Pritch went to the bar, and Dave said, "So, undercover work, how was that?"

"It was alright." She grinned. "Actually, I loved it. It took me all over the Country and once to Italy for Europol. Best job I've had. I'd still be there if not for a media team arsehole. Not that I'm bitter or twisted."

"Yeah, we all googled you when we heard you were joining the team. By the sound of it, you've had a rough few months."

"Onwards and upwards, as they say, but I'm really pleased to be involved in this case. It's a good team, and the DCI didn't bite my head off when I called him out at dark o'clock."

"The team is excellent, not a dud amongst them, and the boss? We couldn't ask for better."

Pritch carried the drinks, the two pints and a bottle of cider, between his hands, using force and friction to hold the triangle together. Dave grabbed his pint and Christine's cider and succeeded in spilling a portion of Pritch's pint.

Dave mouthed, "Sorry," and handed Pritch a paper napkin from the table.

Pritch said, "Cheers all."

Dave and Pritch started to discuss a recent football game. A subject Christine knew almost nothing about. She said, "Someone invited me to an Arsenal home match. I only accepted when I was told I could watch the match from a private box and there would be alcohol and food."

Smiling, Dave said, "Yeah, I've seen those posh people in the fancy boxes. Out of my league, all that."

Christine smiled, "Mine too. Someone knew a friend of a friend who had a box which he wasn't using for the game. Actually, I enjoyed the experience. The only downside was having to watch over 90 minutes of football between courses."

Pritch shook his head, "Philistine!"

Christine drained her glass and interrupted Dave and Pritch's new discussion of a cricket match they had both seen at the Oval to tell them she was off. Both glanced at her and waved hands in farewell without a break in the conversation.

Chapter 13

Three days after discovering Sarah's body, the team had a clearer understanding of her movements on the day of her murder.

At the morning briefing, the DCI did his best to inject some life into the investigation. "OK, let's review what we have so far from her work and colleagues."

Lucy said, "Sarah had been at work as usual on the Wednesday and had attended a few meetings. Lunched with colleagues, during which there was some discussion of plans for the weekend."

Pete chipped in, "I've read a statement from one of her female work colleagues she was friendly with. Sarah said she had no plans for the evening except for a glass of wine, a microwave meal, and a box set on Netflix."

"Thanks, Pete," Lucy continued, "Sarah joined the company five years ago from a rival firm and worked her way up the chain of command until she received a promotion to HR director last year. Her package funded the house and her lifestyle."

The DCI said, "Do we know anything about the ex-husband?"

Ray said, "I spoke with a colleague who said Sarah had been married to a worthless piece of shit. Her words. For three and a half years. Again her words, he cheated on Sarah, and she kicked his arse out. They finalised the divorce two years ago."

"That's when she reverted to her maiden name," Lucy said.

"So, do we think he could be a suspect?" the DCI said.

Pete said, "Dave has an action to interview him. But given what we know about the other killings, I don't think he's a serious candidate."

"I agree. Let's get the interview done and crossed off the list."

After the briefing, Christine walked over to the allocator's desk and picked up her actions from Pete. One of these was to take a quick identification statement and gather some background information from Sarah's father. Whilst there, she mentioned to Pete, Kumar and Pritch's idea about digging further into the previous victims' lives. Pete thought it a good idea and said he'd write up some actions.

On returning to her desk, Christine told Kumar, "I spoke to Pete about your idea yesterday. Pritch had a similar thought in the pub last night. Pete is going to write up some actions. Have a ring around the previous case officers and ask if they delved into the victim's background in any depth. Maybe something will pop. I'm going out to get an ID statement from Sarah's father, but I'll be back later to give you a hand."

Kumar nodded and walked over to Pete's desk.

Christine returned to her desk and dialled Frank's number. He was home, and Christine told him she would be there with a colleague in about 20 minutes.

Christine saw Lucy marking out a statement in yellow highlighter pen and she didn't look too enthralled. She sidled up to her desk, "Fancy a trip out?"

Lucy looked at her like Christine had told her she'd won the lottery. "Absolutely, Sarge, I've been highlighting statements for two days ... I would love a trip out. I'll even drive. Where are we going?"

Christine said, "Bring some blank statement forms, and I'll meet you downstairs in the car park. I'll fill you in on the way."

Christine left the incident room, leaving Lucy to grab the pool car keys and the forms.

Christine needed a bit of fresh air. Recently, she savoured inhaling deep lungfuls of crisp fresh air, well, as crisp and fresh as any South London air could be. Whether because of her recent collapsed lung or some other reason. However, she thought of the anguish Sarah must have gone through in those last few minutes of life, knowing she would never take another breath.

Lucy interrupted her thoughts with a cheerful, "Got the Peugeot, the clean one," as she waved the keys in the air.

They both got in the car. Lucy said, "So where're we going, Sarge?"

"Lucy, I've told you when we're in the office or no public around, call me Christine. We're going to see Sarah's father. I met him at the mortuary the other day, but he was not fit to take a statement from then. He lives in Merton, between here and Wimbledon."

Christine showed Lucy the address in her notebook. "Oh, I know it. An ex of mine lived around the corner from there."

They both buckled up, and Lucy headed out of the building's secure car park and turned left.

As Lucy drove the car, Christine's thoughts revolved around Sarah's last moments. Suddenly, she realised where she was.

Nightmare thoughts came tumbling into her mind like a kaleidoscope on cocaine.

"Christ," Christine exclaimed, not entirely sure if she had said it out loud or not. But when Lucy said, "Sarge, everything alright?" with a concerned look, she knew she had.

In answer to Lucy's question, she said, "Yeah, I'm OK. My sister and me played on those swings when we were nine. Someone took her. She's dead."

Lucy glanced at Christine and said, "Oh my God, what a terrible thing to happen. It must have been awful."

Christine had turned her head towards the side window and didn't reply.

She stared out of the window at the receding swing park.

Fourteen was her age of rebellion. She started smoking with the 'wrong crowd' at school. Later, towards the end of a naff school disco, one of the 'wrong crowd' suggested they go out back for a crafty fag. Her first experience of cannabis. She found pleasure in the illegality, making the joint, and experiencing the buzz. All of it. But best of all, it made the nasty, sister-stealing world disappear for a while.

Everything came to a head explosively, about six months later. Her mum was ranting at her for not tidying her room, not putting her clothes away, not doing the washing, not being Samantha.

She was in Christine's room and picked up her school bag by one of the handles, and some contents fell out. A few exercise books, a pair of gym socks, an overdue library book and her stash. They both stared at the small plastic bag lying on the floor. Even though she was younger, fitter, shorter and therefore nearer to the ground, her mum beat her to it. Then she beat Christine.

She had never seen her mum so angry. "Ungrateful little cow! Bringing drugs into my house! Social services are still hovering, and now you want to bring the police to my door?" Those sentences punctuated with slaps, punches, and the occasional kick. To be fair, her slippered feet didn't hurt so much. But the resentment and disappointment she saw in her mum's eyes did the damage.

Lucy stopped the car alongside the curb outside a small detached house. "Christine, we're here?" she said softly.

Struggling to regain composure, Christine said, "OK, let's do this."

Christine unlatched the wooden gate, and Lucy followed her up the path to the front door. There was a brass knocker on the door, but no bell. Christine knocked. Sarah's father jerked the door open. He must have been waiting behind it. He looked like he hadn't slept since the last time Christine saw him at the mortuary. She reckoned Frank had stood a good six feet tall, but today, he appeared shrunken, as if collapsing in on himself. He wore the same clothes, and from the old people smell they gave off, they hadn't seen the inside of a washing machine in a while. Frank Davies was seventy-two years old and looked every hour of it.

He opened the door wider to allow them in and closed it with a bang once they had done so.

"Sorry, the door's stiff. It needs a hard shove. Come through to the lounge."

He sidled past them in the narrow hallway and opened the door on the left into a typical lounge from the 1980s. Beige, brown, and multiple shades of beige and brown. He offered them the brown sofa and took the brown armchair with beige piping.

Once they were settled, Christine said, "Mr Davies... Frank, we met before when you identified your daughter. I'm Detective Sergeant Christine Woolfe, and my colleague is Detective Constable Lucy Worthington. We need a statement formally identifying Sarah and some background information. Can we make you a hot drink before we start?"

Frank shook his head and said, "I'm all tea'd out, but thanks for asking. Would you like one?"

Christine and Lucy shook their heads. Lucy said, "Thank you, but we had one a little while ago."

Christine said, "My colleague Lucy will write your statement as I ask the questions. Frank, first, can you confirm you identified your daughter, Sarah Jessica Davies, to me at St George's Hospital on the 27th of this month?"

"Yes, I can."

"Can you describe your relationship with your daughter? You mentioned previously you had grown apart."

"No, I wouldn't put it quite like that. We disagreed over her mother's cancer treatment, and her death coming a few weeks after the disagreement led to us not speaking much after the funeral." He paused and took a breath. "Sarah was always a very forgiving young woman, and I could see she was coming around to my way of thinking. We had spoken on the phone and had met up for coffee a few times. She hasn't been back to the house since the funeral, though."

"What can you tell us about James Much, Sarah's ex-husband?"

Frank's mouth tightened, and he took a brief pause before confessing, "To be completely honest, I don't think they were ever a good match. Sarah was always interested in the finer things in life and was prepared to work for them. James liked the finer things, but thought the world owed him a living. He bounced from job to job, often sacked, and expected to live off Sarah. She had a great job as an HR manager at a soft drinks company. Promoted recently, too."

"Yes, we know. Was the divorce amicable?"

"It was from James' point of view. Sarah took out a loan to buy him out of the house, although she had made most of the mortgage payments during their marriage. He had cheated on her if you can believe it, and he got to walk away with cash in the bank. I saw him at the supermarket a few months ago; he apparently lives around here now, and I gave him a piece of my mind. I could tell he regretted cheating on Sarah, or at least not having access to Sarah's wage each month."

"Was he ever violent towards Sarah?"

"Not that I know of. Do you think he may have been involved in Sarah's death?"

Christine could tell Frank had been thinking about it since her conversation at the hospital.

Frank shook his head and said, "I would never have thought it of him. He stayed in this house while waiting for their house purchase to go through. Could I have been such a poor judge of character?"

"No, Frank. Although its early days, there's no evidence to suggest James had anything to do with this. But it's a routine question we have to ask. Can you think of anyone else who may have been in conflict or had a grudge against Sarah?"

Frank shook his head. "No, I can't. Sarah was a wonderful child and grew into a lovely young woman. A credit to her mother in every way."

Christine asked some more standard questions, and twenty minutes later, Lucy compiled the statement, Frank signed it, and they were done. Frank Davies appeared even more diminutive and was sagging into the armchair.

Christine said, "Frank, are you sure we can't arrange for anyone to stay or visit?"

Frank replied, "No, I'm alright. It's the shock of it all coming so close after losing her mum."

They bade him farewell at the door and walked back to their car. The front door slammed behind them. Christine thought the answer Frank had given 'a credit to her mother in every way' was strange. Why not both of us?

Chapter 14

Christine and Lucy entered the incident room carrying several bags of McDonald's burgers and fries. The team looked on enviously as they deposited the bags on a vacant desk.

Lucy said, "Well, tuck in, guys, Christine's treat. Kumar, there's plant-based burgers in there for you and me."

The team fell on the food like a pack of ravenous dogs. Lucy took a meal into the DCI, but he picked it up, wandered over to the desk, and stood around eating with everyone else.

Through a mouthful of burger, Kumar said to Christine, "I brought Pritch in on the action we spoke about before you left. He did his usual tech wizardry, searching databases and registers of births, etc. Well, we had a bit of a turn-up for the books. All the other victims were born in or around Wimbledon. What do you think of that?"

"I think you may have got us our first lead. Have you told the DCI?"

"Not yet. I wanted to tell you first. Not sure what it means, but we know Sarah was also local."

"OK, let's bring him up to speed now."

They both walked to the other end of the desk, where Pete was telling a war story from his uniform days to the DCI and Pritch.

Christine waited for the punchline, and when the laughter had died down, she said, "Sir, Kumar and I were talking yesterday, and Pritch made the point again last night. So, I had Pete write an action to dig deeper into the previous victims. Kumar, tell the DCI what you've found out."

"Well, we were thinking, why was there so much time between the murders and the wildly different geographical locations? We thought maybe either the killer was travelling around the Country and happened upon his victims, or maybe he was searching for them and had come across them in a location where they lived or worked. We thought maybe they all worked for the same company or went to the same pub, gym, or school."

The DCI said, "Interesting, what did you find out?"

"They were all born in or around Wimbledon, thirty-four or thirty-five years ago. Including Sarah."

"Fantastic work, Kumar. Pete, write up actions to discover everything we can about our victims. Where they went to school, etc. Anywhere they could have met their killer. Find out when they left the area, too."

"Christine, can I have a word?"

The DCI walked back into his office, and as Christine entered, he closed the door.

"That's excellent work, Christine. But what impressed me the most was you could have claimed the information for yourself as you're new to the team to curry favour with the boss. But you didn't.

You gave credit where it was due. I liked that. The way you handled the murder scene also impressed me. You're a team player. When this case is over, if you want me to, I will try to keep you on the team."

"Thank you, sir. I really appreciate it."

"Oh, and Christine, all of that lot out there call me boss. I'm OK with it, except in public."

"OK, thank you, Sir... Boss."

Mid-afternoon, the DCI ambled into the incident room to get an update from Pete before the evening briefing. He sorted through the completed and pending actions and gave instructions for the further actions he wanted allocated.

Pritch, in Christine's limited experience, usually sat in the corner of the incident room at a desk, quietly tapping away at his keyboard, always with a large cup of coffee within easy reach, as happy as a pig in shit. That was why everyone turned his way when he shouted, "Fucking hell, boss!"

He had been trawling the web, looking for Sarah's online footprint and any links following her murder.

The DCI looked over to where Pritch was sitting and said, "What have you got?"

"Boss, you have to see this. Our boy has announced himself."

They gathered around Pritch's screens. There was a banner headline that read 'I'm coming out.' When he took his computer off mute, the track of the same name by Diana Ross filled the room.

After a few seconds, Pritch muted the sound again, and they read what was under the headline.

Welcome one, welcome all. A heartfelt special welcome into the light to my loyal fans from the dark side. Those of you following my career so far will have noticed I have irrevocably deleted my posts from the so-called dark web, but fear not expect the same level of detail about the kills and my thoughts here in the real world.

The time has come for a wider recognition of my skills, and it wouldn't have happened if I had continued to hide my light under a bushel, as the good book says. I have kept the counter in the top left of the page, but I have reset it to one, Sarah Davies' death, so as not to give too much away to our fabulous boys and girls in blue.

Sarah was done. The high, the rush, it ended abruptly, like a summer breeze passing by. Lately, I've noticed the buzz didn't last like it used to. Back in the day, a session like that would keep me going for weeks, at least, but not now. Now, I come down almost as I leave them. I keep nothing you see, no little trinket, no lock of hair. Nothing to keep the high going. I need to be careful; I've read so many stories of other less careful practitioners tripping themselves up on forensics or being found with some incriminating keepsake linking them to their previous pleasures. It all makes perfect sense. Despite that, I put myself at risk each time I get payback.

They found Sarah the day after I left her. Some low-life burglar got the scare of his life and bolted straight into the waiting arms of the boys in blue who had been on his sorry tail. Careless, impulsive, stupid. Planning, that's what it takes. What is it the army says proper planning prevents piss poor performance? Too right. Still, ever onwards.

On that note, a heartfelt welcome and introduction to our disparate family to Steve and Christine, who recently joined our merry band of enthusiasts and connoisseurs.

Unfortunately, it's their job to try and stop the fun. What say we roll the dice, ride the rollercoaster and may the best man or woman win?

Keep checking back for future updates. Maybe I'll ring the changes next time to meet the needs of all the special interest groups.

This will be fun.

À bientôt

Christine saw there followed a detailed and graphic description of the actual murder, which matched their thoughts and the timeline they pieced together. A collection of photographs followed and displayed a freshly dead Sarah.

The DCI was the first to speak, "Pritch, get onto IT forensics and work with them to see if you can trace the IP address for this site. Get some of their 'moles' to delve into the dark web. We need to find those supposedly deleted pages. How high was the counter before? We need something. I'm going to see ACC crime, this will go viral. We need a strategy in place. Team briefing, three-line whip, here at 5 pm today." He strode out of the room.

Pritch said, "Fuck me sideways," and picked up his phone. The rest of the team left him to it, went to their computers, and brought up the page.

Chapter 15

Re-reading the announcement didn't make things any better. It told the world we had a serial killer on the loose who was confident enough to post their exploits for all to see.

Why is it so easy? This is a grand house with a private drive, secluded, decent locks, and even an alarm system. Waste of time, of course, if you bring death home with you. Still, you have to give it to her; she's keen, practically dragging me upstairs. And what stairs! They had a sweep, a sinuous curvature, which no doubt a writer would call snakelike or something equally mundane.

The bedroom is her sanctuary, sorry was, all subtle pinks and greys. Deep shag pile carpet, enormous bed; what our American cousins would call super king, with pillows and throws and a little stuffed dog of some kind. Not a real one, you understand; might have had a bit more respect for her if it was, no, some cutesy seen better days kids' toy, probably as old as her.

There's a dressing area off to one side with a sliding door. It's open just enough to show off the expensive cabinetry and hanging arrangement. I can see power suits for work, flowing cocktail dresses, racks of folded tee shirts and fluffy jumpers for those chilly autumn strolls.

"I'll be back in a minute." *And she's gone.*

She's in the ensuite, freshening up and likely slipping into something uncomfortable but very sexy. I have a little nose around. No pictures next to the bed, but a photo of a younger Sarah on the dressing table, darker hair, so not a natural blonde then. Open a few drawers. Hmm, nice underwear collection, all lace and silk. The stuff she uses for when she has the decorators in must be elsewhere. She's calling me — "What was that?"

"I said make yourself comfortable; the electric blanket's on, so we should be cosy."

I undress. She'll want to be furthest from the bedroom door; it's a female protection thing, so I'll slide my little pressies under the right-hand pillow. Wow, this is cosy, must consider one of these blankets for those cold, lonely nights. Great sheets, high thread count, I expect, classy.

The bathroom door opens, and I was wrong. Nothing, not a stitch. She's thirty-four, but she's flawless. The grass has been mown, so the difference in hair colour is not obvious. Her tits have had an expensive helping hand, and I doubt they looked any better fifteen years ago.

She pouts, "Will I do?"

She knows how hot she is. I smile and pat the bed next to me. Instead, she climbs onto the bed and straddles me. We kiss, long and deep. She breaks away, and I raise my head and latch onto one of her dark red nipples hanging within reach. I always go for the low-hanging fruit! She moans, and I take control, grabbing her shoulders and forcing a reversal. Now I'm on top — my rightful place. She's gazing at me with eyes saying, 'fuck my brains out'.

"Just lie there... Close your eyes and think of nothing..." I gently caress her arms, her legs from toes to inner thigh. She sighs. "Let it creep up on you. Don't think about it, don't anticipate it, don't even want it. Leave everything to me." Down I go.

"You have no idea how good that is," *she moans. It's rude to speak with your mouth full, so I think to myself — really, no idea?*

I flip her. Face into the pillows, arse pressing into my belly. As I nibble her neck, she lets out a gasp. I think the lady doth like it. I kneel up and take her bottom in my hands, spreading the cheeks and exposing her to me. More gasps.

I yank her up so she's at the right height for me. The dog in me, that is. I enter her.

"How does it feel?" In answer, she forces herself into my groin like she's trying to stick us together. "Slowly now, slowly, gently."

As we continue, our bodies glisten with perspiration, the rhythmic movements intensifying. I expect Sarah will be a vocal participant - they usually are, after all.

She isn't bad. Tight. Kegel's not a stranger here. She's on her way, her cheeks flush. A light film covers her entire body.

"I want to look into your eyes." I manipulate her onto her back. We've both done this before, although obviously not together. I stay inside her and lose little rhythm.

Quicker now. Suddenly, her legs are over my shoulders, and she's puffing like Thomas the Tank Engine. A loud, drawn-out "Oh God!" erupts out of her. Always with the Deity. I reach under the pillow. It's Christmas! Her eyes close.

They snap open as I shove my present into her left ear. I was right; she screams, confusion and betrayal on her face.

She stares into my eyes, trying to work out what's happening. I stare back, put the nozzle from the expanding foam can into her mouth, and press the trigger.

Sarah can't compute what's happening. Her mouth, nose and windpipe are filling with foam. Moisture makes it expand quicker and stick more. I'm looking into her soul, watching life flee.

I come like a train. The Flying Scotsman, not TtTE.

I come out of her and stand beside the bed, watching her. Sarah, like they all do, had tried to scrape the foam away to breathe without success.

Time to clean up. It's out with the bleach spray and wipes and everything, and I do mean everything gets a going over.

Afterwards, I stand at the foot of the bed, looking down at her. She was beautiful, and I gave her the fuck of her life.

As I leave, I pause. The electric blanket — switch it off or not? Not- she said how cosy it was, and she's getting cold.

Christine likely wasn't the only one in the incident room to have the thought, Christ, he's told the world everything except his name and address. We have nothing to hold back to weed out the weirdos who clammer to own up to murders.

They had tentatively linked 4 deaths via MO, and so far, none of the efforts of four police services had found a decent clue to the killer's identity. In fact, any clue, decent or otherwise. But what worried Christine most was how the killer knew about her. The DCI she could understand, he was the boss, but she didn't recall seeing her name anywhere.

Chapter 16

Another week had gone by, and to say they had progressed about as far as a centipede with 99 broken legs would be to exaggerate the team's achievements. Pritch and his cyber buddies had established our killer, true to his word, had erased any trace of his exploits on the dark web or anywhere else. Of course, they only had his word there was ever anything there in the first place or that Sarah Davies was anything other than a one-off murder. The other three cases linked could be a coincidence, but they didn't think so.

The DCI had set up another room with uniform and civilian staff to whittle out the people calling to tell them they knew the killer or often they were the killer. Some of the police stations in the area and some further afield had people claiming to be the killer presenting themselves at the front desk. Normally, incident room staff would do a PNC check on the criminal history and a quick interview to rule them out of the running. But this time, the killer had posted precisely what he had done, and the only thing they had was the probable use of an ice pick for the ear wound. But at this time, that was a guess.

Pritch had set up an alert on the 'I'm coming out' web page, so anything new added by the killer or any new comments by his followers would ping a message to Pritch. The page gained more viewers by the day, with over 1150 comments recorded and a million and a half views.

He had tried to trace the originating IP address of the page to get a location for our suspect, but as Pritch put it, "He's done a right good 'Thomas Cook' on this." He translated for the non-nerds and the slow-witted as he had been all over the world bouncing from IP to IP location before ending up at a computer in Shetland. The team got excited for about 10 seconds before he explained the computer in question was in the Lerwick Police Office.

The DCI arranged for discreet enquiries to be made. The computer and servers underwent a forensic check, along with those who had access to it. Still, they're not hopeful of any leads coming from it. The website vanished for 5 seconds before reappearing, sending Pritch off on his world travels again.

Of course, we also had to check out the people who had posted comments. Most thought the site was some kind of hoax. A few wanted to know when the film, which the site clearly promoted, would be released, but 270 posted comments making suggestions for the next kill or asking the killer to hurry and post some more pictures: maybe even a video. Of the suggestions for his next victim, two wanted a nun, five liked the idea of a black child, three were eager to see a MILF, and one wanted a double event with a husband killed after watching his wife slaughtered. The rest were various combinations of the same general themes. The world itself may not be sick, but it has to be said many of its inhabitants are a little unwell.

Pritch and his fellow cyber-moles spent a lot of time trying to trace the sicko commenters. Most turned out to be as adept as our suspect at hiding their identities and locations.

At the morning briefing, Pritch said, "I've opened an email from the FBI in Louisiana. It seems one poster on the 'I'm coming out' site was not as good as the others. Drum roll, please... The winner of the 'Wish I had paid more attention in criminal computer classes' award goes to Gerald James Bertram, white, aged 54, married with four children and a good job in St Francisville, Louisiana, USA. The FBI popped 'round to his place pretty sharpish, seeing as how he was one of the commenters who wanted a black child to die and how he was a math teacher at the local high school. It turned out that he was also absent from class on the day they taught 'how to hide extreme child porn on your computer'. Here's hoping for some prison stairs he can stumble down frequently."

"Thanks for that, Pritch," the DCI said, "and I can confirm, as we expected, the Shetland connection to this case is only through an IP address."

The media team at the Yard and the DCI took endless calls from journalists wanting information about the case or if they had any suspects or anything at all. The modern media's a voracious beast, never sated, clamouring for anything to fill the 24-hour feeding frenzy of TV and online news channels.

Chapter 17

The knock on her door came as Lucy put the finishing touches to her makeup. She took a breath, attempting to reduce her racing heart. She nodded at her reflection with a quick glance in the mirror and a smoothing of her little black dress. Well, that's as good as it gets.

She casually walked towards the front door to lower her heart rate. She saw Sebastian filling the doorway through the spyhole even though he was a few feet away from her door. With a jumper draped over his shoulders, he sported blue jeans and a dark blue shirt. He looked like a film star. He stood with an enormous bunch of flowers in one hand and a bottle of red wine in the other. She took a deep breath and opened the door. Sebastian smiled that smile of his, and her pulse quickened all over again.

Sebastian said, "I couldn't remember the number you gave me, so I pressed the first flat, and a nice lady told me you were upstairs and buzzed me in."

"Must have been Mrs Crenden, elderly with a grey bun?"

Sebastian nodded. "Yes, I saw her when she cracked open the door to her flat to be nosey."

Lucy laughed, "I expect so, but where would the police be without nosey neighbours?" She shook her head. "Where are my manners? Come in, come in."

Sebastian held the flowers towards her. "I got these flowers for you do you like lilies or some other type some people think they're morbid as I'm told they have them at funerals they're called Stargazers or so the florist said." He said this in one breath, which left him slightly red in the face.

"I'll put them in a vase, and yes, I love them."

Lucy led Sebastian down the hallway and into the living room.

"Oh, I forgot to mention, do you mind cats?"

"No, I'm a cat person. Not so keen on dogs or land sharks, as I call them. An Alsatian bit me when I was a kid."

"Oh no, I hope you weren't badly hurt. I got bitten by a Pekinese during a search a few years ago. Small but sharp little teeth."

"No, not badly hurt, just mental scaring," he smiled, "and I avoid dogs."

"Actually, it's only one cat, and you probably won't even see DeeJay, as he's wary of strangers, especially men. Take a seat."

Sebastian sat on the sofa and looked around the room. "It's a nice place you have."

"Thank you. Would you like a glass of wine?"

Sebastian stood up like a piston. "Sorry, I meant to give you this when I came in." Handing the bottle over. "Don't know why I didn't. Holding onto it like grim death for some reason. Do you like red or should I have bought white? Or rosé?"

Lucy laughed, "I like all three, but I have a red already open. Want some?"

He was nervous as her, which endeared him to her even more. "Please."

Lucy returned with two glasses of wine. She stopped in the doorway, staring at Sebastian sitting on the sofa. DeeJay was curled up on his lap, purring for all he was worth, and Sebastian stroked him under the chin.

"He has never done that before in his entire life. Last Christmas, when my dad stayed, DeeJay didn't appear until Boxing Day, and even then, he took one look at my dad and ran into my bedroom. He must sense you have a kind soul."

"Is that something you believe in?" Sebastian said, scooching to one side to allow Lucy room to sit down.

She handed him a glass and said, "I think it is. Not necessarily in a religious way, but I believe in good and evil and souls."

Sebastian took a sip of his wine and nodded his head in appreciation.

"I do, too, and Karma. Great believer in Karma."

"I see it all the time in my job. Not everyone gets what's coming to them. At least in this life. It can be infuriating sometimes, but I love my job all the same."

For a few seconds, Sebastian appeared lost in thought and put his wineglass on the coffee table. "I don't think I could do what you do. I'm not a violent person, and I'm not saying you are, but watching criminals benefiting from their crimes and basically getting away with things, sometimes violent things. Well, not sure if I could go to work each day."

"We get a win occasionally, but I know what you mean."

This conversation isn't going in the right direction, Lucy thought.

She took a sip of wine and said, "Didn't you say you lived in Thailand for a time a few years back?"

Sebastian nodded, "I did. Lived in Bangkok for a couple of years and moved to Pattaya. It's a fantastic country. The people are wonderful and friendly. I probably should have stayed there. But I had to come back."

Here goes nothing. Putting her glass down next to his, she took Sebastian's hand in hers and said, "I'm pleased you didn't stay." Lucy could feel her face getting hot. "Sorry, don't know where that came from."

Sebastian smiled that smile of his and kissed her on the lips. Lucy liked it. She liked it very much and kissed him back. DeeJay, sensing the lack of attention, slunk off towards the kitchen. The kiss became an embrace, and before they knew it, it involved touching, feeling, and removal of clothing. Sebastian kissed the top of her breasts as he struggled to find the correct way to undo her bra. She wrestled with his belt and tried to unfasten his jeans. He had a buttoned fly. Who has a buttoned fly on jeans? In the end, she pulled the front apart, and the buttons popped open. She reached down. Oh, my God! Partly because having removed her bra, Sebastian was cupping her breasts, kissing her nipples and gently biting each in turn, and partly because he was a big man in every sense. Sebastian stood and picked her up like a precious feather and carried her into the hallway, trailing bits of clothing in their wake.

"Where's the bedroom?" he asked.

Lucy pointed to a door, and he nudged the handle down with his knee and pushed the door open. He placed Lucy gently on the bed and removed his jeans entirely and his boxers. Somehow, in the same movement, he removed her knickers. Suddenly, she could feel warm breath on her pussy.

Sebastian said, "Is this OK with you?"

"Fuck yes."

She squirmed as his tongue moved around her lips, sometimes touching her clit, sending shivers of pleasure into her belly. Teasing her. He lifted her legs one at a time over his shoulders. Now fully exposed to him, she wanted him badly, but not just yet. There was sucking and licking and blowing and biting. She could feel her swollen pussy come alive with each movement his tongue made. Without warning, Sebastian took her whole pussy in his mouth, his tongue deep, and she came. How she came. Panting, sighing, screaming, crying with the sheer joy of it.

Lucy breathed, "Fuck me," as an exclamation, but he took it as permission.

Sebastian smiled that smile of his and flipped her on her belly. She was wet and swollen, and now she was full of Sebastian. He withdrew, and Lucy waited for the thrust. It came time and time again. He was panting; she was writhing beneath him, almost out of her mind. She had experienced nothing like this before. It was as if he knew what a woman wanted, and he gave it to her. She came again. She let out a moan and buried her face in the duvet. Sebastian's thrusting got more urgent until he, too, reached his climax.

He came out of her and laid on the bed. Turning towards him, she lay with her head on his chest. A few minutes passed before either could catch their breath enough to speak.

Sebastian raised his head and said, "Look at the door."

Lucy looked and saw DeeJay sitting, staring at them both with what Lucy knew was his not-impressed face. DeeJay turned and strutted away. Lucy laughed, Sebastian joining in.

"I've managed to piss off the cat," Sebastian said.

"You didn't piss me off, though, and that's what counts in this flat."

Chapter 18

Four weeks had passed since they had discovered Sarah Davies' body, and the centipede had broken its remaining leg. Nothing, zip, nada. Christine was pretty confident, although only based on MO, they had correctly linked the other victims they had identified to Sarah's killer. They interviewed friends and work colleagues, and re-interviewed the friends, family, and work colleagues of the previous victims. Apart from being born in the same area, there was no link discovered between the victims.

Christine didn't like to think about it, but they were waiting for another crime in the hope the killer would slip up this time.

There had been no further contact via the web, but the page was still gaining views, over 15 million now. How many of those were new or returnees to the site they didn't know? But Pritch couldn't take the site down, although, to be honest, it would likely be the only lead to a new murder.

Christine left a meeting with the DCI and Pete, during which the DCI had canvassed the thought of scaling the enquiry down. Not closing it, but maybe cutting the number of enquiry detectives by half. The Yard was crying out for people to work on other serious incident squads, and the boss had more people than jobs for them.

She looked over the incident board for the umpteenth time, hoping inspiration would seep into her brain. The DCI and Pete walked towards the lift to go to the pub for de-stressing.

Pete called, "Christine, you coming for a drink?"

"Not tonight, Pete. I'll finish up soon and head home."

"OK, see you tomorrow."

Staring at the board, Christine thought about the four women the son of a bitch had murdered. They would never see their family again or be seen by their families. Never have a family of their own. Grow old and reminisce about times gone by. Their lives ended before their allotted time, taken by some sadistic bastard for his sick pleasure. They would have no more history than they had now. The end chapter of their life book would read Murder Victim.

Christine grabbed her bag, switched off the lights, and headed for the stairs. Halfway down, something about old times and history swirled in her brain. Then the thought coalesced, and she ran back into the incident room and fired up her computer. She found a local history site and typed in the dates she wanted. Scrolling through the pages, she clicked on a link. She read the information, printed it off and jogged to the Dragon's Head.

She shouldn't have done that, as she gasped for breath outside the pub. Christine steadied herself and pushed open the door. The pub was packed. Mainly men, she noted, but a few old women dotted around the tables pointedly ignored by the men. The same barmaid was behind the bar, but she had help tonight from a young, skinny lad of about twenty. His face probably had clear, smooth skin, but it was difficult to see for the mounds of fit-to-burst red boils covered in an oily sheen. She shook her head to clear the image and looked around the bar to find Pete and the boss. She spotted them at a far table and squeezed through the crowd.

The DCI looked up as she approached, "Changed your mind?"

"No, boss. I was thinking about the memories and history the women would never have. I realised we've been digging into the past lives of the victims, trying to find where they could have met their killer. But what if they never did? Until he killed them."

Both the DCI and Pete raised their eyebrows, and their faces wore a look of bafflement.

Pete asked, "What do you mean? Are you saying it was random attacks?"

"No. Maybe they couldn't have met their killer because they weren't born. Look at this."

She handed the DCI the sheet she had printed. He and Pete read it, sat back, and looked at her.

The DCI said, "So you discovered a year or so before the four women were born, a rapist attacked women in the area around Wimbledon. You're saying maybe the link they have in common is this person raped their mothers?"

"I know it's a long shot, but we haven't found any other connection, and it might explain why all but Sarah have left the area. If they knew?"

Pete said, "Was the rapist ever caught? He'd likely be in his sixties by now."

"The article didn't say, and I don't have the first clue how to find out. Probably a job for Pritch."

The DCI said, "OK, keep this between us for now. First thing in the morning, I'll set Pritch on it. We can get it checked out fairly easily if it's verified."

Christine looked blank, "How?"

"They took blood samples from all the victims and stored them. A DNA test will prove or disprove your theory. It's quite a leap, but a potentially good one."

Pete asked, "Staying for a drink?"

Christine felt she had intruded on man chat and said, "No, I'm off home. See you in the morning."

The DCI said, "Good work, Christine. My old boss used to point to his head and say, 'Up here for thinking and down there for dancing whenever he had an idea'. Maybe you have your thinking head on tonight. Let's find out."

"Fingers crossed I do, boss. Bye, Pete."

Christine was in early but saw Pete, the DCI, and Pritch were already in the boss's office with the door closed. As she looked, the DCI waved for her to come in.

Pritch said, "Morning, Christine. The boss was telling me about your idea. I should've thought about it. But I'm glad someone did."

The DCI said, "Pritch assures us he can easily check if the rapist was caught. He should be able to get the information before the morning briefing. We then need to decide what we should do with it. I still think it's a long shot, but as you rightly say, we haven't anything else to connect them." He paused, then said, "Pete, what's your thinking?"

Pete said, "I'm inclined to run with it. Yesterday, we had a meeting to discuss reducing the team working on this. Today, we have a possible new lead."

"OK, I'll authorise the expenditure for the four DNA tests. I agree it's our best lead yet. OK, Pritch, carry on with what you do best. I'll arrange for the blood samples to be brought to the lab by courier and tested. It should be a few days before we have a result."

Christine said, "Thank you, boss."

"OK, briefing in 45 minutes when the rest of the team should be here. But let's keep this under our hat for now."

They all agreed and left his office.

The briefing was routine, and very little came out of it.

Pritch reported back to the boss, Pete and Christine. "As far as I can tell, they never caught the rapist. Of the three women who reported a rape to police, all three told the officers they thought the rapist was trying to get them pregnant. I spoke to a retired Collator, Ted Johnson, now we'd call him an intelligence officer. I tracked him down via an old sweat at Wimbledon nick. He was a young PC at the time and, by chance, was actually first on scene to one of the rapes. The story the woman told him said the actual offence took about a minute, but he kept her with her backside raised at an angle for over two hours. As far as he recalls, all three women were offered the new morning-after pill, and they all took it. None, as far as he could tell, were mothers of the victims."

The DCI said, "OK, let's park this line of enquiry until we have the DNA results. If we're not sure, we could cause a tsunami of grief for the families."

They all agreed.

Pritch had requested for the rape files to be sent over to the incident room. "It'll take a few days, maybe a week. In the meantime, I'll continue to dig."

The DCI said, "Thanks Pritch. I'll let you know when I have the DNA results."

Chapter 19

Two days later, the boss called Christine into his office.

"OK, looks like your shot in the dark paid off."

"Really?"

"All four victims have a familial DNA match on the male side. Basically, they all have the same father. Almost certainly the rapist. But we must remember when talking to the families any male of the right age, probably fifty-five and up, could be our man."

"When I spoke with Sarah's father at the hospital and told him I would be in touch for an identification statement and some family background, he was polite, but I got the impression he didn't relish the idea. Still, if he knew Sarah's history and his wife's, he probably wouldn't want it broadcast."

The DCI stood up, "Ok, let's tell the team. I want you to take Frank as you've met him. We need a DNA swab from him. What other family do we have still around for the other victims?"

"If I remember correctly, Gillian Michaels from Leeds, five years ago, still had a mum and grandfather living. Rachel Evans in Edinburgh had no living family they could find. Maybe we could get Pritch on it?" The DCI nodded. "And Jennifer Simkins has a mum."

They both walked out into the incident room where the team had gathered for the evening briefing.

"OK, ladies and gents," the DCI said, "gather 'round. We have a new line of enquiry. The other day, Christine was thinking about our victims and how they were all born in and around Wimbledon. She researched and came up with a mad idea for how they could connect to our killer. She found out a serial rapist was terrorising the area about thirty-five years ago. Her theory was they had never met their killer until they died because they hadn't been born. Now, as outlandish as it seems, it was correct. I've got the DNA results for all four victims. They all share their DNA with their father."

Murmurs of "Well done, Christine," and "Way to go, Sarge," from the team.

"Christine and Lucy, as they've already met Frank Davies, will interview him at his house and take a DNA swab. The other victims, we'll ask the local force to interview relatives and take sample DNA. If we can prove a familial match to a family member, we'll have at least identified the rapist. OK, get on with what you were doing."

Chapter 20

The following day, Christine grabbed Lucy, and they headed back to Frank Davies' house. Christine said, "I haven't called. I want to surprise him. Put him on the back foot. I don't think he's involved, but he should have told us."

"I can understand why he wouldn't," Lucy said.

"I do, too, but holding things back in a murder investigation makes our job so much harder. I'm not going to go in heavy-handed, though. Softly, softly, catchy monkey. If there is a monkey to catch."

They drove a few miles, with Lucy uncomfortably shifting in her seat.

Christine said, "You OK, Lucy? I can see you fidgeting."

Lucy said, "Do you mind if I ask a personal question?"

She chose not to let anyone in. She liked Lucy and wanted to know her better, so give something to get something, "Ask away."

"The other day, you mentioned something about your sister getting abducted. You've been through a lot. What with your sister and getting shot?"

Christine sighed. Should she tell Lucy? Very few people in the job or outside it knew her story, but she could see a bond forming between them. Lucy was nice people. She made her decision.

"My sister was why I became a police officer. I was nine. My sister, Samantha, and me went to those swings we passed the other day. I haven't been back there since. That's why I reacted the way I did. I was on the roundabout, doing some stupidness or other. Samantha was going towards the swings. Then I lost sight of her.

"I jumped off the roundabout, fell, grazed my knees and started running all over, dripping blood, calling out her name. A woman came up to me and calmed me down. I was going nuts, and she told her husband to call the police on his mobile. After about ten minutes, a patrol car turned up, and they took Samantha's description. But I never saw her again."

"Oh, my God. What did your parents do?"

"Dad wasn't in the picture. Mum went mad, almost literally. Took to the bottle and blamed me."

"But it wasn't your fault. It was the bastard who took her."

"We both probably knew that, but she blamed me. I was supposed to be the sensible one. We snuck out of the house. Mum didn't know we were going to the swings. I blame myself, too."

"I can't begin to imagine how you felt. How old was Samantha?"

"Same age as me. Twins."

"I'm so sorry. I can understand why you're so driven. Thank you for sharing. You OK to do this interview now? We could grab a coffee?"

"No, I'm OK. We can have a coffee after."

They drove in silence until Christine pulled up outside Frank's house. Christine knocked on the door. After a couple of minutes, Frank pulled the door open. They could tell the door had worsened since the last visit, as Frank had struggled to open the thing. Probably the damp weather. As he stood there gasping for breath, his eyebrows shot up when he recognised them and a smile came to his lips. "Is there news?"

Christine smiled, "Can we come in, Frank?"

Frank had pulled himself together, changed into fresh clothes, and the musty smell was gone from the house.

"Of course, of course. Go through to the lounge. You know the way."

They walked down the hallway, and Frank slammed the front door behind them.

They waited until Frank joined them before sitting on the sofa.

Once they were all seated and Lucy had taken out her notebook, Christine said, "Frank, something has come up in our enquiries into Sarah's death. I'm sorry, but there's no easy way for me to ask this... are you Sarah's biological father?"

Frank snapped his head up as the colour drained from his face. "So you've found out our secret. We didn't tell anyone, ever. Was it this new-fangled NDA thing?"

"DNA, yes. Can you tell us about it?"

"I need a drink. Would you like one?"

"No, we're fine."

"Well, I'm having one."

He got up and opened a small drop-down cabinet filled with glasses, a bottle of whiskey, and another of sherry. He reached for the whiskey, poured what must have been a quadruple into a whiskey glass, and sat back down.

Lucy and Christine looked at each other but made no comment.

"I met Sarah's mother at secondary school. We became friends, then boyfriend and girlfriend. She was in my year, but in a different class. Anyway, after secondary school, I went into the army and Janet, who had the brains, went off to university. And I'm sorry to say we lost touch." Frank took a large slurp of whiskey before continuing. "I met and married someone else, but it didn't work out. We realised in the end we didn't actually like each other. It was convenient, and that's no way to build a relationship. When I left the army, I moved back to Morden to be closer to family." He took another drink of whiskey. "Then, one day, I was coming out of Wimbledon tube station, and I saw Janet walking towards me. She was hurrying to get somewhere, but we spoke briefly and met in a local pub the next evening. The rest, as they say, is history."

"OK, did Janet have Sarah when you met?"

"No, after meeting a few times, we knew we wanted to be together. She told me one night what must have been the hardest thing she ever had to tell me and definitely the hardest thing for me to hear. About a month before I met her outside the tube station, someone had raped her in her own home.

Lucy said, "Did she report it to the police?"

"No, she was too ashamed. I tried to persuade her, but she was adamant. We found out a few weeks later she was pregnant. We had fallen back in love and agreed to get married and bring the child up as our own."

Christine said, "Not many men would have done that. At least not any I've met."

"I told it matter-of-factly, but there was much soul-searching on both of our parts. I never considered having children with my first wife. After the divorce, I put the thought out of my mind, as I never believed I could meet someone and love her enough to want children. But I loved Janet, and she needed me. I was there when Sarah was born and throughout her life." Frank stared into his near empty whiskey glass. "We always dreaded her getting ill and needing something medical which would give the truth to our lie, but she remained healthy. We never told her."

"Do you recall what Janet told you about the assault, Frank?" Christine asked.

"I remember. How could I forget? I was so furious with what she went through I was ready to kill. I'd trained in the army, so I knew I could do it, but she didn't know who it was and didn't even see his face."

"Go on, Frank."

"She said he wore a black knitted balaclava; the kind made infamous by the IRA. He had a big knife, which he used to persuade her to do what he wanted."

Both officers could see his arm gestures getting stiffer and his colour, which had returned, drain again.

Christine asked, "Did she tell you how he got into the house?"

Frank nodded. "She was walking home alone from a night out with friends and unlocked the front door when he grabbed her from behind and shoved her into the hallway. He took her straight upstairs. Janet said it surprised her he appeared to know where her bedroom was. He made her get undressed and raped her."

"Thank you, Frank. It must have been very difficult for you to hear all those years ago and we made you dredge it all up again. I hope it hasn't re-opened old wounds."

"Of course it has, but if I could deal with it then, I can deal with it now."

"Is there anything else you think we should know?"

"The hardest part for me to hear was he kept her on the bed, naked, for over two hours. Staring at her. Janet believed he wanted her to get pregnant. I thought he was a sick bastard and wanted to gloat at what he'd done. But Janet was right as usual."

Christine said, "Did you discuss terminating the pregnancy once you knew?"

Frank grimaced at the thought. "It almost split us up. I thought it was the best idea. I told her if she wanted children, we could have children. Janet was a practising Catholic and wouldn't hear of it. We didn't realise then, as my army friends would have said, I was a Jaffa. So, our own child wasn't on the cards. We only found out when we tried for a brother or sister for Sarah."

"Thank you for telling us your secret, as you described it. I'm sorry to ask this next question, too. We need to take a DNA sample from you. I have the kit with me. It's just a swab test."

Frank stiffened. "Do you think I raped my Janet?"

"Not at all. We have to carry out the test to cross the T's and dot the I's. For elimination purposes."

Frank nodded, and his face softened. "No, I can see that. Will it help to catch Sarah's murderer?"

"It may do. We're currently following a line of enquiry, and the more information we can obtain, the better chance we'll have."

"OK, what do you need me to do?"

Christine explained she needed him to rinse the whiskey out of his mouth with water a few times, and she would take a swab from inside his mouth. Frank agreed, and a few minutes later, Lucy and Christine were walking back to the car.

Lucy said, "Wow, what a story and a half."

"It certainly was. I hope it's true, and if it is, I feel sorry for him. To find schoolday love again after all that time, make a commitment like he did and lose both his wife and daughter within two years. Neither in a good way."

"What's a Jaffa?"

Christine smiled, "Jaffa oranges have very few pips. So it's seedless."

"And so... oh, I get it now. Another blow. They really must have had a strong relationship."

They got in the car, both looked back at the house and saw Frank staring a thousand-yard stare from a window as they drove away.

Chapter 21

After the evening briefing, Pritch was about to close his computer when an alert popped up on his screen. New content on the 'I'm coming out' page. The DCI had walked out to the lift to go home. He shouted to Christine to fetch the boss. She ran to the door but had to run down two flights of stairs as the lift doors had closed. She caught him as he was going through the security door.

She panted, "Boss, new content on the murder website."

In unison, they turned and crowded into the small lift to ascend to the incident room.

Pritch had the page up on his screen, and as they walked in, he said, "Boss, he's claiming another. With pictures."

They read over his shoulder.

"Welcome, welcome, welcome. Roll up to see all the fun of the fair. This ladies and gentlefolk is the late, fantastic Jasmine."

Below this headline was a picture of a young Asian, Black or mixed-heritage woman, naked, kneeling on the floor at the foot of her bed. Her torso rested on the bed, and her hands zip-tied out in front of her. Her face looked away from the camera, but they saw smeared yellow expanded foam as if she was trying to clear it from her mouth and nose using the sheets. There was a detailed account of the murder below the picture.

I fucking hate nightclubs! Discos, jazz clubs, music venues or live music pubs. Loud, incessant music, often with a mind-numbing beat. Men viewing their best of a bad lot via beer goggles. Yet, deep in their hearts, they know it's just a shag. Nothing more, nothing less. A chance to boast to the guys around the office coffee machine in the morning and move on to the next meaningless encounter. But, and here's the rub - there's no better stalking ground. Too crowded for anyone to clearly remember anyone else. Alcohol, maybe illicit substances, hot, sweaty bodies, most looking for a hookup, some looking for the one. Like flies buzzing 'round shit. With me as the giant turd.

Problem is I'm picky. I know what I like, and I know what I want. And as I sip my drink and glance up from my table, I see Jasmine.

Jasmine and I have met before, although she won't remember when. You could say we go back a long ways. Jasmine's pixie cut dark hair shines almost black as the glitter ball lights bounce off it as she sways her head in time. She has a great body and good genes. Black catsuit, cut, so it emphasises her fantastic, gym-toned arse. Not too much in the rack area, just a gentle pubescent swelling. She wears a silver cross high on her throat. Making a statement?

I see Jasmine, like me, is also picky. I've counted three guys she's turned away in the last 45 minutes. If I was a person who enjoyed betting, I would go up to those guys and bet I could leave the club with Jasmine. Stereotypically, they have all decided Jasmine is a lesbian. How could she not be after turning down the elite of Dalston men?

They would bite my hand off to take the wager. Thing is, I know she's not. In fact, I know a lot about Jasmine.

I know she works as a childminder at a local kids' nursery, in her head, practising for motherhood. She won't make the same mistakes her own mother made, like committing suicide. Her foster mother treated her well and brought her up to be a good, kind, God-fearing young woman. Shame. It's the other one she needs to be afraid of.

Tired or fed up with dancing, Jasmine wanders up to the bar, coincidentally (not really), as do I. I get there just before her but let her order first from the barman who I caught the eye of. Thanks, she says. Not a problem, I say; it's my last one before I head off. Steve, I say. She looks me over before saying, Jasmine. We talk, we find we have a lot in common. I tell her I'm a supply teacher at the local infant school. First placement after training college. She says she works with babies at a nursery. Wow, we both like children. What are the odds?

We talk. My last drink turns into three. We respectfully/accidentally touch each other in non-sexual ways. Neither demurs. I put my hand on her shoulder as I guide her to a table. She touches my knee to emphasise a point. Jasmine is a little unsteady, but still thinks she's in control. In fact, she hasn't been since she left her house earlier this evening.

I say I should go; little ones won't teach themselves when school opens tomorrow. She laughs. Jasmine, I say. Can I get you a cab? No, she says, I only live a couple of streets away from here. Well, I say, in payment for your company, let me escort you safely home. And so, we leave the club. I will take her home safely. I didn't promise she would be safe once we got there.

I took her to her door. I kissed her goodnight, and as I turned to walk away, she called me back. Hey, she said, one last drink? We never had the drink, but I had my fill of Jasmine. We kissed, we fondled, I nibbled. She loved it. We reached the bedroom; we got naked. I felt pumped. I cupped her breasts and gently bit the nipples. Then pushing her hands above her head went down on her. I blew and teased and nibbled and stuck in my tongue. She writhed and panted and came and came again. I turned her over and pulled her to the end of the bed. I had to take a picture of her phenomenal arse. Firm, exquisitely shaped, and so ready for penetration.

On the screen was a picture of the victim's bottom between the text.

As I rode her, I held her wrists above her head, and she started to struggle. In one smooth motion, I put on the zip tie I had at the foot of the bed already looped and stuffed some of the sheet into her mouth. I think she liked it. I rode her doggy style as she writhed beneath me. Also at the foot of the bed was my little friend, say hello to my little friend Jasmine. I shoved the blade into her ear. She stiffened. I felt her muscles contract around me, then relax. Then the application of the 'shut the fuck up foam'. After a while, I withdrew both the blade and myself. Sorry to say, Christine, bleach spray and wipes again.

I gave her the fuck of her life and the last one she'll ever have.
Until next time!

They studied the pictures, looking for clues to where Jasmine's body might be located or who she was. Was Jasmine even her name? While Pritch went off on his virtual holidays once again, the DCI authorised an urgent internal bulletin to be sent throughout the

Met and surrounding police services, Kent, Surrey, Essex, etc. He wanted to be notified about the murder asap, in case there was any forensic, CCTV or hopefully a signed confession bearing the home address of the killer.

After a few hours, Pritch's on-line travels led him to a computer in the CEO's office of a well-known national high-street bank. Obviously, we checked him out, but we knew our suspect was making us do 'busy work', chasing our tails.

Chapter 22

A day later, the DCI and the team were heading to an address in Dalston, East London. The DCI got the call at 1.23 pm on Friday from Stoke Newington CID. Apparently, the nursery manager where Jasmine worked had been concerned when she didn't arrive for work. She hadn't answered her phone when the manager called, and one of her colleagues had popped 'round during her lunch break and found the front door closed. However, when she knocked, it opened. She called out Jasmine's name but got scared and called the police. The DCI had received the call swiftly after the uniforms had arrived on scene, not because the officers had read the bulletin but because one officer had seen the 'I'm coming out' website.

The DCI decided to split the exhibit officer's duties. This was a different murder, and he wanted nothing to compromise any conviction down the line. So Ray Finn was the XO for Jasmine's case. Christine managed the phones, dealt with anything that came in during the team's absence, and kept Pete and Pritch company.

The DCI called her about three hours after the team arrived at Jasmine's address. As usual, he was direct.

"Christine, we may have a break. I need you to arrange for a traffic biker to attend the scene and pick up a package for the forensic lab. There was the usual bleach smell when we entered her bedroom, but the scenes of crime techs have found what they believe to be semen in her anus. The lab has agreed to do a rush job on the sample if we can get it there before six."

Christine said, "Fantastic, I'm on it."

As she dialled the control room number, she mused how far down she had stepped into the gutter. How could she be saying fantastic when a young woman had been anally raped and murdered? She told herself normal feelings would resume once they caught the bastard. Her emotional wall would protect her from the crap of the job. She would deal with it later.

The team returned to the incident room by 8 pm. Scenes of crime were still processing the scene, but the DCI wanted everyone to know where they were at with the investigation. Once everyone had their beverage of choice, he stood and addressed the team. "Local uniform alerted us to the latest crime scene. They had viewed our suspect's website and recognised the murder scene from the pictures displayed. We got lucky. The victim's name is Jasmine Cooper, a nursery nurse. Some of you also know we found semen inside the victim. We have sent this to the lab and expect something concrete by the morning or the next day. Tomorrow, there will be actions for most of you to dig into Jasmine's life. That's it from me. Questions?"

Pritch raised his hand. "The website has over 25 million hits and rising. We've been fielding calls from the media team clamouring for something to tell the press."

"Good call, Pritch. The Commissioner had one of his deputies call me earlier. I've called a press conference for eleven tomorrow morning. I've got to attend morning prayers at the yard at nine, so I'm hoping we get a DNA hit on the semen first thing. Then, at least, I might have something positive to say."

The DCI, looking visibly tired but still managing a weary smile, took a seat and addressed the group, "OK, ladies and gents, thanks for the excellent work you've done today. Head off home now. Back here at 8.30, please."

The team quickly headed off home.

Christine hung back.

"Boss," she said, approaching his office, "Can I have a quick word?"

"Of course, Christine, take the weight off. What is it?"

"Well, not wishing to be a 'Debbie Downer', but it's a real stroke of luck him leaving the semen, don't you think? When you called, I was excited, but I started thinking about it afterwards. At least four murders we can reasonably put to him with no forensic trace. Then he forgets he anally raped her without a condom this time? I also thought he was almost pointing us to the semen in his description of Jasmine."

"I didn't want to voice it to the team just yet, but the same thought had occurred to me." Putting some papers in his briefcase, he said, "We might be lucky, but the way this guy has handled things so far, I think a softly, softly approach will be the way to go if we get a DNA match. There's nothing we can do until the results come in, so let's get some rest. Tomorrow could be a busy one."

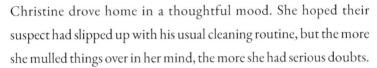

Christine drove home in a thoughtful mood. She hoped their suspect had slipped up with his usual cleaning routine, but the more she mulled things over in her mind, the more she had serious doubts.

The Gods, who look after hungry and knackered police officers, were smiling. Her parking space was empty. She swung around and reversed in so she could make a quick getaway and trudged up the two flights to her flat.

She threw her coat on the bed and went to investigate the fridge. Eggs, bacon, bread and a tin of baked beans in the cupboard. So, a second breakfast it is.

After a hearty breakfast and a glass of Sauvignon Blanc, Christine prepared for bed. But sleep eluded her. The case played on her mind, especially the killer's mention of her name. Why was she involved? How did he know her name? They echoed in her mind, intensifying the questions.

She drifted off to sleep while her brain was still running through those thoughts.

Chapter 23

Christine's mobile woke her at 2.25 am. Not the alarm she had set, but the ringtone.

She groped for the mobile, knocked a tumbler of water onto the floor, and accepted the call. "Christine, sorry to wake you," the DCI said before she could say hello. "We have a DNA match. I need you to mobilise the team to be in the office by 4.30 am while I make excuses for not attending morning prayers."

Rapidly blinking sleep out of her eyes, she asked, "Who's the match?"

"I'm sending the details to your phone, but it's a guy arrested for drunkenness when he was 22. We need a full background and arrest plan, but remember what we discussed last night. I don't think he has come to our notice since."

"OK, boss, I'll see you in the office."

The DCI hung up. She headed for the shower.

Christine arrived at the incident room 45 minutes later. Pritch was already there, as well as Pete, Dave and Ray. Over the next 30 minutes, Lucy and Kumar arrived and grabbed coffees to kick-start their day. She said nothing, as she wanted the boss to put his take on it. Besides, she was busy sorting out the arrest and the SOCO teams.

Their suspect was Simon Harry Jessop, born 6 June. He was white and 5'10. Back when he was twenty-two, he was 12 stone. He was born in Wimbledon but now lives in Battersea. His mother had died a few years ago, and father not in the picture. As Christine read the details, a worm started wriggling in her stomach. He was born to a single mother in Wimbledon thirty-five years ago. He was more or less the same age as the female victims.

The DCI walked into the incident room and beckoned Christine to follow him into his office.

As she followed him, she asked, "How did your not attending morning prayers go down?"

He looked over his shoulder and said, "About as well as expected. The DNA match helped, but they still want this solved the day before yesterday. Also," he added, "I intend to announce at the press conference we have arrested a suspect. I'll not name him, but if we suspect Jessop is not our man, it will keep the ruse going for a while for the actual killer."

Christine remained in the incident room, coordinating things. Ultimately, the raid on Simon Jessop's residence was a bit of a damp squib. The boss went to the front door with Dave Wilde while another couple of officers went around back to prevent Jessop decamping over the garden fence. Dave was an excellent wingman to have, as he was one belt away from a black in judo. The rest of the search and forensic teams were on standby in their cars and vans further up the road. Jessop opened the door after about 30 seconds, and the DCI introduced himself. After ascertaining Jessop lived alone and there was no one else in the house, the boss briefly explained why he was there and arrested him. Dave cuffed and transported him back to the station.

The forensic team entered the house and expected to spend most of the day there. After the team was done with each room, the search team would take over, looking for any evidence to prove or disprove Jessop was our guy.

While Christine fielded media interest with Pete in the incident room, the DCI attended his press conference. The press was out in full force, with TV crews from all the main channels and national and local newspaper reporters. Several independent Internet news reporters had signed in. Pete, Pritch and Christine watched it live on BBC News.

There was a buzz of anticipation as the DCI stood at the front of the room.

He raised his hands for quiet. "As you will know, my team has been searching for the suspect who killed Sarah Davies in Wimbledon. The suspect may also be the person who has posted details of the murder on the 'I'm coming out' website, which I'm sure you've all seen.

"You will also have seen a new post on the site claiming to have killed a young woman called Jasmine. We have now found and identified this woman. We are withholding her identity until any next of kin have been informed. As a result of our enquiries, we arrested a suspect this morning. He is being held at an undisclosed location and will be interviewed regarding the young woman's death. I will take a few questions, but you understand I am limited in what I can say at this time, and I need to get on with the investigation."

Almost every hand in the room shot up, and those online showed they had questions.

The DCI pointed to a local reporter.

"Jonathan Pointer, BBC London. Are you linking the two murders now, and if so, why?"

"We are not ruling it out at this time because there are similarities in the method of how both women were killed. Next, the lady with the red scarf."

"Jessica Small, Guardian crime reporter. You have released little information to the media, even after the 'I'm coming out' website got millions of hits. What is being done to protect women in London? Are you content for the killer to have the only voice and control the narrative?"

"We do not know if the same person committed the two murders or if they're linked. The identity of the person behind the website, whether the perpetrator or an accomplice, remains unknown. The murders are in two separate areas of London, and at this time, only the website and maybe the method link them. We urge everyone to be extra vigilant, especially women. When we learn anything else the public should know to keep them safe, we'll let them know. I'm sorry, but I must go. When we have any further information, we will call another media conference."

There was a cackle of questions yelled after him, but the DCI ignored them and strode out of the door.

Chapter 24

The DCI returned 20 minutes later and asked Dave Wilde to join him in his office.

"Dave, I want you to ask the awkward questions in the interview. I want to be his friend. You're more his age, so he'll think he can relate to you. It'll keep him off balance."

"OK, boss, will do. Any awkward questions in particular?"

"All the sex stuff, and don't ask it nicely."

Standing up, the DCI said, "OK, let's do this. Pete told me when I got back he has a brief here already."

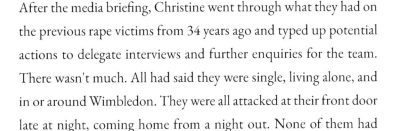

After the media briefing, Christine went through what they had on the previous rape victims from 34 years ago and typed up potential actions to delegate interviews and further enquiries for the team. There wasn't much. All had said they were single, living alone, and in or around Wimbledon. They were all attacked at their front door late at night, coming home from a night out. None of them had boyfriends at the time. This pointed to the rapist spending time on each victim. It wasn't random, in the sense of spur of the moment.

He must have researched and followed each woman for some time to learn their habits. The problem was all the known victims had opted for the no-baby option, so none of our victims resulted from the rapes they knew about, except Sarah.

Simon Jessop was already in the interview room, seated on a chair bolted to the floor in front of a desk. Sat next to him was the duty solicitor, who opened his briefcase and took out a legal notepad and a pen as the DCI and Dave Wilde entered.

The DCI nodded to Jessop, and he and Dave sat across the table. Dave switched on the audio and video recording.

"Mr Jessop, as you know, I am Detective Chief Inspector Stephen Balcombe, and my colleague is..."

"Detective Constable David Wilde."

The DCI said, "Say your name for the recording?"

"Simon Harry Jessop."

"And your legal representative?"

"Robert Southgate, from Paterson's Solicitors."

"I must caution you again. You do not have to say anything. But it may harm your defence if you do not mention when questioned something which you later rely on in court. Anything you do say may be given in evidence."

In response to the caution, Jessop said, "Mr Southgate has advised me to say no comment to all the questions you may ask..."

Dave's mouth went tight, and he slowly shook his head.

"But I have decided to answer your questions as I haven't done anything wrong. I want to clear up whatever this is and go home."

That turn of events clearly shocked Robert Southgate who said, "Simon, I strongly advise you to make no comment until we have a better idea of the charges and evidence against you."

Jessop shook his head and said, "I just want to get this over with. This is a nightmare."

"Do you know why I arrested you?" the DCI asked.

"You told me it was for the murder of someone called Jasmine? I don't know anyone called Jasmine. When did the murder take place? I was at a conference most of the week in Weston-Super-Mare."

"OK, we'll get into all that. The young woman's name was Jasmine Cooper. She lived in Dalston, East London."

Jessop said, "No, I really can't recall ever meeting anyone with that name."

Dave placed a headshot of Jasmine on the desk. "Please look at this picture?"

Jessop leaned forward, studying the picture. After about ten seconds, he leant back, shaking his head. "No, I don't think I have ever seen her."

The DCI said, "You don't think you've seen her, or you haven't seen her?"

"Sorry, just a figure of speech. No, I haven't seen her before."

"You said before at the house you had just got back from a few days of training for your job. What do you do?"

"I work in sales for a Mercedes dealership in Central London. We had a training conference Wednesday through to Friday on the MBUX system."

"MBUX?"

"Oh, it's the updated version of the infotainment system. You can talk to it to navigate to your destination or control certain aspects of the car—"

Dave interrupted. "Do you go clubbing much?"

Dave saw the question surprised Jessop, as it appeared he'd lapsed into his sales pitch.

"Sometimes, but I don't enjoy it. I think it's the worst place to meet anyone, if that's what you go for."

The DCI said, "Is that what you go clubbing for? To meet women?"

"No, I generally just tag along with a couple of the guys from work. Have a few drinks and then leave them to it."

"When was the last time you had sex?" Dave asked.

"What?"

"It's a simple question. When was the last time you had sex?"

"Actually, if you had asked me before last week, I would have said about six or seven months ago. But I think I had sex on Wednesday night."

The DCI frowned and said, "You think? Is that another figure of speech?"

"No, I'm just not sure."

"Explain?"

"After the training finished late Wednesday afternoon, our team went to the hotel restaurant for dinner and then to the bar. The guys can get a bit rowdy, so I slipped away and found a wine bar down the street. It was much quieter."

"Go on."

"Well, I was two glasses in when I noticed this stunning woman with red hair who came in and sat on a stool next to me at the bar. She was a looker."

It appeared Jessop was lost in the moment.

Dave said, "Go on."

"She wore a short green dress and had forever legs. I knew I was 'punching', but I had a bit of Dutch courage in me, so I asked her if I could buy her a drink. She looked me over and nodded. She had a glass of Chablis, and I had another Sauvignon. We talked, don't ask me what about because I can't remember, and then moved to a small booth.

"She insisted on buying the next round and went to the bar to get them. I'm not much of a drinker; now four glasses of wine to her two. I remember, sort of, walking back to her hotel with … Julie? Maybe. I know we went to her room because that's where I woke up in the early hours. Julie was still asleep, and I felt weird, so I left. When I got back to my hotel, I fell asleep again. I was late to the training session and felt really muzzy-headed all morning."

"Hangover?" the DCI asked.

Jessop nodded and replied, "Maybe, but the mother of all hangovers."

The DCI paused for a moment and said, "So what made you think you had sex with this Julie?"

"I don't exactly remember, although I've tried. There was stickiness on my... cock. You know." Looking around the other three men. "The last of the spunk that dribbles out."

"But you can't actually remember having sex with her?"

Jessop shook his head. "I really wish I could. I was a lucky man if the body matched the legs and face."

Dave said, "So, how do you explain your semen in Jasmine's anus?"

"What? I've never..." Jessop turned to his lawyer and said, "What are they talking about? I don't know the girl and I've certainly never had sex with her. And I've never done it that way."

The DCI said, "DNA. Do you know what that is?"

Now visibly shell-shocked, Jessop appeared close to tears and said, "Yes, I do."

"Well, the scenes of crime officers took a sample of the semen and transported it to the forensic science laboratory, and they compared the DNA sample to yours, and it matched."

Jessop immediately stood up. "I haven't given a DNA sample. How can they match what they don't have?"

Robert Southgate reached up and touched his shoulder. "Simon, sit down. Let the officers explain."

Jessop sank back into his chair, tears welling up in his eyes.

"Simon," the DCI asked, "do you recall being arrested for drunkenness a few years ago?"

"I do, but what's that... oh, the swab they took. Is it still on file?"

"Part of the National DNA database."

Without pause, Dave read out Jasmin Cooper's home address. "Have you ever been there?"

"No. I don't even know where that is. Dalston is not somewhere I usually go."

"So if the forensic team finds evidence of you being there, fingerprints, trace evidence or door-to-door enquiries, finds a nosey neighbour who saw you. How will you explain that?"

Before Jessop could answer, his solicitor put a hand on his arm. "I would strongly advise you not to answer. The officer is fishing."

The DCI said, "What was the name of the hotel you stayed in at Weston-Super-Mare?"

Jessop told them.

"Will your company corroborate your attendance at the training sessions and stay at the hotel?"

Jessop looked shocked, and the tears came again. "They will, but do you have to? I paid for the hotel myself and will claim it back on expenses. I like my job; no one wants to employ a car salesman accused of rape and murder."

"We didn't accuse you of raping Jasmine."

"Really, REALLY. Someone murdered her, and you claim my semen was found in her anus. Sorry, I just put two and two together and made four."

Jessop looked around the room wildly, hyperventilating. Standing up, he said, "I need to get out of here."

He moved to the door and tried the handle, which didn't open. He banged his fist on the door.

The DCI said, "Simon, calm down. I think this is a good time to take a break. We'll get you a hot drink and revisit this later. Dave, can you escort Simon back to his cell and give him a drink?"

Dave stood as his boss pressed the button to release the door. As Dave led Jessop out of the interview room, his solicitor said, "Simon, I'll come and see you in a little while."

The DCI escorted the solicitor to the reception area. He said, "We'll probably interview him again tomorrow morning. But you're welcome to take further instructions from him. But probably best to let him calm down and have something to eat and drink first."

Robert Southgate nodded and headed out of the station.

Chapter 25

Christine looked up as the DCI and Dave walked into the incident room. Neither looked overjoyed at how the interview had gone. The DCI beckoned Pete and Christine into his office and shut the door.

"We'll have everything he said to us checked out, but my gut says he didn't kill Jasmine. During the interview, he described a classic case of being 'roofied'. He describes a gorgeous woman coming on to him, and at one point, she bought them drinks. If Rohypnol or something similar was used, it may not show up in his blood after this time. But we'll take a sample. Pete, can you arrange that?"

Christine said, "Sounds like a setup boss, a professional maybe?"

"You could be right. Jessop claimed he woke with a banging head the next morning in his hotel room."

"Damn. That means we're back to square one."

"I know. Look, I need someone to go to Weston-Super-Mare and check everything out. Ray is the XO on this one, so I'd like you to go. Take Lucy with you. Both of you watch the interview before you go. Alright?"

"Of course, boss. I'll ring Ray and tell him, and I'll also let Lucy know. She's outside now, so we can watch the interview and then get going."

Christine hurried over to Lucy, who was talking to Pritch, "The boss wants us to go to Weston-Super-Mare to check out Jessop's alibi. That OK with you?"

"Of course. Are we leaving now?"

"He said we should watch the interview first. Don't think it went too well."

Pritch said, "I'm not surprised. Semen a red herring?"

Christine said, "I thought so last night, but the boss didn't say. Just said to watch the interview and check out his alibi."

As they moved to Christine's desk, Pritch called, "Bring me a stick of rock, will ya?"

Christine and Lucy watched the Jessop interview, and Christine thought the DCI's gut feeling was correct. By the time they had finished, Ray was back, and after briefing him on the exhibits on Sarah's case, Christine and Lucy picked up the keys to the Peugeot again and set off to Lucy's home.

As they arrived at Lucy's flat, Christine noted the block was much better laid out than hers. Shrubs and small trees everywhere you looked and gaps where she guessed bulbs would grow in the spring. It would be a riot of colour. A proper intercom system for the entrance and garages. She thought the ground rent must be enormous.

"Nice looking flats, Lucy."

"Thanks. My dad was on the building team and got me a discount. Come up, I'll make coffee while I throw a few things into a case."

As she followed Lucy into the block and up to the first floor, 'on the building team' most likely didn't mean a brickie or plasterer. As Lucy unlocked the door, she noted Lucy had two Banham locks on her front door. She had been thinking of getting those for her flat, but like everything else, she hadn't done it yet.

Lucy said, "Go through to the living room, pointing to a room off to the right, I won't be long."

Christine could see a separate kitchen at the end of the hall. Nice, she thought, but not decorated in her own unique minimalist style. Lucy had clearly desired and acquired most of the Laura Ashley catalogue. She saw a large bookcase in the living room with a few photographs in frames and masses of paperback books. Left alone in someone's personal space, she loved nothing more than perusing the bookshelves. You could tell a lot about the person from the books they read. In Lucy's case, lots of Chick Lit romance and a few Mills and Boon. Plus, a copy of the latest Blackstone's. So Lucy had ambition to move up the ranks.

Christine went to sit on the sofa when she heard a loud screech. A large tabby cat scooted out of her way and was now glaring at her with indignant eyes.

Lucy was instantly at the door. "Sorry, should have warned you about the cat. You OK with cats?"

"Yes, I like them. They don't like being sat on, do they?"

"DeeJay, DeeJay, where'd you go?"

A very disgruntled DeeJay approached Lucy from behind the sofa and started to purr and rub against her leg. Lucy reached down and scratched behind his ear.

"OK, coffee coming up, two ticks."

Lucy returned with a mug of black coffee and gave it to Christine. "Almost done."

Christine said, "Do you live here alone? Sorry, am I being too nosey?"

"No, you're alright. At the moment, but I've been seeing someone recently."

"Lucy, you dark horse. Is that why you've not been coming to after-work drinks?"

"Mmm. Sebastian, tall, blond, and handsome. Blue eyes and a dazzling smile, but shy like you wouldn't believe. I don't even have a picture to show you. He works in graphic design in the West End. He's intrigued by my job and finds it fascinating."

"Wow, I'm pleased for you. I hope it all works out. I thought there was more of a spring in your step the last few weeks. Are you done?"

"Almost. Just need to get stuff from the bathroom. Go down to the car, and I'll meet you there in a couple of minutes."

When Lucy came to the car, they headed to Christine's flat. Lucy was driving, which gave Christine time to decide how to prevent Lucy seeing her place. She doubted Lucy would appreciate the packing box aesthetic she had going on. Then she remembered the GO bag left over from her undercover days. Sorted.

As they pulled into the parking area of Christine's flat, she said, "I have a GO bag ready. Be two seconds. We need to get on."

Lucy looked disappointed but said, "OK, I'll keep the car warm."

When Cristine returned to the car, she said, "You alright to drive? I checked, and it'll take about three hours to drive to the nick. I've booked us into the same hotel Jessop stayed in."

"I'm OK to drive."

"We can stop off for a coffee halfway, and I can take over if you like."

As they drove, Christine reviewed the case file. Two murders, a killer posting details of his crimes on the internet for all to see and claiming more killings than they knew about so far. Maybe the links to the three deaths linked by MO were his, maybe not.

"When we arrive at Weston nick, we'll let them know we're on the ground and ask them if they recognise the woman's description. From what Jessop said, I don't think the woman was a street prostitute. I think someone paid her a lot of money to seduce Jessop and get his semen. Hopefully, she's local, and we can interview her and get a description of the killer."

Lucy said, "Let's hope so. We've got nothing so far. I know the boss is getting frustrated and is he's feeling pressure from the higher-ups to solve this."

They drove in silence for a while before Lucy asked, "When I knew you were joining the team, I googled you. I hope you don't mind?"

Christine glanced up from the file she was reading, "Of course not. I would."

"So someone shot you? In the chest? And declared dead?"

"Yes, to all three."

"Were you scared?"

"No, there wasn't time. The protection team running down the alley scared the scumbag. He grabbed me, and the gun went off. At least, that's what I've been told. Memory is a little hazy."

"Do you miss it?"

"Getting shot?"

Lucy laughed. "No, undercover work. Playing a character?"

"I do, but if I'm honest, remembering a lie 24/7 takes its toll on you. When the mobile rings at five in the morning and someone calls you Carrie instead of Christine, you have to wake up quick."

Lucy shook her head. "I don't think I could do it. Really I don't."

"You'd be surprised at what you can do if you put your mind to it. I saw the Blackstone's in your bookcase. Are you studying?"

"You're sharp. Yes, just started. Not looking forward to the traffic stuff, but the crime stuff is OK. Bread and butter really, or I shouldn't be doing this job."

"Yeah, everyone hates the traffic stuff," Christine smiled, "even traffic officers."

Lucy laughed and took the slip road to the services. "Fancy a coffee and a snack?"

Over coffee and sandwiches, Christine asked where Lucy had met Sebastian.

"I know it's a cliché, but he was behind me in the queue at Starbucks. An old lady three in front of us was having trouble deciding what drink to have, and Sebastian said, 'They have too many choices, don't they?' I looked over my shoulder to see who had spoken. When I looked into those bright blue eyes and saw that smile, I was lost." Lucy flushed. "I went there for the next two days around the same time to bump into him. Not something I've ever done before. On the third day, he was there. I was behind him this time and I said, 'They have too many choices, don't they?' He was smiling that smile when he turned. We grabbed a table, and as they say, the rest is history."

"Wow, Starbucks has a lot to answer for. Good for you. Well, we better hit the road."

As they walked back to the car, Lucy said, "He really is a unique and special person. I don't think anyone has understood me as a woman the way Seb does."

Christine shook her head. "You got it bad, girl!"

Lucy laughed like a giddy schoolgirl. "I do, and I'm proud of it."

Christine grabbed the keys, and three hours and forty minutes after leaving her flat, they arrived at Western-Super-Mare police station. It was closed. According to Google (which she should have checked beforehand), the station was closed Saturday and Sunday. She knew small 'County Mountie' stations could close to be covered by a larger station. Even some smaller stations in the Met had met such a fate, but it rarely worked. A few officers already stretched thin on the ground get spread so thin they become transparent and invisible to the public. No longer patrolling looking for miscreants but what she called fire brigade policing. Officers rushed from one call to the next, relying on the public to be their eyes and ears on the ground.

As they stood shaking their heads, Lucy said, "There's a marked police car coming towards us."

Taking her life in her hands, Christine stepped out in front of it, waving her Met warrant card. The patrol car stopped, and the driver lowered his window.

Christine showed them her warrant card and said, "Sorry to stop you, we're from the Met. I'm working on a murder case and wanted to have a quick chat with your local CID, but the stations closed?"

The driver checked her warrant card, checked her face, satisfied himself the two matched and said, "The murder teams in Bristol. Have they seconded you here?"

Christine and Lucy both looked puzzled.

"No, we're from a murder team in London. We may have a link to Western-Super-Mare. I wanted to let the local detectives know I'm on their patch."

The driver nodded and smiled. "Sorry, we had a woman murdered here in the week, and I thought you were here for that. I can give you a number for the CID; you might get hold of someone."

The worm in her stomach wriggled. It's been very active of late, "The woman killed. Was she a redhead?"

The driver switched off the engine. "Can I see the warrant card again, please?"

Christine gave it to him, and he studied it even more thoroughly. When he gave it back, he said, "Yes, she was. Apparently, a woman from London. Never seen anything like it, we took the call. An old lady walking her dog found her. She had yellow expanding—"

"Foam in her mouth." She finished his sentence for him.

The passenger nodded, "Not something you to see every day, but if I'm honest, I'll be a happy man if I don't get to see anything like it again. What a way to go. I've used the stuff on my house extension. Sticky as hell."

Christine said, "I need to speak with the murder investigation team."

The passenger wrote the incident room number down for her and gave the address of the incident room in Bristol, about an hour's drive away. They thanked the officers and walked back to the car.

Christine called the DCI on her mobile. It went to voicemail.

"It's Christine, boss. Call me back as soon as you can. I'm in Western-Super-Mare and I think we have another related body. I don't know the details yet, but I'm going to call the incident room up here and head over." She ended the call.

Christine rang the incident room in Bristol and got an answering machine. Frustrated at not speaking to an actual human, she said, "Hi, this is Detective Sergeant Christine Woolfe from the Metropolitan Police Major Incident Team. I'm currently in Western-Super-Mare, where I've spoken to a couple of uniform constables here who told me about your murder. I'm heading your way, but can someone please call me back?"

She recited her mobile number and hung up. Christine started the car and headed towards Bristol.

Lucy said, "What do you think this means?"

"I think it means the killer is several steps ahead of us and is clearing up. We need to get to the incident room and find out where they're at with their case."

The DCI called back about twenty minutes later.

He said, "Got your message; what have you got?"

"I spoke to a couple of uniforms. There was a bit of confusion about what I wanted. They thought we were somehow seconded to their incident room. When I heard a female with red hair, found dead in an alley with yellow foam in her mouth—"

The DCI interrupted, "OK, that's a twist. We've got the blood results. There were traces of Rohypnol in Jessop's blood sample."

"I called the incident room and left a message, but no one's called me back yet. We're about 40 minutes away. I don't see it being Jessop. If you like, it's too easy. First, forgetting the anal rape, giving us his semen, then putting himself in the frame for another murder. Nah, I'm not really buying that."

The DCI said, "I'll make some calls, try to get hold of the SIO there. Let them know you're coming. Be circumspect about what you share at first. We should have a heart-to-heart before we enter 'I'll show you mine if you show me yours' territory. As far as I'm concerned, this could be another serial kill for a case we started. I'll call you back, hopefully, before you arrive in Bristol. Drive safe."

He hung up.

Chapter 26

Christine decided against her better judgment to take the M5 to Bristol. She preferred the A and B roads. Motorways are so boring, but if you're in a hurry, which she was, they made sense. Well, that was her plan. If you want to make God laugh, tell him you have a plan! It was why the roadworks and three lanes reduced to one and the 40 miles an hour speed limit (really 10) pissed her off. They were almost stationary when the DCI called back.

"Hi Christine, I've spoken to Detective Superintendent Harry Jones. He's running the incident room and heading up the murder team. From what he's told me, I don't think there can be any doubt his woman, Charlotte Ann Seymour, by the way, is connected to our case. The scene was forensically clean, sprayed bleach and the yellow expanding foam. I've told him about the link to the other murders. When you get there, tell him about the killer's website."

"Thanks, boss. Do we know her?"

"I did a quick check on Crimint. Two convictions for cheque fraud back in the late noughties and soft intelligence says she's moved into high-class prostitution. Got an address in Highgate, London. Harry Jones is expecting you. See what they've got and report back. I'm heading home now, but call me anytime. We're going to re-interview Simon Jessop in the morning."

Christine and Lucy arrived at Bristol nick, for some reason called the Bridewell, twenty minutes after clearing the roadworks on the M5. Parking in the marked loading bay just down from the Bridewell, she put the Met police log book on the dashboard in case any eager beaver traffic wardens put a ticket on the windscreen, and they both walked into the station.

A uniformed officer escorted them to the murder incident room after they showed their warrant cards to the reception. Their escort knocked on a half-glazed door through which Christine watched a fifty-plus, thin and balding man shouting into the telephone. Looking towards the door, the man beckoned them in, saying into the phone, "At last. Thank you so much."

He came from behind his desk with his hand outstretched. "Superintendent Harry Jones."

Christine shook his hand. "DS Christine Woolfe. And this is DC Lucy Worthington."

Having shaken Lucy's hand, he returned to his chair and sat down, waving his two visitors into chairs in front of his desk.

"Sorry about the shouting. I try not to do it too much, but sometimes people need a rocket up their backside. Anyway, I've spoken to DCI Balcombe, and he's filled me in on what you have in

London, and it would appear to connect with what we found here on Thursday morning."

Christine said, "Yes, sir. We stopped a patrol car when we found Western-Super-Mare station closed. By happenstance, they were the first officers on scene and told us about the plumber's foam."

"Yes, nasty business. Not seen anything like that before. A bad way to go. How far have you got? Why are you over here?"

"We have a second body, and we found some semen. That led to us arresting a suspect this morning. He claimed to have been here for a Mercedes dealership training session. We think your victim roofied him, and his semen planted in our second victim. We came over to check out his story and to identify what we believe to be a high-class prostitute hired to get his semen. It would seem the killer disposed of your victim after the job."

Superintendent Jones shook his head. "Callous bastard." Realising what he said, "Sorry, excuse my French."

"That's alright, sir. I've said worse lately on this case."

"What can I do to help, and how can you help us?"

"We'd like the Holmes case number so we can go over the statements and forensic reports. Were there any other injuries on your victim?"

"No, nothing. Why do you ask?"

"Have you heard about the 'I'm coming out' website?"

"Should I have?"

"Probably not, but we think it's a website put on the internet by the killer. Type it into Google and take a look."

Superintendent Jones woke his computer and typed in the details.

"Ok, this is a first for me."

He scrolled down the page, reading swiftly. He glanced at Christine; she knew he had got to the bit which mentioned her by name. He continued to scroll, reading as he went until he reached the end.

He sat back in his chair, looking towards them but focused on the door behind them.

"Are you over run with crazies? He's blabbed every detail. What do you think he's using for the wound to the ear?"

Christine said, "Something like an ice pick. Did you find anything like that on Charlotte Seymour?"

"No, just the foam." He shook his head while smoothing his hand through his thinning, dark hair. "She was a beautiful woman, but she died ugly. Whatever you need, I'll give you the Holmes case number. Anything else, just ask."

"Thank you, sir. We're staying in the same hotel, our suspect, or whatever we're calling him now, stayed in and we still need to check out his story. We can ask around at the bar and the hotel tonight, but we may be on your patch tomorrow as well, to bottom his story out."

"Not a problem. If you like, tomorrow I can give you a Western DC to help and smooth any ruffled feathers."

Christine stood, and Lucy followed. "Thank you, sir. That would be very helpful."

She handed the Superintendent her card, "Ask the DC to meet me after ten tomorrow morning, and we can make a start."

As they walked down the stairs to the front office, Lucy said, "Why ten?"

Christine smiled, "Hotel breakfast. Not to be rushed."

Chapter 27

DCI Balcombe arrived at the incident room early. He wasn't often the first to arrive. He wanted some time to himself to think about the case. Dave Wilde and he were planning to re-interview Simon Jessop. Which, given what they had found out yesterday and what Christine had told him from Western-Super-Mare, wouldn't take long. The problem was without Jessop as a suspect; they were sliding down the snake with no sign of a ladder. Damn. The killer was taunting them. Parading his crimes on the web for all to see.

Like Christine, he had thoughts about why she was so prominent in the case. First at the murder scene, mentioned twice in the online 'I'm coming out' page. He didn't like to think it, but either there had been an internal leak, which was possible with all the police officers, scenes of crime techs and members of the public involved. Or maybe someone from his team? No, he put the thought out of his head. He knew and trusted them all. Maybe Christine was in danger in some way. Lucy appeared to be getting close to her. When they returned, he would have a quiet word with Lucy. Ask her to stay close and look out for anything suspicious. But in the meantime, there was something he could do.

He heard some noise and chatter outside his office and saw Dave and Pete strolling into the incident room with takeaway cups of steaming coffee.

"Morning boss," Pete said, "want a coffee?"

"Yes, I do. Thanks. How did you know I'd be here?"

"Didn't, got it on the off chance. If not, you could have nuked it later."

"Thanks again. Step in here, both of you. I want to talk over the case and the Jessop interview?"

Both did as instructed and seated themselves opposite the DCI.

The DCI sipped his coffee. Still too hot for him, but he appreciated the thought. Setting his coffee cup on his desk, he looked at both men.

"I'll tell the others at the morning briefing, but as you're early birds, you get the juicy worm. Christine and Lucy went to Western-Super-Mare to check out Jessop's alibi. Well, the local station was closed, and they flagged down a passing patrol car to ask where the local CID were. There was a bit of confusion as the officers thought they were there for the body they found Thursday morning. A good-looking redhead suffocated by plumber's foam."

Dave said, "What? Same MO? That can't be a coincidence."

"Very unlikely to be. My take on it is this; our killer hires a prostitute in London. Her name was Charlotte Seymour. Hires her to get jiggy with Jessop and get his semen. Remember, we found faint traces of Rohypnol in his blood yesterday? It dissipates quickly. She hands the condom or whatever over, and he kills her. Tieing up the loose end. He returns to London, murders Cooper, plants the semen and, like good little coppers, we follow the false trail and arrest Jessop. To make it even more interesting, the killer couldn't have known Jessop would blab the whole story to us about him sleeping with the woman."

Pete said, "Fits with Jessop's story. Was the ice pick used in the Western murder?"

"I'm not sure yet. Christine and Lucy were heading over to the incident room in Bristol when I last spoke with her. I expect they were busy, and she'll call this morning. What's your take on this case?"

Pete was the first to speak. "I've gone through everything we've got so far. Jessop was looking good as our suspect, but he's fading now. The killer is baiting us, almost daring us to catch him. I think he feels he's the smartest guy in the room. He's forensic savvy. Does that mean he works in a related industry? If I'm honest, his whole spiel on the web describing how he carries out his kills and the last one when he talks about Jasmine at the nightclub. Not sure I buy it. Something seems off."

The DCI said, "Christine mentioned something to me at the Davies murder scene about how he couldn't ask to check out their shed before they had sex. So either he must carry the tools of his trade with him, or they are already there. The chances of two women who live alone having readily available an ice pick and a can of plumber's foam... Well, the chances must be extremely unlikely."

Dave chipped in, "Boss, the same thoughts have been going through my mind. He must have a way of knowing they lived alone and with no partner or boyfriend around. Wouldn't want to be surprised. He must be keeping them under some sort of surveillance, tailing them, learning their routines."

Pete interjected, "But nothing came up from the Davies house to house, even when Ray and Kumar went back. James Menday, the lad who was the local liaison for the first few days, I asked him to trawl the CAD messages for a month before the Davies murder. Nothing."

"OK," the DCI said, "do we still have access to the Davies' house?"

Pete said, "Yes, what are you thinking, boss?"

"Maybe the crime scene investigation team missed something. Get a team back there to look for anything to indicate any signs of covert entry and surveillance. If they find anything, send them over to Cooper's house, too. We don't know what his agenda is, and there's no way to know if he's targeting another woman right now."

"OK, boss, I'm on it."

The DCI's phone rang. Pete and Dave stood up to leave.

"Dave, stay. I want to discuss the Jessop interview."

"DCI Balcombe. Oh, hi Christine, how did it go last evening?"

Cradling the phone under his left ear against his shoulder, he took down notes.

"Thanks, Christine. See you when you get back."

He replaced the phone on its base.

"Christine says there was no ice pick used in the Western killing. They asked around the hotel bar where Jessop was staying for the conference. The bar staff confirmed, as best they could, he was there for a while. His colleagues were getting loud, and he said his goodbyes and left. They will try to find the wine bar later with a local DC who knows the area. But Christine has looked at the hotel car park CCTV and confirmed Jessop's car was in place the whole time from when he arrived for the conference until he left to come home."

Christine and Lucy finished their second cup of coffee, pushed their breakfast plates away, and each gave a long sigh of contentment.

Lucy said, "I do so love a hotel breakfast. Once, my dad took me to stay at Claridge's for two nights to see a show. We went to the dining room on the first morning, and the breakfast was lovely. But on the second morning, we ordered in our suite. I had fresh fruit salad, lightly scrambled eggs, bacon, two sausages and hot toast. With a carafe of orange juice and a pot of coffee."

Christine had been right. No brickie could afford a suite at Claridge's, and the matter-of-fact way Lucy spoke about it and her use of the word carafe gave the game away. Lucy came from money. So why had she joined the Old Bill?

"Well, I can't top that, but whenever I stay in a hotel, I always make sure I'm up in time for breakfast. Not fussed about lunch or dinner."

She glanced at her watch and waved at a waiter. "Another cup of coffee, please. Lucy?"

"I'm OK. I think my caffeine levels will do for now."

"The detective Superintendent Jones promised us should be here in ten minutes. We'll give him the description Jessop gave the boss.

If it reminds him of somewhere, we'll ask to see their CCTV. If it doesn't ring any bells, we'll have to try all the wine bars within walking distance."

Her coffee came, closely followed by a young man in a beige trench coat with the look of a lost sheep on his face. He scanned the dining room, saw two women, and walked over. Overhearing him asking two random women if they were DS Woolfe and DC Worthington, Christine took pity on him and called him.

He approached their table. "Sorry, I just got the names from my superintendent. I'm DC Giles Trevor."

Christine stood and extended her hand, which he shook.

"DS Christine Woolfe and DC Lucy Worthington, Met Police Major Incident Team."

DC Trevor was still shaking her hand. She gently pulled it free and said, "Coffee?"

"Yes, please. Thank you."

He sat at the table, and Lucy asked a passing waiter for another coffee.

"Superintendent Jones said he was sending someone who knew Western-Super-Mare well."

"Lived here my whole life, born here, went to school here and policed here."

"Great, right man for the job, then?"

Christine explained their task and noticed the frown on DC Trevor's face.

"What's wrong?"

"Well, I don't drink, never have. In uniform, I went to a few pub fights, but the wine bars, I don't think I've ever been inside one."

The disappointment must have been clear on Christine's face as he said, "I know where all the wine bars are. I just can't recognise the description of the inside."

Christine rose wearily and said, "OK, wait here with Lucy. I'll be back shortly."

She walked to the hotel bar, where she spied the barman she spoke with last night stacking cases of beer.

He glanced up at her approach. "Oh, hello again. Need something else?"

Christine smiled, "I do as it happens." She described the wine bar as Jessop had done.

Returning to their table in the restaurant, she said, "Colin, the barman, thinks from the description it sounds like the Western Winery, about half a mile down the road."

DC Trevor perked up at once. "I know the place, always a quiet and sophisticated crowd. Lots of fancy cars parked outside. One night in uniform, I spotted a Ferrari with a bald tyre and—"

Christine said, "Let's go, times marching on."

Chapter 28

Once again, Jessop and his solicitor, Robert Southgate, were already waiting in the interview room. Dave switched the recording equipment on, and the DCI recited the caution again. They all identified themselves for the recording as before.

The DCI placed a picture which he had printed off Crimint in front of Jessop. "Is this the woman you met in the wine bar and had sex with?"

Jessop looked at the picture for a few seconds and nodded.

Dave said, "Please answer for the recording."

"I think so. She may be a few years older than the picture now. But yes."

The DCI asked, "When you left the wine bar, which hotel did you go to?"

"I told you yesterday, I can't remember. It wasn't too far from the bar and not too far from my hotel. But I had to ask someone on the street where my hotel was as I couldn't place it."

"Can you remember what time it was you left the woman's room and hotel?"

"Not really. Bit of a blur, as I told you yesterday. I crashed when I got back to my hotel and was late for the conference."

"Yes, you mentioned it yesterday. You said yesterday you thought her name was Julie?"

"I did say that, but now I think it could have been Julie, Jane, or Janice. I think it started with a J. You've got her picture; you must know her name."

"We do. It's Charlotte Seymour. Police discovered her body in an alleyway in Western-Super-Mare last Thursday morning."

Jessop looked genuinely shocked, and his eyes filled with tears. "Nah, nah, I had nothing to do with that. Why would I do anything to someone I just met the night before? You can't do this to me." He turned to his solicitor. "They can't accuse me of this, can they? I never, would never, ever kill anyone." He looked at the video camera and said, "I never did this thing."

Robert Southgate said, "Is my client going to be charged with this woman's murder and that of Jasmine Cooper, Detective Chief Inspector?"

Ignoring him, the DCI said, "Mr Jessop, the blood sample we took from you with your consent yesterday has been analysed, and it contained traces of Rohypnol. The so-called date rape drug. At present, we will not be bringing charges, but please stay contactable, and I will make it a condition of your bail we retain your passport."

"So my client is free to go?"

"Yes, DC Wilde will take you both to the custody sergeant, who will arrange bail. Let's say six weeks from now, you will return to this station to answer your bail unless we contact you beforehand. Interview stopped."

Jessop said, "You need my passport, you said."

"We already have it," the DCI said, "we found it during the search of your house yesterday."

Both officers stood. "Dave, I'll see you upstairs once you've sorted his bail."

Chapter 29

The Western Winery was closed when they arrived, but some judicious and heavy knocking got a response. The door opened on a chain, and a young woman of about twenty-five peaked out. DC Trevor showed his warrant card and said, "DC Trevor, Western CID, can we come in, please?"

The woman looked at the card, then at Christine and Lucy and said, "Who are they?"

"They are colleagues from the Metropolitan Police, and they need to ask you some questions."

Christine and Lucy showed their warrant cards. The woman closed the door, slid the chain off and opened it to allow them in. She closed and locked it behind them.

"What can I help you with?"

Christine said, "What's your name?"

"Sandra, Sandra Duncan."

"Are you the manager here?"

Sandra nodded. "For the last six months, after Sid left. I have a brother in London; nothing's happened to him, has it?"

"Not as far as we know. We're here to ask you about Wednesday evening and your clientele. Do you have cameras?"

"We do, one on the front door, one which covers the general room and one which covers the doors to the toilets and private areas. Sometimes, I'd like cameras in the toilets, especially the ladies. Stuff goes on in there, you wouldn't believe. Or probably you would." She looked around the wine bar. "Sorry it's a bit dim in here, but if I put the lights on, eager customers will be banging on the door. We don't open for another hour."

Christine took to this woman instantly. Controlled, sensible and to the point. A clone of herself.

"I'd like to show you a couple of pictures. Were you here Wednesday evening?"

"Yes, it was quiet. Mid-week in Weston tends not to set the world on fire."

Christine showed the picture of Simon Jessop to Sandra. "Do you recognise this man?"

She looked intently at the picture and nodded, "He sat at the bar on a stool," She pointed to a stool about halfway along the bar, "he had one, maybe two glasses of wine before a woman with red hair wearing a green dress joined him."

Christine said, "You have an excellent memory. Any reason you recall so much?"

"As I said, Wednesday was quiet. We got chatting, in between me serving other customers. I took to him. Then this attractive redhead came in, sat next to him, and that's all she wrote. He hardly glanced my way after that. I think they moved to an alcove seat over there. The woman came to the bar for wine refills, and when they finished their drinks, they left together."

"Did you get the impression the man knew the woman?"

"I don't think so. In fact, if I'm to be honest, I she was a brass. High-end, but a brass all the same. Was I right? That why you're here? Are you from vice?"

Christine took out a second picture given to her last night by Superintendent Jones. "No, we're not from vice. Sandra, is this the woman?"

Recognition was almost instant, "Yes, that's her."

"Sandra, can we see the CCTV recordings?"

"Of course, this way."

She led them to the office behind the bar and booted up the computer. Christine was pleased to see it was a digital system. It would make getting copies of any recordings easier.

Sandra first brought up the door footage and speeded through until she caught sight of Simon Jessop walking towards the bar stool. She rewound a few seconds and played the clip.

At 20:36:25, they could see Jessop enter the wine bar via the front door. He headed towards the bar but went out of shot. Sandra switched to the bar camera and whizzed through until she found him sitting at the bar. She rewound it, and they all watched as Sandra and Jessop chatted and ordered his first glass of wine. They chatted some more, and he ordered another glass. When he was partway through, Charlotte Seymour joined him at 21:14:11. She didn't look at him and appeared to be waiting to order a drink. He took a gulp of his wine before he spoke to her. She smiled, nodded, and Jessop waved at Sandra to order a glass of wine for her.

At 21:29:36, they both got up and headed to an alcove booth. They appeared to be deep in conversation.

At 21:48:06, from Jessop's body language and his interview, this was when Seymour insisted on buying a drink for both of them. It looked like Jessop resisted, but he eventually capitulated as Seymour stood and walked towards the bar. She returned a few minutes later with two glasses of wine.

At 22:19:37, Seymour was very touchy-feely with Jessop, and she whispered in his ear. He nodded, and they both stood up and headed towards the door.

Sandra brought up the door camera, and they saw at 22:20:45 Seymour and Jessop walking out of the wine bar. Jessop had his arm around Seymour's shoulder, and she had hers around his waist.

They hadn't had to sit through almost two hours of video as Sandra had shuttled through, stopping when she or the others saw something they wanted to see.

Christine said, "Thank you, Sandra. How do we get copies of the footage?"

"I can put it on a USB key."

"OK, but can we replace the hard drive?"

"I don't think the owner would like that."

"Sandra, unfortunately, this is a murder investigation. The red-haired woman was killed sometime on Wednesday night or the early hours of Thursday morning."

Sandra's hand went to her mouth. "By that guy?"

Christine said, "We don't know yet. Have you seen either of them in here before?"

"I don't think so. Oh God. That poor woman. Is it the woman in the local papers? Did they find her in the alley?"

DC Trevor said, "Yes."

Christine said, "Thinking about it, I'll need to seize the NVR, sorry."

Sandra said, "NVR?"

"Network Video Recorder. It's a common type. DC Trevor here will track another down for you and hopefully get it back soon. In the meantime, could you dump the footage onto a USB key for us? Giles, is there a local CCTV shop or PC World?"

"There's a CCTV outlet on the industrial estate outside town."

"OK, take my corporate card and head over there. Get a replacement for this NVR and bring it back here. It should work once you connect the cameras. We'll meet you back at the incident room in Bristol."

She wrote the PIN on one of her business cards. She smiled at DC Trevor. "Don't get carried away with the spending. Just the NVR."

"Of course not." He smiled back and hurried out of the bar.

Sandra handed the USB key to Christine, who said, "DC Trevor will probably be back shortly after you open. I'm sure he'll help you set everything up and get it running. I'll give you a receipt for the NVR. Thank you so much for your time and recollection. You've been a big help."

Lucy and Christine left the wine bar, Christine carrying the NVR under her arm.

Lucy said, "Well, everything we saw there backs up Jessop's account of what happened, doesn't it?"

"It does. Do you mind driving us back to Bristol? I want to bring the boss up to speed before we get back to the Bristol incident room."

Chapter 30

DCI Balcombe put his phone down and strode into the incident room. Pete, Dave, Pritch and Ray were present.

"Ok, listen up, guys. I've heard from Christine. Lucy and her found the wine bar Jessop mentioned in his first interview. Thanks to a very observant barmaid, she can put Jessop in the wine bar at the appropriate times. What's more, she has seized the digital CCTV recorder and is bringing it back here once she drops off a copy of the footage on a USB stick to the incident room in Bristol.

"Basically, Jessop's story checks out. They saw the woman come into the bar, drink and talk with Jessop, as he described, and they left together. I imagine Harry Jones, the local detective superintendent, won't be too pleased Christine is taking the whole video recorder. Still, she'll tell him we'll send him a clone of the whole hard drive in the next day or so. Hopefully, that will ease his misgivings."

There were mumblings of back to square one, and where do we go from here? Which he ignored.

"Pete, any news from the scenes of crime team?"

"Early days, but they rang a short while back and said no sign of anything on the front door, potential signs of covert entry on the rear door. They're now checking the rest of the house for cameras or recording equipment."

"Thanks, Pete. Anything from anyone else?"

Pritch said, "Nothing new on the website, boss, but if you're thinking about covert surveillance, I've got a little do-hickey at home would pick up any signals coming from the house. I could do a sweep at Cooper's place, as it's the most recent?"

Dave, smiling, said, "Do-hickey? Is that a recognised term?"

Pritch grinned. "Probably not. Not sure where that even came from."

The DCI said, "OK, Pritch, take Dave with you, collect the do-hickey from home and check out Cooper's place. In fact, take the keys and use the thing inside, too."

He returned to his office. There was a mound of non-related paperwork he wanted to complete by the time Christine and Lucy returned from Bristol. He woke his computer, opened his emails, clicked on the new message, read it and said, "Shit," to his empty office.

Chapter 31

As he drove their pool car towards Pritch's flat, Dave said, "You know, mate, we really need a break on this case. Every which way we turn, we come up with shit!"

Tapping on his mobile, Pritch said, "I know what you mean. Forensically, we're screwed with no leads. The suspect must be getting his info from somewhere. He knows his stuff, though. You know, I know my shit, but this guy has the edge on me. I don't think the IT skills are from a sixty-plus-old man. He's right up to date. Using the latest code. He must be getting help, or someone younger is pulling our chain."

"I know, just doesn't feel right. Rapists are not usually the sharpest tools in the box. Cunning as fuck, but not up to running rings around you." He smiled, "But if you eat any more of those chocolate shortbread cookies, anyone could?"

Pritch punched Dave on the arm. They both laughed. Something neither had done much of lately.

Pritch directed him to the entrance to the car parking area.

Getting out of the car, he said, "Won't be long."

Dave waited outside the block of flats while Pritch collected his 'do-hickey'.

A few minutes later, he returned, clutching a small black plastic case like the ones used by professional photographers, and jumped into the car.

Chapter 32

When Lucy and Christine arrived back at the Bristol incident room, they showed Harry Jones what they had found. They also gave him a second USB stick with footage from the hotel Jessop had been staying in, which showed him staggering, as if drunk, along the corridor and entering his room at 05:16:39. She had made a copy for the London team.

Superintendent Jones said, "So, you've found Charlotte Seymour, our victim, and your previous suspect, Simon Jessop, met, as he claimed. We still don't know where Seymour was staying or have any idea who arranged for her to come on to this Jessop."

"No, sir. Hopefully, the clear photo from our Crimint system will help your team locate the hotel. Stupid question, but I take it there was no CCTV in the alley where she was found?"

Superintendent Jones shook his head. "No, and the cameras nearby had been 'adjusted' to not show the street. Whoever this killer is, he's thorough."

"OK, sir. My boss will keep in touch with you, and I'll get our IT department to copy the hard drive from the recorder and have it couriered over here. We'll wait for DC Trevor to return with my credit card and head back to London. Thank you for all your help."

"No, thank you. I'm sure we would have eventually found the wine bar, and no doubt wasted a lot of time tracking down Jessop. You have taken us a step closer to catching this person. I'll keep in touch with Steve Balcombe."

Christine stood and joined Lucy by the incident room coffee machine. "We'll wait for Giles to return here with my card and head back. But first, coffee."

Chapter 33

On the drive to Dalston, Dave kept glancing at the piece of tech Pritch had removed from the case. It was about eight inches long, three inches tall, and roughly one and a half thick. It had a built-in screen and several accessories in the foam-lined case. Pritch was busy attaching what looked like an antenna to one side and a flat, pointy arrow-type thing to the other. He booted it up and started playing with the settings.

"That looks like an expensive do-hickey. What does it do?"

"I'm in the trade, so I got it at cost, but it was still close to two grand."

Dave whistled.

"But if Cooper's house has any nasty electronic bugs, this'll find them."

They arrived at the small house Jasmine Cooper had called home about an hour after leaving Pritch's flat and saw the forensic team was still there. One of the team recognised them and waved.

"We're almost done packing the vans up now. Nothing else to report, but your boss will get a full report later."

Dave said, "Do a couple of you mind hanging on for a while. Pritch here has a bug finder, and the boss had an idea. Maybe that's how our killer knows about the women."

"Well, we have another job to get on to. But I could leave Sarah Russell here. She has her own van and can join us after."

The tech called Sarah over, and Dave explained what they were going to do.

"It shouldn't take too long, and if we find nothing, you can be on your way."

She smiled, "On one condition. Can I watch what you're going to do? I'm fascinated by anything spy-related."

Dave smiled back, "That's not a problem Miss Moneypenny," he said in the worst impression of Sean Connery anyone had ever heard, "Sorry, should have practised that a bit more."

Sarah grinned, "Ya think?" and went off to finish loading her van.

Pritch came over and told Dave he was ready to go around the front and rear of the terraced house. Dave explained Sarah Russell from forensics was going to join them. Sarah wandered over, and Dave introduced Pritch.

Pritch said, "So I'm first going to do an external sweep front and back on all bands just to see what's there. Likely to be lots of Wi-Fi and mobile signals, but we can narrow it down to a single band if we're lucky."

Sarah said, "What are we looking for, exactly?"

"Something you wouldn't notice normally, or maybe the transmitter could be inside something already here, like a telephone box, where the cable comes into the house. If the suspect has put any kind of surveillance inside the house. It will need to transmit the signal data to the outside box, which will either contain a recording device or piggyback to a mobile, which could be anywhere. But if we find any bug, we will know how he gets his info on the women."

Pritch switched his do-hickey on. Lots of lines danced up and down the screen.

"As I thought, lots of signals."

He twisted a small knob on the unit and moved the joystick, and the signals diminished to a few.

"I'll do a few passes out the front here on the various bands. Keep your fingers crossed."

Pritch worked his way carefully along the front of the terraced house and back and forth.

After about ten minutes, he said, "OK, nothing so far. Let's try the back."

They all walked through the house and opened the back door. Pritch went through the same procedure, but again, with nothing definite.

He said, "Unless he has managed to locate a bug with a large battery within the house, the only other explanation is it may be outside the houses on either side. But let's check the inside first. Where's Cooper's bedroom?"

Sarah said, "Top of the stairs and the door on the right."

They followed Pritch upstairs and into the bedroom. Pritch started his twiddling of knobs and joystick and grinned.

"Gotcha."

He appeared to be using the pointy arrow flat thing Dave had seen earlier on the machine as a pointer to where the signal was coming from. He focussed on the small bookshelf Jasmine had placed right across from her bed. It was full of mostly paperbacks, with a few magazines and a couple of library books.

Pritch said, "I think we have a winner."

He pointed to a copy of a chick-lit novel by a well-known author. Dave took pictures on his phone.

Sarah said, "I've read that one and a couple of the others in the series. I see Jasmine also has them, too."

Pritch said, "Probably why he chose this one, as very few people re-read books, especially if they're following a series."

All three crouched to study the spine of the book. Pritch was the first to see it. "There, in the black letter h. A pin hole lens. OK, Sarah, over to you. Be careful; there may be a wire coming out of the back of it."

She carefully removed three books on either side of the suspect novel with gloved hands. She shone a light from her torch along the top edge and either side of the book.

"I can't see anything, no obvious prints or wires. I'll try UV before I dust."

She did so, but shook her head. She reached into her bag, retrieved her fingerprint kit, and dusted the outside of the book in situ.

"That's suspect in itself, no prints. Nice glossy surface, ideal for fingerprints. Nothing. Grab me an evidence bag, will you, Dave?"

Sarah inched the book towards her. She checked behind and again saw nothing. She lifted the book to place it in the evidence bag.

"This is far too heavy for a paperback. Dave put some gloves on and spread the sterile sheet on that table."

Dave did as he was told, and Sarah placed the book on the sheet. She lifted the front cover with tweezers. All that remained of the book was the external cover, front, spine, and back. Where the pages should have been was a black metal box. The top of all the pages from the book were still there, but only one-centimetre deep to give the illusion of a regular book.

Pritch was the first to speak. "Right, this is the hub. I'm guessing we'll find others in the living room, hallway, bathroom, and maybe the kitchen. This is custom. The battery is in here, and if I'm not mistaken, a mobile chip. He could receive data from this and the others anywhere in the world. If he programmed it correctly, and I'm sure he did, he could have been watching Jasmine for at least a month, maybe more. You bag that one up. I know the frequency now, so I'll get on finding the others."

Pritch left the bedroom, leaving Dave and Sarah to bag the prime exhibit.

Within minutes, Pritch called, "Found another in the bathroom."

They joined him, and he pointed to an electric shaver socket next to the bathroom mirror.

"I think you'll find a camera and transmitter behind there. Be careful; the socket will probably be live. The killer wouldn't want Jasmine or anyone else poking around."

Dave noted Pritch had started to call the victim Jasmine rather than Cooper. It was becoming personal for him.

Sarah went through the same routine as before. This time, she found some partial prints in the places you would get if you plugged a shaver in. They would be examined, but no one thought they belonged to anyone other than Jasmine. She undid the two screws and withdrew the body of the socket. As Pritch had said, the transmitter and camera were wired into the power.

Dave looked at the tiny camera which came from the transmitter on a short length of wire and picked up one of the screws, which looked stunted, more like a bolt with a flat end. He studied it and held it up to the bathroom light.

"There's a hole drilled in this all the way through."

Sarah and Pritch looked.

Pritch said, "Clever bastard. The glass of the camera lens would have appeared to be the same as the silver of the screw. I knew it was there because of my device. I'll look for others."

Pritch found another in the hallway smoke detector. No prints. The only difference from a standard smoke detector camera was you couldn't see it even when Sarah removed the detector from the ceiling and opened it up. It looked normal.

The last one Pritch found was in the light switch in the living room. Again, it used the power from the switch. Dave spoke with Pritch, and they rang the boss.

The DCI picked up on the first ring, "Hi Dave, found anything?"

"We have boss, four sophisticated surveillance cameras. Pritch thinks they transmit to a mobile. So our suspect could receive the feed anywhere."

"OK, take pictures, get someone from forensics to collect them and get over to the Sarah Davies scene."

"Boss, the forensic team was packing up when we got to Jasmine Cooper's place. Sarah Russell stayed with us. She's got everything."

"Excellent work. Call me when Pritch has done a sweep at Davies' place." He disconnected.

Dave turned to Pritch and said, "The boss was over the moon the hunch turned out—"

Pritch interrupted him. "Shit, call the boss back. I just thought of something."

Dave did as requested and handed Pritch the phone.

"Dave?"

"No, boss, it's Pritch. I just had a thought. The gear we've taken from Jasmine's house is not cheap. He probably wants it back. The fact it's still here a few days after the murder means he wants to see what we do. Once we're fully clear, he'll return everything to normal. No trace. I think we missed a trick. Now we've taken the cameras out, he'll know we found them, and he's unlikely to return here. Although, I suppose I could put a couple of my cameras in, just in case. What do you think?"

"I agree. Damn. We didn't think it fully through, did we? Anyway, no use crying over spilt milk. Put the cameras in, and we can hope for the best. Still, take a look at Sarah Davies' place. The forensic team might still be there. But we've been clear of the place for a while now, so he's probably retrieved his surveillance equipment."

"OK, boss, will do. See you soon."

Turning to Dave, he said, "You heard most of that? I always carry a couple of small covert cameras under the foam in the case. I'll stick those up, and we'll get to Sarah's place."

Dave smiled to himself. This case was definitely getting under Pritch's skin.

Chapter 34

Pritch and Dave returned to the incident room in time for the evening briefing. Pritch busied himself by uploading pictures of the surveillance cameras they had found to his system. He turned one of his large monitors around so it faced into the room and waited for the DCI to start.

"OK, quieten down, everyone. Nothing further from Christine and Lucy, but they should be back here soon, so they may have an update. Dave and Pritch have been out at both the Cooper and Davies scenes. I was wondering, as I know many of you have been, how the killer knew so much about his victims. He must have stalked them for a while. I sent a forensic team to the Davies scene earlier to check for any signs of covert entry and surveillance. All I can say is they found possible tampering with the back door lock. So maybe signs of covert entry by our killer. But I'll hand over to Dave and Pritch."

Dave said, "Thanks, boss. We went to the Jasmine Cooper scene first, but I'll come back to that. We then went to the Sarah Davies scene and found no evidence of electronic surveillance devices still in situ. So, back to the Jasmine scene. Pritch, who has an entire box of tricks I didn't know about, found four electronic digital covert cameras. The main one in her bedroom, and others in the bathroom, hallway and living room. Pritch?"

Pritch woke his monitor. "OK, this is the bookcase in Jasmine's bedroom. My bug-finding device indicated a bug in this book. When Sarah, the forensic tech, removed the books on either side, as seen here, there were no fingerprints at all. Which is suspect. When she removed it, we found this inside."

Kumar said, "What the hell is it?"

"This is a very high-end, self-contained covert surveillance hub. Basically, it contains a long life battery, a mobile chip so it can send data anywhere in the world, a camera and microphone, and the capability to receive signals from other covert cameras and transmit them via the mobile network."

Pritch moved on to the bathroom. "As you can see here, the device indicated the shaver socket. Once Sarah removed the socket, Dave noticed our killer had drilled out one screw and cut off the pointy end."

Dave took a bow.

"Thank you, Dave. This meant the camera was virtually invisible as the lens blended with the silver of the screw. Moving on, I found another camera in a light switch in the living room and a camera in the smoke detector in the hallway, pointing at the front door. The interesting thing about this one is when Sarah took it down, we still couldn't see the camera. Again, high end."

Looking around the room, Pritch could see he had their rapt attention.

"So, what does all this mean? Well, my take, and I think Dave agrees, our killer knows his tech stuff. As evidenced by his website and the sophisticated nature of the products he uses. It also means he did at least two covert entries into Jasmine's house to scope out where to put his cameras and note which book to use, what make of shaver socket, light switch and smoke alarm. I suggest he did not do any of the work on-site. The drilling of the screw would take precision tools. Dave and I think he leaves the kit in place to watch what the police do when the scene is discovered."

Ray said, "So he's learning all the time."

"Yes, that's right. We think he waits for all the forensics to be finished, and the scene shut down before he returns, removes his gear, and replaces the originals. As you know, we went to Sarah Davies' house after Jasmine's and found nothing. But that scene shut down weeks ago. Questions?"

The DCI spoke first, "You said the hub thing will send the data to a mobile. Could we trace the mobile and pinpoint where he is?"

"We could if he routed it to his personal mobile, and he may have done. However, if this case has taught us anything, we won't be that lucky. I suspect it'll be a burner and get bounced around a fair bit. Oh, I forgot to say, we realised seeing us removing his gear most likely means the killer won't return to Jasmine's place. But just in case, I put in a couple of my cameras in her bedroom and the hallway." Pritch brought up the feeds on the monitor. "Fingers crossed."

Kumar said, "So, he stalks these women. He knows them, he finds them, and he kills them. If it's not an old rapist from back in the day, what's the killer's motive? What's driving him?"

Pete said, "That's a good point. I'm veering away from the original rapist committing these murders. But why does it matter so much to the killer? What's his interest in Simon Jessop, or was he a random?"

The DCI said, "Actually, I can answer that. Jessop shares the same paternal DNA link with the other victims. I found out earlier, and I've been thinking, having ruled him out as a suspect, should we put him into protective custody? Thoughts?"

Pete said, "The killer could have closed this case down by leading us to Jessop, finding him dead with a remorseful suicide note telling us some cock and bull story about why he did it. We would have wrapped the case up double quick. But he doesn't. He gives Jessop an out. Whatever we know now, I think there's more to come."

Pritch was looking at the DCI when Pete said this, and it seemed Pete had never said a truer word.

The DCI said, "OK, food for thought. I need to make some calls. Christine and Lucy should be back soon. Briefing in the morning, as usual."

No one was going anywhere. They all crowded around Pritch's computer and bug-finding gadget, asking questions about it and why their killer didn't kill the boy child of the rapist.

Fifteen minutes later, Christine and Lucy bowled back into the incident room clutching the NVR and a box of twelve Dunkin' Donuts they picked up at the last service station they stopped at for a comfort break and more coffee.

Lucy said, "Doughnuts for anyone not watching their waistline."

The entire team rose as one from their chairs to grab a doughnut. Christine went over to the boss's door and knocked gently. He beckoned her in.

Leaning around the door and smiling, Christine said, "Dunkin' Donuts outside, boss."

The DCI's face was grave and said, "Maybe later. Christine, come in and sit down."

She did so. "What's up, boss?"

"Like you, I've been thinking about why our killer mentioned you on his website. I've done a press conference. My name is out there. Why is yours? To be frank, it has got me worried. Maybe I should have asked you, but I wanted to protect you and the team, so I did it anyway."

What the fuck had he done? Was she off the team?

"What did you do, boss?"

"You know each officer has their DNA added to the National database?"

She didn't like where she thought this was heading. Not one bit.
"I do."

"Well, I asked for your DNA to be compared to the DNA of the rape suspect. I got the email back this afternoon. It matches the paternal strand, the same as our victims. I'm so sorry, Christine."

She felt a sinking feeling. She knew what it was. It was the feeling of having the rug pulled from beneath your feet. The feeling your world will never, ever look the same. The feeling you wouldn't recognise your reflection in the mirror. Everything you thought you knew about yourself gone in an instant. She had felt the same thing once before. When Samantha was taken. She realised the DCI was looking at her with concern in his eyes. She had to say something.

"I never knew; mum always said it had been a brief thing with my dad, but she got two beautiful girls from it, so that was OK with her. She said she hadn't seen him since..."

"I'm sorry, Christine. If I could have told you differently, I would have. There's something else I think we need to discuss. Simon Jessop, he's also related. In effect, he's your half-brother."

For Christine, the world stopped spinning, but she carried on moving. It jerked her. She almost toppled on to the floor. On reflex, she put out her hands to grip the chair. Her protective shield, which she had relied on most of her life, was down, no matter how much she wished it wasn't, and for the first time in a long time, she was vulnerable.

"So that makes eight children we know of, eight children of rape." Tears were welling up; she tried to blink them away, but they flowed even more. The DCI passed a box of tissues towards her, and she took a couple.

"I'll grab us some coffee. Leave you alone for a few minutes."

OK, need to start processing this shit. The rapist's my dad; five of my half-sisters have been murdered, six including Samantha, and the previous suspect's my brother. Whether it's dear old dad or some sick fucker who knows about all this, they needed, she needed, to stop him. Dead.

The DCI returned with two mugs of black coffee and placed one in front of Christine.

"We can talk about this tomorrow if you'd prefer? But we do need to talk about it."

She felt her shield begin to materialise in her chest, "No, I'm alright. It was a lot to take in, but we can talk."

"You mentioned before I went out to fetch the coffees there were eight children of rape? So far, we have five murder victims with positive DNA. Simon Jessop and now you. My count is seven?"

"I don't tell many people, as it's private and not in my file, but I was a twin. Mum named us Christine and Samantha. Dad was never in the picture, and now I know why. When we were nine years old, Samantha and me took ourselves off to the swings on Tooting Bec Common. Samantha was abducted from there. No one saw anything; we never heard of or saw Samantha again. I think she was killed; at least, I hope so. We all know what can happen to young girls taken by paedophiles. Is it bad of me to say I hope she's dead?"

"Knowing what we know and see in the job, probably not. But it's sad to lose hope at such a young age. I'm sorry for your loss and having to give you bad news, but—"

Christine cut him off. "Sorry, boss, but I think I know what you're going to say. I think the core team should know about me. I won't say I'm keen, but they might make connections they wouldn't if they don't know. Just ask them to respect my privacy as much as possible and not gossip about it outside the team."

The DCI nodded, "I'm sorry you're having to semi-publicly out yourself, but I respect your decision and think it's right for the investigation. Are you happy with me talking them through everything? If you want to think about it overnight?"

"No, the sooner they know, the more able they'll be to make intuitive connections. I think it will carry more weight from you with the privacy warning."

"If you're sure, the team's all here now?"

"People keep popping up from back then into now. No more secrets."

The DCI stood up, "Agreed, OK, let's do this. Do you want to be there or go home and process all this?"

"I'd like to stay and get all the 'sorry to hear that's' out of the way tonight."

They walked out into the main incident room as Lucy brought the team up to speed about Western-Super-Mare.

The DCI stood at the front and announced, "OK, quieten down. We have a major update on the case, and as a result, I need to bring you all in on something relating to one of our own I have been holding back. What I am about to tell you is not to be discussed outside this incident room. Nor is it to be gossiped about to other colleagues, family or friends now or when this case is solved and over. I will hear about it and come down on you like the wrath of God."

That got their attention.

"Now you all know Christine discovered during a burglary surveillance operation Sarah's body. And you know it was the first time we saw the 'I'm coming out' website. You also know our suspect mentioned Christine's and my name on the site. What I withheld until I spoke with Christine just now was Christine's DNA shares a paternal link to the rapist, the same as the other victims."

Sharp intakes of breath from the team, then silence in the room while the detectives processed the information.

"Keep in mind Christine did not know any of this until five minutes ago, so please give her some space, as I know you will."

The DCI turned to walk into his office when Christine cleared her throat, "Boss, we should also mention my sister Samantha."

Turning back, "Yes, that's right. Christine was born a twin. Her sister, Samantha, was abducted at Tooting Bec swings on the common not too far from here. She was never found. It's too early to tell if her abduction has anything to do with our case, but keep it in mind."

As Christine expected, the team crowded around and offered sympathy and support. She hadn't expected Pete and Pritch to give her the biggest hugs she had ever had. She was overwhelmed, made excuses, and dashed to the women's toilets to spruce herself up. Lucy came in and put her arm around Christine's shoulder. "I'm here if you ever want to talk; the whole team is too. Want to slip away for a quiet drink?"

"Thanks, Lucy. Another time. I want to go home, wrap myself in the duvet and start processing. Say my goodbyes for me?"

Chapter 35

The following day, the DCI called Pete into his office.

"I'm thinking about getting Simon Jessop back in here with his solicitor and telling him what we discovered about his parentage. I'm also considering offering him protection or suggesting he go away until we've cleared this case. What do you think?"

"He was pretty upset when you interviewed him. Can we trust him not to go to the press? Also, telling him something like that in front of his solicitor may not go down so well. We could release him from his bail, notify the solicitor, and speak to him privately."

"Yes, that's not a bad idea. I'll ring Paterson's and talk to Robert Southgate. It's not the weekend, so Jessop should be home after work. Are you free to come with me later?"

"I'll make a call to the missus. Should be ok."

Christine woke up on the sofa in her living room. Her tongue was stuck to the roof of her mouth. When she breathed out, she could smell how bad her breath was. On the floor was a half-eaten naan bread next to a bowl that contained the remains of a prawn vindaloo.

She groaned and rolled onto her back. A hard lump turned out to be an empty litre bottle of Liebfraumilch. Well, that explained why she felt like shit. A takeaway Indian and a large bottle of sweet white wine will do it every time.

A chasm opened in her head as soon as she sat up. She immediately laid down again. She needed water, but how could she get it? Standing wasn't an option. Crawl to the sink. No, crawl to the fridge. She had bottled water there. She rolled off the sofa but wasn't quick enough to put her hands out, and her chin struck the edge of the curry bowl. Now, she had curry sauce over her face. This was why she lived alone.

She almost made it to the fridge before the vomit rose. Kitchen sink or toilet? With superhuman will, she got to her feet and, in a quick staggering shuffle, got to the toilet almost in time. Some of the projectile vomit went into the toilet bowl. The rest, not so much. Christine embraced the toilet and let rip again. It felt better, good in fact, but the universe has a way of not letting you get away with stuff. The doorbell rang.

Play dead was a good plan. She felt like it anyway. Play dead, and they would go away. But the universe was against her. The doorbell rang again. Then her mobile started its Sweeny theme tune. So, someone she knew. She heard knocking and a woman calling out her name. Lucy!

Christine wanted to shout, "Be right with you." But what came out sounded to her like Wookie speak.

It must have sounded the same to Lucy as she knocked again and shouted, "Christine, are you alright?"

Getting her mouth to articulate English words took an effort, but she managed, "Be there in five."

Christine grabbed the hand towel and wiped her face. She raised herself to sink level and ran the cold tap. She rinsed her face and took sips of water. Then she noticed she was naked from the waist down. She staggered into the living room and picked up her trousers and knickers from where she had flung them. They were wet. She really hoped they were wet from wine, but it was a faint hope. Shivering, she edged into the bedroom and wrapped her thick dressing gown around her.

Christine eased open the front door. Lucy took one look at her and said, "Coffee?" She walked past and said, "Where's the kitchen?"

Christine pointed down the hallway. Christine heard her filling the kettle, opening cupboards, placing mugs on the worktop, and spooning coffee into the mugs. In fact, her ears were hyper-sensitive to every single bit of noise.

She clung to the living room doorframe and said, "I'm taking a shower. Won't be long. Make yourself comfortable."

Christine realised she couldn't stand the drumbeat of the overhead shower on her head. She switched to the handheld spray and stood there for what seemed like hours, but in reality was perhaps ten minutes. Why hadn't mum told her, especially after Samantha was taken? She was all her mum had left, after all. No other family. It had been unfair the way her mother could blame a nine-year-old for Samantha being abducted. It had been a joint decision to go to the park. If anything, she had agreed to Samantha's suggestion. Although, now she was older, she realised she was the only one her mother could blame. Most people she found don't relish blaming themselves and are more than ready to attribute blame to others. Even their own daughter.

Christine turned the shower off. She wouldn't allow herself to wallow. What was done was done. Mum was dead. Samantha was dead. She was alive and needed to deal with it.

A few minutes later, dressed in a sweatshirt and leggings, she joined Lucy on the sofa.

Lucy spoke first. "Sorry for just turning up like that. I knew the DCI had texted you to take a couple of days, and I wanted to make sure you were alright. It can't be easy hearing what you heard yesterday."

"It wasn't. Thanks for coming over. You've seen me at my worst now. An Indian and a litre bottle of Liebfraumilch."

"Oh, my God. I hate that stuff!"

Christine laughed, which made her head hurt, "So do I. But it was the only thing I could find in the packing boxes."

"So, what's the plan now?"

"Well, I need to go through these boxes and find Samantha's stuff. I need to get it tested for DNA."

"I can help if you want me to?"

"Thanks, but I need to do this myself. I haven't opened most of these boxes since I packed them. There'll be some memories I need to deal with my way."

"Of course. I understand. I'm a phone call away. Look, I can tell the boss I've seen you. I'll get into the office. Anything comes in, I'll let you know."

"Thanks, Lucy."

Lucy stood and walked to the front door. "See you when you're ready."

Christine closed the door behind her and stumbled her way to her bed. Packing boxes could wait.

The DCI and Pete walked up the front path of Simon Jessop's house just after 7 pm. Earlier, the DCI spoke to Robert Southgate and told him they were releasing Jessop from his bail. And considered him a victim rather than the perpetrator. Pete rang the doorbell and waited. He was about to ring again when he heard someone coming down the stairs in the house. Simon Jessop opened the front door, and Pete could tell he wasn't pleased to see them.

The DCI said, "Mr Jessop, can we come in?"

"Why? My solicitor called me at work earlier and said you were dropping any charges and treating me as a victim rather than a suspect."

"That's true, but we think you may be in danger. Please, can we come in?"

Jessop moved back from the door and allowed them to enter. He pointed to a room on the right, and they walked ahead of him into his living room. Jessop gestured towards the sofa whilst he flopped down into an armchair.

"Ok, what's this about?"

"Just over thirty years ago, there was a rapist active in the Wimbledon area. We now know the murdered women we have identified shared a paternal link with that rapist. He fathered all the children, and someone, maybe the rapist, but he would be old by now, is killing those children, now adults."

"And what has this got to do with me?"

Pete could almost see the cogs whirring behind his eyes.

"Wait, are you saying I could be one of those children?"

The DCI lowered his voice and said, "We know you are. The same DNA test we originally linked you as a suspect. I had it confirmed you share a paternal link with the murdered women."

"But my Gran always said my dad was a navy sailor my mum met on a trip to Liverpool."

"You didn't live with your mother?"

"No. Complications during childbirth. Gran took me in."

"As we discussed previously, DNA doesn't lie. Maybe your grandmother didn't want to tell you what happened, or maybe the sailor was your father. But he was also a rapist."

Pete could see the news had shaken Jessop. His face was ashen, and when he put his hand back down on the arm of the chair, he noticed a slight tremor.

Jessop stood. "I need to process this. If that's everything?"

The DCI said, "Unfortunately not. We believe you could be in danger and are here to offer you protection."

Jessop sat back down. "Why would you think that? When the woman roofied me would have been the ideal time to kill me. In fact, he tried to set me up for his crimes. I don't buy it."

He stood again. "Could you leave now?"

Both officers stood. The DCI said, "Please think about the protection. It may only be for a short time. In the meantime, I'd like my officers to visit you to do an electronic sweep for cameras and listening devices?"

"What?"

"We believe our killer keeps surveillance on his victims before he attacks them. It would be two officers, one of which you already met, DC Dave Wilde. They would do a sweep with a device to trace any bugs."

"Alright, they can come tomorrow evening after I get back from work. But now, can you go?"

The DCI held out his hand, but Jessop didn't notice or ignored it. Both officers followed him to the front door and left.

As they drove back to the incident room, Pete told the DCI, "Well, he took that better than I would have."

"Yes, he did. None of us know how we will react to situations, and he didn't know his father or mother. I'll sleep happier after Pritch does the sweep. I don't think he's going to accept protection."

Chapter 36

Lucy's mobile pinged. She opened the app. A message from Sebastian. She read it, 'Sorry running a bit late. Be about 10 minutes.' She let out the breath she had been holding. He wasn't cancelling. Get a grip. He likes you, loves you. Stop behaving like a lovesick schoolgirl.

She glanced around the sandwich bar. The tables were filling up as the lunchtime crowd descended. The woman behind the counter kept looking over to her table between take-away customers. Lucy sensed she was estimating how long Lucy could take to drink her cup of coffee before the table became free.

Salvation arrived with a flustered Sebastian. Lucy thought he had been running. His face was red and his hair awry.

"I'm so sorry," he said breathlessly, "My meeting over ran. Have you ordered?"

Lucy smiled, "No. But I was getting a 'hurry up' vibe from the woman behind the counter."

Lucy stood, and Sebastian hugged her and kissed her. The kiss lingered. She felt her neck and face warm up. Maybe she was a lovesick schoolgirl, after all.

"I'll go order. Another coffee? What do you fancy to eat?"

Lucy wanted to say, "You," but restrained herself with, "a cream cheese and avocado panini, please."

Sebastian joined the queue and a short while later, carried the tray back to the table.

"How have you been? It's been frantic at work. Sorry for dragging you up to the West End, but we haven't seen each other for a long time."

Lucy said, "I've been busy too. In fact, I just got back from a work trip."

Sebastian lowered his voice. "Connected to the murder you're working on?"

"Yes, it's now three."

"Please tell me you're not working on the case people are talking about. The serial killer with the website?"

Lucy nodded while taking a bite out of her panini.

"Oh, that must be terrible. One of my colleagues brought up the website, and I saw some pictures before our head of design told him to switch it off. Awful." He shook his head. "How could someone do that? I'm worried about you. He reached out across the table and held her hand."

Lucy blushed again. "Don't be. My team is the best, and we're the police and there are thousands of us."

"But there's only one of you."

Lucy made a retching face and smiled.

Sebastian admitted, "Too Much?"

Lucy grinned. "I appreciate the thought behind it."

They ate in silence for a while.

"You said the trip connected with the case? If you can't tell me. I'll understand, but I'm fascinated with how it all works. How you build a case?"

"Team work mostly. You know I mentioned Christine? I went with her to Somerset to check something out and found a murder team from there investigating a murder like our two. Anyway, it was just follow-up stuff."

"Please be careful. Don't put yourself in harm's way unnecessarily."

"I won't. I'm not brave enough." She smiled. "What's the rush at your work?"

"Nothing compared to what you're involved in. A big client who produces breakfast cereals rejected our pitch last week. We don't want to lose them, so it's all hands to the pump." He chuckled. Lucy liked the sound. "There's only so many ways you can convince the public to buy a box of cereal."

Lucy thought she could listen to him talk all day. His voice was light, yet masculine. He could read her the phone book, if they still have them, and she would like it.

Sebastian finished his coffee. He smiled that smile of his. "Sorry, I have to dash. Next time I'll come to you."

They both stood and walked outside. They hugged, a long kiss, and Sebastian walked away. She needed to return to the incident room, but she felt lighter in her soul as she sauntered towards the tube.

Chapter 37

A day later, Pritch and Dave reported during the morning briefing, they had visited Jessop's home and found no trace of any electronic surveillance devices. The DCI had also instructed them to sweep Christine's flat. Which thankfully also came up empty.

Christine was back in the incident room. She had found nothing which might contain Samantha's DNA. She had been sure there was a box of her sister's stuff; clothing, hair brush, toys. But she couldn't find it. Maybe she had thrown it when she moved in ten years ago. But she couldn't understand why she would have done it.

Christine spent the day catching up on the case, reviewing statements and the pictures of the surveillance bugs Dave and Pritch had found. She knew she had been right. He stalked his victims and learned all about them, their habits, their vulnerabilities.

At 5 pm, the DCI had started the evening briefing when Pritch got a ping on his computer announcing an update to the web page. They all gathered around his monitors. The killer had written two paragraphs in what appeared to be French. Christine only had language skills left over from her school days, but even she could pick out her name in the text.

Pritch highlighted the text, and after Google translate worked its magic:

Good afternoon, one and all,

I've been reading your comments on my last outing, and I must say some of you are more impatient than I. But I have made my decision. Although giving too much away just now would spoil the surprise. And the surprise is everything. The look, the panic, the sheer terror when they realise what's happening to them. I can tell you, there's no rush like it. Their last fleeting thoughts about their complicity in their own death.

Anyway, time marches on, and I would like a minor task undertaken by one of our new journeymen, or in this case, journey woman. Christine, my dear, I need you to revisit the head of the family. I know it's been ten years since you last had a little chat, but I really do feel you would profit immensely from getting reacquainted. In fact, I will make it one of my little conditions for continued admittance to the funfair. You, Steve, and the rest of the merry band will go back into the dark. So, Hi-Hooo, Hi-Ho, Hi-Ho, it's off to work you go. Don't forget your bucket and spade.

Following behind the technician, Christine knew her appointment with her maker was not far off. At 5 am that morning, they exhumed her mother's coffin and brought it to the hospital. The mortuary tech shuffled in front of her as they moved down the hospital corridor. Her faded green scrubs, hiding a fuller than-average 50-year-old's figure and blood-spattered Crocs, screamed, 'I've been here too damn long, and I really don't give a rat's arse'. A phrase Christine always thought too long for the indolent to actually use. She watched the taut, paler green fabric covering the tech's inner thighs meet with each step. Swish, swish, swish. Hypnotic.

Christine suddenly realised her brain was playing catch up with her ears; "Sorry, what did you say?"

The tech repeated, "How long since you lost your mother?"

Christine wanted to reply with sarcasm to the attempt at polite mortuary chat. She didn't understand? For the last ten years, she had known exactly where her mother was, to the millimetre, for every second. But she complied with, "Just over ten years," adding, "it was her heart" to stop further inquiry.

"Shame," the tech said. Swish, swish, swish.

As she approached the mortuary, the familiar scent of hospitals filled the air, growing stronger with each step. Despite their efforts to mask it, the unmistakable smell of death invaded her nostrils, reminding her of the sombre reality within. They arrived at a battered wooden door with 'Viewing Room' in barely legible gold signwriting.

The tech opened the door and said, "You understand you're here as a private witness, not a police officer?"

Christine nodded.

"Wait in there. I'll let the pathologist know."

The room was dimly lit. She saw nothing in the room. Her eyes remained locked on the viewing window on the opposite wall. The DCI, the pathologist and the tech who escorted her were in the post-mortem area. Four feet from her, separated by the viewing window, was the coffin she buried her mother in. It drew her in. She bashed her hip into a table with pointy corners. She rubbed where it struck distractedly. The noise of the table moving caused the DCI to glance into the viewing room.

Her mother wanted a solid oak coffin. From the look of things, it had served her proud. When her mother died, it was only Christine and the vicar at the graveside. The grave digger kept a respectful distance until the mound of earth needed to be shovelled back into the hole. No one else came to pay their respects. No one else sent flowers or a condolence card. Samantha's abduction should have been a catalyst for change and it had been, but negatively. Her mother and her argued constantly, usually about nothing. But when her mother died, she had never felt so alone in the world.

A speaker high on the left wall crackled into life. "DS Woolfe, I'm Professor Dixon. We spoke briefly on the phone two days ago." She gave Christine a grim smile. "I need you to identify this is the coffin interred during your mother's funeral service. Are you able to do that?"

Christine started to speak, but Professor Dixon gestured to the left and she noticed a small microphone with a push-to-talk button. Pressing the button, Christine said, "I can."

Professor Dixon confirmed the details and said, "You can wait outside now. You know I need to extract some material from a tooth for a DNA comparison? Kathy," pointing to the tech, "will let you know when I've finished."

Christine didn't need telling twice. With a nod, she was out of there. She had said her goodbyes ten years ago. She wasn't keen on playing catch-up.

Christine was sitting on the low wall outside the mortuary, getting some fresh air, when she heard tech Kathy's familiar, but now accelerated swish coming up behind her. She looked flushed, and by the way, she was sucking air not long from making Professor Dixon's work list.

"DS Woolfe, sorry. Can you come, please?"

She wouldn't tell Christine what was going on; she kept repeating Professor Dixon needs to speak with you. In fact, the DCI waylaid her before they had got too far. He beckoned her to follow him and walked ahead to a side corridor.

"Christine, grab a pew," he said, guiding her to a bench.

What the hell had happened now? She sat down like the bench was a life raft bobbing on the ocean.

"We've not known each other too long, but I sense you prefer plain speaking. From the hip, as they say." He fidgeted with a pen he took from his suit jacket and kept looking over her shoulder, not making eye contact with her.

Christine said, "What's wrong, boss?"

The DCI took her hand in his. Whoa there, Steve, personal space. Or, holy shit, this is gonna be bad!

"Christine, did you see your mother in the coffin before they screwed down the lid?"

"Yes, I was there when they did it; what's the matter? Isn't it her coffin?"

The DCI released her hand and used it to nervously smooth his hair, front to back. Fuck, it's the holy shit version.

"OK, all the news in one hit. Yes, it's your mother's coffin." He still wasn't making eye contact. "It contains most of your mother and a couple of bits not from her." His throat moved as if he was trying to swallow a couple of Lego bricks. He coughed and tried swallowing the Lego bricks again. "I'm sorry to tell you her head is missing, and in its place is one from a man probably in his late fifties..."

"You said a couple of bits," Christine blurted.

The hand was back. "Yes, I did. There was also a castrated penis shoved into the man's mouth."

OK, didn't see that one coming; no pun intended. WTF, no, really WTF.

"Forensics will run tests on the head, the genitals, and your mum's remains to cross the t's and dot the i's."

They had asked Christine if she was OK with viewing the contents of the coffin. She agreed, but approached with trepidation, not knowing how her mother's body would have fared over the ten years. The oak coffin had done a good job. Her mother's body looked like a mummy without the wrappings. The head and the penis, well, they were greasier looking.

"I'm sure the torso is mum's; she had an appendix scar on her stomach there and a double mole on her right arm. The head and penis? Not a clue."

Christine declined the DCI's offer of a lift back to the incident room and hit a local bar hard before the tube journey back to her flat. The alcohol cosh worked. It made the journey completely numb, and thanks to an off-licence top-up once she got home, it wasn't until she woke the following day she thought about things and stuff.

What did this mean for the case? The killer obviously wanted her to see Frankenstein's monster, but to what end? The penis in the mouth was possibly sending a message this guy was a sexual deviant, rapist, or a literal dickhead. Maybe our rapist?

Things were getting much too personal. Given the family connections, the DCI told her to take a few days off while he decided if she should continue on the case. Honestly, she was OK with the time out, but wanted to stay involved. She was there at the start and fully intended to be there when they caught the bastard.

Chapter 38

Christine slept late on the third morning of her enforced break. She realised she had raised her protective shield the day of the exhumation. She built her shield without conscious thought and it offered protection when Samantha was taken. It got reinforced when her mum turned against her, and during other times in the job when she had to see and deal with some of the nasty shit most coppers experience. It was now in full protection mode, raised without conscious thought, and as long as it remained in place, she could deal with whatever the world threw at her.

Christine swung her legs out of bed and sat staring at nothing but thinking of everything.

She knew the compression of the anguish, and sometimes the horror, into a little box in the back of her brain had consequences. Many of her colleagues turned to alcohol as a release valve, swapping one demon for another. It never worked, but they convinced themselves it did until the box leaked, releasing the demons into their normal relationships and work. So far, in Christine's case, it meant she appeared cold and unemotional to her partners, focused on the job and not giving of herself. And they all walked. Some after a short while, sometimes they lasted a while longer. But they all left.

Still, she would have to deal with it when the time came, but not now. Now she needed to focus on the job. As usual.

Retail therapy was the answer to the unasked question, sealing the lid of her little box. And so, while she adjoined the battle in the Colosseum of the 21st century, Primark, her mobile rang.

She answered, and before she could speak, the DCI said, "Christine, can you come down to the Forensic Science Lab at Kennington." He gave her the address and rang off. Something in his voice caused her little worm to become active again.

Forty-seven minutes later, as Christine approached the office, she saw the DCI sitting at a desk in conversation with John Tweed, the DNA forensic lead. He noticed and waved her in, pointing to the vacant chair next to John.

Christine had worked with John on a couple of her larger cases before getting shot. He was late forties, slim, wore glasses and had a tangle of dark hair, which he must style each morning with a live 240-volt cable. He blinked rapidly every 20 seconds and had a speedy and to-the-point way of talking. Like he didn't have the time. In short, your stereotypical movie mad scientist. Except, he dressed superbly. Today was a tailored dark grey Ozwald Boateng suit, matching shirt, and a slim pink tie. He looked the crazy bollocks. He was also very good at his job.

The DCI started speaking, "This case keeps getting weirder. John, can you break it down for Christine, starting with the head?"

John pulled a sheet of A4 from a document folder on his lap, glanced at it and began, "OK, Christine. We pulled DNA from teeth in the man's head and got a system match. As you know, in the area around Wimbledon about thirty-four years ago, there was a series of rapes. Three women reported being attacked in their homes. The incident team at the time suspected there might have been more victims, but no one else came forward. After a thirteen-month spree, there were no more reports, and the trail went cold. Since then, no other matches have come to light, and the rapist is still unidentified. Although you know all the recent murder victims share his DNA."

"Sounds like someone knew or found out," Christine said, "Was he decapitated at the same time my mum died? Anyone reported missing? Was the penis his? Any headless bodies turn up around the same time?" The words flowed effortlessly, delivered as a stream of consciousness.

John smiled at her. "Ever thought of becoming a cop, Christine? You have a flair? I agree, around the same time is more than likely, no, yes and no."

Christine processed the answers before saying, "So, we're in deep shit with no clue which way is up, would be my guess?"

The DCI smiled and said, "Well, yes."

His face turned serious, and he told Christine what he hadn't wanted to say to her over the phone.

And the hits kept on coming. Leaving the forensic lab, Christine meandered around Central London, turning over information and remembered conversations, family interactions, and her entire life. Her inner anti-collision detector took over as she ghosted through the London crowds. Having to speak to anyone would have broken her loose grasp on reality.

After about two hours, Christine stopped and, for the first time, took notice of where she was. Maybe her wanderings had not been so aimless after all. She stood outside Somerset House on the Strand.

The DCI had told her they had extracted viable DNA from her mother's remains. He also reminded her each Met officer had a DNA sample taken and stored. So they did a comparison, but there wasn't one. Christine's mother... wasn't.

Sooo... They replaced her 'not the mama's' head with a dead dick-sucking unidentified rapist active thirty-five years ago. Aaand... the information which led to the joyous discovery was from a yet-to-be-captured or identified serial killer still very much active and taunting them on the wicked wild web. Where the F.U.C.K did she fit into this crock of shit play? She hadn't auditioned for the role. She just improvised her lines as she stumbled through each scene.

There had been conversations with the boss about how, should, could she remain on the investigation? He had his view; she had hers, and in the end, she was no longer the exhibits officer. She found herself relegated to the tasks of background resource and tea maker. Yes, the Gofer once more, but in her mind still involved. The worm in her stomach was correct. Smart little invertebrate. Honestly, you couldn't write it.

Chapter 39

The Detective Superintendent had told the DCI to hold another press conference, which hadn't gone well. He had nothing to say, or rather, he had nothing he wanted to share with the press. They asked questions about the previous suspect. He informed the reporters he was released and excluded from the investigation. Eventually, he had ended the debacle and turned to leave. Several reporters shouted questions at him. They still wanted answers he hadn't given them.

One question stood out, "I'm told you dug up the body of DS Woolfe's mother. She's on your team. What did you find?"

The DCI didn't break stride and left the conference room.

He hustled into the incident room, "Did you see who asked the last question about your mother's exhumation?"

"We did," said Christine and Pritch in unison. They had been watching on the 24 news channel, "Jake Turner, from the Sun."

The DCI told Pritch to find Jake Turner's contact details but not to make contact or to say anything to the press about his question.

A few minutes later, as the DCI walked back to his office with a mug of coffee, Pritch stood and said, "Boss, got Jake Turner's number for you," and handed the piece of paper over.

He took it, closed the office door, and prepared to grill a reporter. He had just dialled the number when Pritch burst through the door.

"Boss, we've got movement at Jasmine's house."

He slammed the phone down, leapt up, and followed Pritch back to his computer.

As he did so, he called out, "Pete, get onto the control room. I want officers at Jasmine Cooper's address ASAP to detain anyone they find inside. Tell them to secure the front and rear. They have my permission to enter. Tell them to be careful and take all precautions. They could be confronting a serial killer. Christine call up Dave, Ray, and Kumar tell them to drop everything and get over to Cooper's house."

Arriving at Pritch's desk, he said, "What have we got?"

"This is streaming live."

The DCI looked at the screen and saw a man in dark clothing and a balaclava moving around Jasmine's bedroom. He noticed he was wearing gloves.

"Pete, what's the update on the arrest team?"

"Currently, there are no units available. I've tried to stress the urgency of this, but they haven't anyone to send."

"Get me the control room manager."

Pete spoke into the phone and held the phone out, "Boss, Inspector Roberts."

Taking the phone, the DCI said, "Inspector Roberts, this is DCI Balcombe of the Major Incident Team. We are watching a serial killer suspect streaming live from a previous victim's house at the address you've been given. I need officers on scene immediately to surround the house and arrest the suspect."

He listened and said, "I understand, but there must be someone, Armed Response, DPG, foot patrols, someone for God's sake?"

He listened again. "OK, I'll send some of my officers, and please send someone to the house when you can, but not alone. If the suspect leaves, I'll let you know." He cut the call.

"Unbelievable. Thirty-four thousand officers in the Met, and no one's available to arrest a serial killer. Pritch, what's the guy doing now?"

"He's come down the stairs and appears to be heading for the back door, boss."

"Fuck! Sorry, just frustrated. Have you got it recorded?"

Seeing Pritch's look, he said, "Of course you have. Christine, call Dave. I want him to wait for the others and then enter the house to see if anything has moved or changed from when he was there a few days ago. Where's Lucy?"

Pete said, "She ran something to the Yard for me. She'll be back soon."

"Call her. Get her over to Cooper's place as well. If the suspect's gone, which I'm certain he has by now, tell her and Kumar to look for CCTV in the locality. The guy wore a balaclava in the house, but I bet he didn't walk around the streets with it on. And call Inspector Roberts back."

Pete said, "Right, boss, and picked up the phone."

Christine and the DCI watched the replay on Pritch's computer. He stepped from the kitchen into the hallway, always looking around. Stopped at the foot of the stairs and appeared to be listening for something. He opened the door to the living room and went in.

Christine said, "He's being careful because the house is empty. It's a terraced house, and he doesn't want to make any noise for the neighbours to hear."

The DCI said, "I think you're right. Neighbours are used to noises from next door, but anything will register when they've stopped for a while. He obviously doesn't suspect we have replaced his cameras with our own. That was a fantastic call, Pritch."

"Thanks, boss."

After about two minutes, the man came out of the living room and walked wide-legged up the stairs, planting his feet on either side of the treads next to the wall and the bannisters. They lost sight of him then until he entered Jasmine's bedroom. He looked at the bookcase where Pritch had found the main hub camera and stood in front of it with his back to the bookcase as if seeing what the camera would see. He squatted down and into a press-up position to look under the bed. Standing, he left the bedroom, and the hall camera picked him up, coming down the stairs. With one last look around, he walked towards the kitchen and the back door.

Pritch said, "And that's the lot. Eight and a half minutes start to finish. I don't get it. He must have known we found his cameras. Why return to the house?"

Christine said, "I can't wait to ask him. But it is weird."

The rest of the team made it back for the evening briefing, and they all watched the footage. Christine noted everyone made comments, primarily about the Wooden Tops not being around when you needed them, except for Lucy.

Dave reported nothing appeared out of place or missing from the last time he was there. He and Ray had then knocked the neighbours to ask if they had seen or heard anything. They hadn't. Kumar said he and Lucy hadn't found any CCTV or none that actually worked, and no one seemed to even have a video doorbell.

Christine saw Lucy nod, but Kumar told what they had done. Something was up with Lucy. She resolved to ask her when the briefing finished.

The DCI said, "I eventually rang Jake Turner at the Sun. He said the tip came to him from a switchboard call to his desk phone. A male voice said, 'They have dug up DS Christine Woolfe's mother. It may do you some good to ask about it this morning.' He tried to trace the number, but the switchboard said the caller withheld the number."

At the end of the briefing, Pete called Christine over to his desk to discuss an action she had filed. When she finished talking with him, Lucy was gone.

She asked Kumar, "Do you know where Lucy is?"

"She said her boyfriend was coming over tonight and had to get off."

"OK, I think I'll head off too. See you tomorrow."

Chapter 40

Christine stepped into the shower and turned the water on, full and hot. She tried to steam the sense of unease out of her. There was definitely something wrong with Lucy. She replayed her thoughts. When Lucy returned to the incident room, she seemed to be her usual self. She was laughing with Dave about something or other. They all gathered around Pritch's computer to watch the footage of the suspect. She realised now Lucy changed as she watched the footage. Had she recalled something, or was she reliving the crime scene? She was with the team at the house, and Christine had seen the photos of Jasmine. She would call her. Night out with her boyfriend be damned. She needed to make sure she was OK.

She dried herself, slipped into her newly washed fluffy dressing gown, and padded barefoot to her bedroom. When she picked up her mobile, it was on silent. She saw a missed call from Lucy and a voicemail. She tried calling Lucy back, but there was no reply. So, she left a voice message asking Lucy to call her again. Then she listened to Lucy's voicemail.

She rang the DCI as she was getting dressed. When he answered, she gabbled her words. To the extent, he asked her to slow down and repeat what she had said.

She took a deep breath and said, "Boss, I knew something was wrong with Lucy at the briefing. I thought she was thinking about the Jasmine scene. But she left me a voicemail a little while ago. She recognised the man in the video. She thinks it's her boy—"

She heard the DCI calling her name. "Sorry, I was trying to put my jeans on, but I got tangled and fell. She thinks her boyfriend, Sebastian, is the killer. I'm heading over to her place right now." She recited Lucy's address. "Get me some backup. I'll keep calling her. I'll let you know what I find. She hung up."

Grabbing her coat, she headed for her car. She pressed Lucy's number on speed dial. It went straight to voicemail.

Christine skidded to a stop outside Lucy's block of flats. She ran to the marked patrol car with two officers inside. Flashed her warrant card and called for the officers to follow her. She reached the electronic front door and pressed all the buttons except Lucy's. What sounded like an old lady was the first to answer.

"I'm Detective Sergeant Woolfe; I think one of your neighbours is in trouble. Please open the door."

Through the glass door, Christine noticed the door on the left crack open a little, and an elderly woman peered out. Seeing the two uniformed officers standing behind Christine, she pressed the button inside her flat to open the door. As Christine and the other officers ran past, the lady said to their backs, "I hope she's alright."

Christine pressed Lucy's doorbell and began pounding on the door. She stopped and listened. Nothing. She banged the door again.

She turned to the officers. "Do you have an Enforcer in the car?"

One of them nodded.

"Get it." She banged the door again and shouted, "Lucy, it's Christine. Let me know you're OK." She listened. The only sound was the door opposite opening and a male neighbour asking what was happening. The uniformed officer told him it was a police matter and to close his door.

The officer returned with the big red key, and Christine stepped to one side to give him room to swing it at the door. It burst open on the third blow. The lights were on in all the rooms, but the flat was silent. Christine inched down the hallway. Something caught in the back of her throat. She knew what it was, but didn't want to acknowledge it. The door to the kitchen was open, and appeared empty, as was the bathroom. She pushed open the living room door. DeeJay had yellow plumbing foam protruding from his mouth and nose.

"Fuck, fuck, fuck."

She spun and faced the officers. "This is a crime scene. One of you stay by the door. Nobody gets in. The other speak to the neighbour across the way and ask if he heard or saw anything. Then, speak to the old lady who let us in. I told her one of her neighbours might be in trouble, and she said, 'I hope she's OK'. Ask her what she meant. And make notes."

Christine stood outside the bedroom door. She suspected what she would see when she opened the door. Yet she knew she had to do it. Slowly, she pushed the door open.

She gasped, and her sharp intake of breath stung the back of her throat. Bleach. She could taste it in the air.

Lucy was on her bed naked, lying on her back, head turned towards the door so her dead eyes were staring right at her. Two large cans of plumbing foam and two long tubes filled with foam were lying discarded on the floor.

Lucy's ears had foam, her mouth and nostrils had foam. Lucy's legs were spread wide, and when Christine positioned herself to see, foam was coming out of Lucy's vagina and anus. The killer had filled every exit or entry on her body.

Christine ran to the bathroom and threw up in the sink. She should have trusted her gut or the worm, or just her common sense. Out of everyone, she knew Lucy wasn't right. No one else picked up on it. The bile came again. She ran the tap to clear her shame away, wiped her mouth and resolved again to nail this fucking prick.

As she came out of the bathroom, she heard the DCI telling the officer on guard at the door to let him in. Christine walked towards them both and said, "It's OK. He's my boss."

The DCI walked a little way down the hall, and Christine stopped him.

"He's killed her. Why, boss?" Christine could feel tears welling up, and she did nothing to stop them.

"Where is she?"

"The bedroom. He really went to town on her. He also killed her cat, DeeJay. What kind of sick fuck are we after here?"

The DCI looked into the bedroom, shook his head and reached for his mobile.

Chapter 41

The forensics team arrived about an hour later and started working the scene. The team kicked Christine and the DCI out, leaving the uniformed constable on the door. There was a constable on the main door, and uniform had taped the entrance to the parking area off. The entire team, including Pete and Pritch, gathered together in the car park. Christine brought everyone up to speed.

She played the voice message - 'Christine, I think I've fucked up. I recognised the man in Pritch's video. It's Sebastian. He's the killer. I thought he was just interested in my work. He was asking questions about how the team was doing and about you. I'm sorry for being so stupid. Call me back when you get this, please.'

"In addition, when the old lady let us in, she said as we passed, 'I hope she's alright'. I tasked a constable to speak with the neighbour opposite Lucy's flat and the old lady. The neighbour opposite took the three wise monkeys' approach. So was of no use at all. The old lady, Mrs Mavis Crenden, said she heard some shouting about two or three hours before I arrived, which she thought was coming from Lucy's flat. She heard someone running down the stairs maybe twenty minutes later. That's it. All the other neighbours were out."

The DCI spoke, "I know this is difficult. I had a conversation with my boss. He knows the team can't walk away from this, but he insisted DC Phillips from team 3 become the exhibits officer for Lucy's murder. We can investigate, and we will. What do we know about Lucy's boyfriend?"

He went around the team, and no one knew anything much except Lucy had a new boyfriend. Most hadn't even heard his name.

The DCI looked at Christine who had said nothing. "She called you. You must know something?"

"She mentioned the new boyfriend on our trip to Western-Super-Mare. I think she met him before the Sarah Davies murder. If I remember correctly, she was in her local Starbucks, and this guy behind her in the queue made some joke about the amount of coffee choices they had. Lucy liked him from the get-go and went to the coffee shop over the next few days, hoping to meet him again. Eventually, he was there, and they sat and drank their coffees together. She was smitten with him. I got the impression they were becoming an item. She confided in me he had been to her flat, and they had made love..."

Tears came again, and Christine brushed them away. "The only solid information I have is his name was Sebastian. He told her he was a graphic designer at a firm in the West End. I have no details. Also, he told her he lived in Thailand for a few years and travelled back to the UK via Europe. He speaks several languages."

"Thanks, Christine. Pritch, I want you to take Lucy's mobile as soon as the techs have finished with the flat. We need to find any details about Sebastian. If possible, get a picture and sweep the place with your gadget. The rest of you get canvassing, talk to neighbours, look for CCTV on the roads leading here. Christine, if you're up to it, speak with the old lady. She seems the nosey type. She may have seen Sebastian. We can estimate his height from Pritch's video."

"OK, boss. But I remember Lucy saying Sebastian was shy and didn't like to have his picture taken."

The DCI called Pritch over, "First thing in the morning, get along to the local Starbucks and see if you can find Lucy and Sebastian on their CCTV system. We need a picture."

"Sure thing, boss. I'll nip back to the incident room and grab my do-hickey so I'm ready for when the forensic techs have finished."

Christine knocked on Mrs Crenden's door, which opened immediately. She looked Christine up and down. "You're the young woman who rang my bell earlier."

"Yes, I'm Detective Sergeant Woolfe. Christine. Can I speak with you about Lucy and her boyfriend?"

"Well, I know you're from the police, but I don't think I should without speaking to Lucy."

"Didn't the uniformed officer who spoke with you earlier tell you? I'm afraid that's not possible. There's no easy way for me to tell you this, but your neighbour, Lucy, died tonight."

Mrs Crenden looked as if she was going to collapse, and Christine held her arm and guided her into her living room.

Mrs Crenden muttered, "Sweet Jesus, sweet Jesus."

Christine settled her into an armchair. "Can I get you a hot drink?" Christine asked.

"I wouldn't mind a cup of tea. Milk, no sugar. Lucy was a police detective, she told me. I felt safe knowing she lived here. Did you know her?"

"Yes, she was on my team."

Christine went into the kitchen and a short while later, returned with two cups of tea on a tray. She handed one to Mrs Crenden and took one for herself. She sat on the sofa with the coffee table between them.

"Mrs Crenden."

"Oh, call me Mavis, and you're Christine. Mrs Crenden makes me feel old. I may look it, but in my head, I'm twenty-one again." She smiled at Christine.

"Mavis, did you ever see Lucy's boyfriend?"

"Oh yes. A nice young man. Are you saying he killed her? I wouldn't have thought it. He was big enough, but he had a gentle way about him. And very polite."

"It's too early to say, but we want to inform him of Lucy's death before he hears it on the news."

Mavis gave Christine a shrewd look, "If you say so, dear."

Christine could tell there was a lucid brain behind the old biddy facade.

"Could you describe her boyfriend to me?"

"Well, he was big. At least bigger than Lucy and me. And broad-shouldered. He had blond hair, like yours, but shorter, and swept to his left in front."

Definitely more Miss Marple than old biddy. Lucy was 5'2 in shoes, so big was relative.

"Did he have a beard or moustache? Or glasses?"

"No, nothing like that. He had very smooth skin." Mavis gave an embarrassed smile. "Sorry, got a bit carried away there. He was handsome. If I'm honest, Lucy was a lovely woman, but they must have connected on another level, if you know what I mean."

To her shame in the moment, Christine did know.

"How was he dressed? Can you remember?"

"Casual, I think they call it. Blue jeans, a dark blue shirt and a pullover draped over his shoulders. He was carrying a bouquet of lilies and a bottle of wine. When he rang my bell, I thought my luck had changed. But he couldn't remember Lucy's flat number, and mine is the top bell. So I always get callers."

"What age would you put him at?"

"Now, I'm not very good with ages. Police officers look like school kids, and don't get me started on doctors. I would say late twenties, maybe early thirties."

"Did you only see him the once?"

"No, dear, I saw him this evening. I heard the shouting as I told that young officer in uniform and heard the front door close. I peeked out; my window overlooks the front path. And I saw him walking from the flats towards the main road."

"What was he wearing?"

"I couldn't tell. He had a dark long coat on. But the light caught his blond hair. It was him."

"What time was this?"

"I'm not sure. What time did you ring my bell the first time?"

"About half-past nine?"

"Then it may have been an hour or two before that."

Christine reflected on the time Lucy had called her and left the voicemail time-stamped 19:37. She processed her thoughts. Sebastian came over. Lucy confronted him about being in Jasmine's house. They argued. Then it got fuzzy. Did Lucy call her while Sebastian was still there? If so, it likely prompted the attack on Lucy, or did she call after he left? Did he come back? He must have done if he was the killer unless he killed her after she made the call when he was still here. It made sense. Befriend someone on the squad who will investigate your first London kill. Lucy lived alone, and any surveillance would give him enough information about the team's inner workings. And he could ask innocent-sounding questions.

Mavis was talking, "Penny for them?"

"Sorry, thinking about anything else I need to ask you. Did you see anyone else come into the flats tonight, or did anyone else ask to be let in you didn't know in recent weeks?"

"No, dear. I can't think of anyone."

Christine stood, "OK. Thank you very much for your time and your recollections. Someone will be round to take a formal statement from you at some point. If that would be alright?"

"I'd be pleased of the company. I'm sorry for the loss of your friend."

"Thank you. I'll see myself out."

Pritch approached Christine as she walked out into the car park area.

"Christine, we found three cameras in Lucy's place. The techs have removed and catalogued them. They were like the others at Jasmine's house. The hallway, living room and the bedroom."

"Did you see her?"

"No, thank God. I don't do dead people. Especially friends. They put up a screen. How are you holding up? You got close to Lucy, didn't you?"

"Yes, I did. You know, only two women on the team, girl bonding."

She started to cry, and Pritch held her.

Christine blubbed, "I knew something was wrong as soon as she watched the video. I should have said something or called her. Maybe I could have stopped this if I had seen the missed call and the voice message."

"You can't blame yourself. This killer is a bastard. For some reason, I think Lucy's death was personal to him. He wanted to make her suffer and inflict pain on us...You. I saw her cat. What the fuck!"

Christine eased away. "Thanks, Pritch. I needed that."

She wiped her eyes with a tissue.

"Any luck with her mobile?"

"No pictures, but a number. I'll run it, but given the runaround so far, it'll be a 'pay as you go' or a burner as the Yanks would have it."

The rest of the team drifted back to the car park, and the DCI held a mini briefing. So far, they had gathered no information from talking to neighbours or reviewing CCTV footage on roads leading to the flats. Christine related Mrs Crenden's description of Sebastian and the timeline from her point of view. Pritch revealed he had found three surveillance devices, like those at Jasmine's house. After that, the DCI sent the team home to return to the incident room for an update briefing at 9 am.

Christine drove the short distance to her flat on auto-pilot. Thinking about coulda, woulda, shoulda. She couldn't get the image of Lucy out of her head. Whoever this Sebastian turned out to be, she would avenge Lucy's death and those of her half-sisters. When she finally got into bed, the rage reduced to a certainty, which allowed her to sleep.

Chapter 42

Christine walked into the incident room just after eight. She glanced at Lucy's chair and desk, and the anger and guilt returned. Over the next twenty minutes, the rest of the team arrived, and the DCI started the morning briefing.

"It won't surprise you to learn I spent much of the night talking to senior officers and the press team. I can't hide it from you, and I know you're all invested in solving this case, especially after Lucy's murder. Still, pressure is being applied to take the case away from us."

There were grumblings from the team and shaking of heads.

"It will happen if we don't crack the case, or at least have a named suspect by the end of next week. So that gives us a maximum of seven days. I have made the arguments. I know the dedication you will bring to getting this solved, and the person convicted, especially now, will be unsurpassed. But a fresh pair of eyes will view what we have done by next weekend. Pritch is not here; he's gone to Starbucks to find CCTV of Lucy and Sebastian. Remember, the one advantage we have is we're now also investigating the murder of one of our own. We can pull in favours owed, and people will help if they can. We need to make use of that.

"Sam Phillips is attending the PM this morning. The pathologist is the same Professor Grace who has done the previous two. For those of you who didn't view the scene, the difference was like the Western-Super-Mare victim, Lucy, had not been penetrated by the ice pick or whatever he uses. The killer left two clear plastic tubes full of foam next to the two large cans of plumber's foam."

Dave chipped in, "You get those when you buy the large cans. The tubes enable you to direct the flow of the foam better." He paled when he realised what he had said. "Sorry."

"OK, give me an hour to discuss things with Pete, and you can collect your actions, get back to the scene, and re-canvas."

Dave and Ray offered to go to the local cafe for sausage or bacon butties and coffees for everyone. Kumar said he'd pass unless they had plant-based sausages. But he'd have a coffee.

Christine spent her time reflecting on what she knew about the case and trying to think about any morsel of information about Sebastian. She looked at graphic design companies in the West End and at the About Us pages to see if she could spot anyone in the corporate photos who matched Sebastian's description. She also searched for email addresses, starting with Sebastian at those companies and others that didn't have staff photos. Before she knew it, Dave and Ray were back, and she had got nowhere.

Eating the sandwiches and drinking coffee was without the usual banter. A sombre affair, eating and drinking for sustenance's sake only. They had lost one of their own, and that was unacceptable. But, and it was a big but, they weren't any further forward than when they started. Christine felt precisely the same as the others, but with added guilt. She was the only one to pick up on Lucy's mood as she watched the video; she was the only one to miss her call and not see the voicemail until hours later. Lucy's death was her fault.

Pritch returned shortly after and tucked into the bacon butty and coffee Dave and Ray had got him. Through mouthfuls and slurps, he conveyed Starbucks was a bust.

"They have enough CCTV storage for two weeks, and it gets recorded over. Obviously, if something happens, they can download the footage. I asked if anything had happened around the timeframe we had interest in and was told nothing did. So, I asked if anyone recognised Sebastian's description and showed a picture of Lucy. The staff on duty vaguely recalled Lucy as a semi-regular customer, but couldn't remember her meeting or sitting with anyone. And no one recognised the description. It's a busy place."

The DCI walked into the room and caught the tail end of Pritch's update.

"OK, listen up. I want Pritch to go home with each of you today and use his gadget to check out each property. Lucy's death means the killer is not above targeting police officers. Pritch, that includes your place too."

"I sweep mine weekly anyway, boss."

"Paranoid much!" Dave said, which drew a couple of chuckles.

Pritch said, "Boss, now I'm back; I'll chase up Lucy's mobile number for Sebastian."

"Thanks, but don't delay getting the bug sweeps done. Those of you with someone at home, if they know Pritch and are comfortable letting him wander, I could use you here. Otherwise, do it thoroughly, but get back here as soon as possible. We're up against the clock, as I said this morning. Christine, can I have a word in my office?"

The DCI walked into his office, with Christine following. He closed the door behind her and indicated a chair.

"Christine, if Lucy's death has taught me anything, I should have cared more for my staff. Especially you."

"I don't need any special treat—"

"I think you do. From the first contact via the website, the killer mentioned you by name. We now know you share the same DNA as the other victims and a previous suspect in this case, and now we know the person who you thought was your mother was not. Like it or not, you are deeply involved in this case. This Sebastian, whoever he may be, I believe he will be a DNA relative."

"I've been thinking the same thoughts too, boss."

"I know you haven't any relatives you know of. So, I'm suggesting we put you up in a hotel. Leave your car here in the secure car park and take a different pool car each day. And I'm going to make further stipulations. I want you to team up with Dave Wilde. He'll pick you up and drop you off at night. I don't want you going anywhere by yourself. If that's acceptable to you, you can stay on the team. If not, I'll put you in protective custody until we catch this person."

"I think it's a bit OTT, but I want to stay on the investigation, so reluctantly I agree."

"OK, thank you. Ask Dave to come and see me, will you?"

Christine left and told Dave the boss wanted to see him.

Dave knocked on the boss's door and was beckoned in.

"Dave, I have a job for you. I know it will impinge on whatever spare time you have these days, but it's important."

He outlined his plan to keep Christine safe.

"That's no problem, boss. I was thinking about Christine as well. Her name keeps appearing in this case. I was thinking, I have a spare room at mine. If she's OK with it?"

"Talk with her. The hotel offer still stands, but I would be happier with your suggestion. I know that sounds sexist, but this killer has overpowered seven women, including a trained police officer."

"OK, boss. I'll talk to her."

Pritch knocked on the door.

"Boss, as I predicted, Sebastian's mobile comes back to a pay-as-you-go first activated a couple of years ago. So, no likelihood of any CCTV from where he bought it. I've spoken to the provider, and with your signature on this form, we should have access to mobile and location data by the end of the day."

"Excellent work, Pritch. Christine is moving into a hotel or in with Dave for the time being, so tag up with them and give Christine's flat the once over and then Dave's place. Liaise with the others. Sorry, I should have asked, but I thought you wouldn't mind."

"Not at all, boss. I'll get right on it."

Pritch found Dave and Christine in conversation around the coffee machine.

"The boss has asked me to sweep your place first, Christine. OK?"

"Of course, Dave has kindly offered me his spare room rather than a hotel. So I'll be staying there."

"Yes, the boss mentioned it was a possibility. I'm to go yours first and after, sweep Dave's hovel."

Which earned him a swift slap to the back of his head from Dave.

Chapter 43

Pritch decided it was best if he took his own car, as after Dave's place, he had to go to the home addresses of the rest of the team. Dave drove Christine in his car.

He said, "Look, if anyone has been watching you, he knows the car you drive. Leave it here. When we get back from mine, I'll grab a pool car and swap them out. When we leave yours, we'll take a circuitous route to mine. I learnt a bit about anti-surveillance when I worked drugs."

As they drove, Dave glanced over at Christine. She was staring out of the passenger window.

"You can't blame yourself," he said. "There was no way of knowing. If anything, we were all a bit on the slow side, not realising he might watch us. Thinking about it now, right from the start, when the 'I'm coming out' website appeared, the killer picked you out and mentioned you by name. None of us thought a police officer would be in the firing line."

She turned to face him. "But if I had heard the call, listened to the voice message sooner. Maybe I could have saved her. It seems I'm destined to lose people I care about."

"We all do. This thing we call life, none of us gets out of it alive. It's the way of things."

"But not before their time by another's hand. I want to look into this Sebastian's eyes, if that's even his name, and ask him why. What has my extended family done to him? And what the fuck had Lucy done to deserve what happened to her?"

"I think that's easier to answer. If Lucy confronted Sebastian and told him about seeing him at Jasmine's house, she was a liability. If he'd left her alive, we'd have him in the cells by now."

"I know, I know." Christine sighed, "There's a lot of planning gone on here. Research into the victims and interest in who would likely investigate Sarah's death. Remember, Lucy met Sebastian a few days before we found Sarah's body? Oh, left here. The entrance to my flat is second on the right."

Dave signalled the turn to avoid catching Pritch off guard. A minute later, they arrived outside Christine's building.

Christine opened the door to her flat. "Don't judge."

Dave and Pritch followed her in. Looking around the small flat, Dave said, "It's lovely. There's a lot you could do with it," with a smile on his face, "of course, you haven't, but there's potential."

Christine glared at him in mock outrage. "I'll put the coffee on. But no biscuits for you. Pritch gets Chocolate ones."

Dave laughed. Christine joined in. Tension relieved.

Coffee drunk, Pritch fired up his gadget and started sweeping the flat. There weren't a lot of places to hide cameras. He made a comment on the pile of paperbacks next to her bed.

"I expected them to be detective novels or chic lit. To my surprise, when I last swept here, I found Huckleberry Finn, Tom Sawyer, and the author's biography. But thinking about it, I saw your screensaver the other day."

Christine said, "It's my favourite quote of Mark Twain's. I started reading them at school. Tom and Huck Finn took me far away to Missouri, over two hundred years before I was born. Rafting down the big river on a journey of adventure. The stories were my escape. Took me away from my angry and disappointed mother. Introduced me to Mr Twain, a man so full of quotable quotes he has an entire book."

Pritch found the first camera in the bedroom light switch. The killer had done the trick with the left side screw, as in Jasmine's bathroom.

The second was in the living room light switch. The third, the hub relay, was in the hallway smoke detector. He left them all in place.

Christine shuddered. She hadn't said a word since Pritch had found the bug in her bedroom. She understood. The killer, this Sebastian, had been watching her every move. Seen her naked, drunk and heard everything she said in the flat on her mobile. He had violated her, stripped her, and he revelled in it. Took some sick pleasure from what he was doing. He was in her mind. Had dragged her into his world, his abyss, his Hell. But she saw him now. The veil swept from her eyes. She would have him. Or die trying.

Pritch said, "OK, I've put up a camera above the front door. He'll see it if he looks, but we should see him first. I covered the smoke detector camera while I placed it."

Dave said, "Don't go straight to my place. Head as if you're returning to the incident room and then come to me. I'm going to take an anti-surveillance route, just in case. Especially after what you found here."

They left the flat. Christine said goodbye to her home for the last ten years. She wouldn't live there again. She stared out the side window as they drove, and Dave was savvy enough not to interrupt her.

Pritch was already waiting on the doorstep when Dave and Christine arrived. Dave had taken precautions, such as going around roundabouts a couple of times, jumping traffic lights just as they changed to red and parking on a clear stretch of roadway. No one had followed them home, or at least he hadn't seen anyone.

Pritch said, "Christine, why don't you wait in the car until I do the sweep? If he's bugged the place, he'll see you here."

Christine agreed. Dave approached her twenty minutes later and said, "No cameras here. It's safe to come in."

Christine grabbed the GO bag from the back seat and walked up the path and into the house. Pritch said his goodbyes, and Dave showed her around.

"Kitchen, door to back garden. Living room," he pointed up the stairs, "Upstairs, bathroom and separate toilet, my bedroom and yours is at the end of the landing."

"Dave, thank you so much for doing this. I really appreciate it."

"It's no problem. I'll be glad of the company if we actually get any time here. Go get yourself settled in, and I'll put the kettle on. Do you want a sandwich?"

"Please, whatever you're having."

Christine walked up the stairs. She peaked into the bathroom. Surprisingly clean for a man living alone. Shower over the bath and sink with a mirrored cabinet above. Next door a toilet, well stocked with toilet paper and clean like the bathroom. She opened her room door. A single bed under the window, pine wardrobe and dressing table, padded pine chair, a centre ceiling light and a bedside light on a small pine table. By the side of the bed, a natural sheepskin rug. Yes, this will do. She dropped her GO bag beside the bed and headed downstairs.

Dave had prepared proper filtered coffee and cheese and ham sandwiches with seeded bread. They sat in the living room.

Dave said, "Everything OK?"

"Lovely, thank you."

"Stop thanking me. We need to circle the wagons. He's taken one of ours. We'll get him. He'll make a slip, and we'll have him."

Christine sighed, "He hasn't so far. But you're right."

"He has. He went back to Jasmine's place. Even after he must have seen us take the cameras out. That was stupid. A slip."

"No, you're right. Let's get back to the incident room. I want to see what data we can get from Sebastian's call logs."

Dave collected the plates and mugs, placed them in the dishwasher, and they left.

When Dave and Christine arrived, Pete was the only person in the incident room.

"The DCI, Ray and Kumar have gone home to wait for Pritch. My wife was OK with Pritch going over the place, but the DCI's and Kumar's wives were at work. Ray is single, so it's just me."

Christine asked, "Anything on Sebastian's phone yet?"

"Some location data. We can place him near Jasmine's house and Lucy's flat last night. But it appears he switched the phone off when he left. There was nothing after 19:29. Some text messages between Lucy and him. But he spent a lot of his time somewhere in the Fulham area. Cell tower detail only, but it narrows it down to a few hundred yards' radius."

"Can I see the texts?"

"I'll print them off for you. Lucy was definitely smitten. But he appeared to be, too. When the boss comes back, we'll get house-to-house underway in Fulham. But you'll see from the texts the other week Sebastian invited Lucy to a fancy restaurant in the West End. I've written an action up. Do you and Dave want to take it?"

"Absolutely. Tell the boss there were three cameras at my place, but Dave's was clear."

She collected the printout and found Dave by the coffee machine.

"We have an action. Sebastian and Lucy went to a restaurant in the West End a few weeks ago. Grab a pool car, and we'll head over."

"Do you want a coffee to go?"

"No thanks. I'll meet you in the car park."

Chapter 44

They drove towards the West End and the Italian restaurant where Lucy and Sebastian had their date night. Christine found it hard to curb her excitement. Fancy restaurant, high prices, most people would pay by card. Hopefully, good CCTV coverage and storage. She read over the text messages as Dave drove. Pete had been right. In fact, Lucy had fallen head over heels for Sebastian. In her latest messages, she signed off with 'Love you.' But so had Sebastian. How could someone be so callous? To say those things and yet do what he did to her. Evil exists in the world; every copper knows it, but Lucy had come into direct contact yet not recognised it. The Devil's greatest trick is to make people believe he doesn't exist, so they say. Christine now knew differently. She hoped for the opportunity to reunite Sebastian with him.

Dave and Christine entered the restaurant and flashed their warrant cards at the first waiter they saw. He swiftly led them to the manager's office as if he didn't want the two detectives smelling up the place. As they moved through the restaurant, Christine caught wafts of expensive perfume mixed with Parmigiano and olive oil.

She saw only sparkly people. A date who wanted to impress her had taken her to the Ritz Hotel's restaurant a few years ago. If his credit card had worked at the end of the meal, she would've been more impressed. Instead, she ended up footing the bill, an eye-watering amount. There was no second date. But while she sat there using her surveillance skills to observe the other patrons, she realised they were sparkly people. They didn't exist in her world, only in places like the Ritz or Saint-Tropez or Monaco. On the next table was a group of young girls celebrating an eighteenth birthday of one of them. She heard them talking and moaning. They had been at the Ritz so many times, but daddy insisted as he could put it on his expense account. Next generation of sparkly people right there.

When they got to the manager's office, it was empty.

The waiter said, "The manager is away today. I am Giovanni, the Maître d'. How can I help you?"

Christine introduced herself and Dave. "We're here on a murder enquiry. Do you have CCTV?"

She knew they did because she and Dave had spotted cameras on the front door, behind the bar and dotted around the restaurant.

Giovanni said, "We do, state-of-the-art, as you might imagine. What do you need?"

"We need to look at the footage for this date from about 7 pm, she said, showing him the date on the action form she had brought. Problem?"

"Not exactly, but you have to understand we have a lot of important people who come to this restaurant and not all of them come with who they should. If you understand?"

Christine took a breath. Fucking sparkly people.

"We do, but this is a murder investigation. On the date in question, this woman came here to meet someone." She brought up a picture of Lucy on her mobile. "We need to find out who he was. That's all we're interested in."

"I was off that day, but let me see."

He went over to the bank of CCTV recorders at the far side of the office and switched on the monitor. He tapped a password on the keyboard and entered the date and time Christine had given him.

Dave said, "There, go back a bit."

Giovanni moved the trackball, and the image slowly reversed.

Christine, who had the first pricks of tears in her eyes, said, "That's her. Can we move forward so we can see who she meets?"

Giovanni played the video at half speed. Lucy was looking around as if searching for her date when he stepped up behind her. Dave and Christine stared at the monitor. This was Sebastian. They had him.

Christine made Giovanni scroll back to where Sebastian had entered the restaurant and play it at double speed until he and Lucy left. Giovanni could zoom in to isolate their table. Their system was genuinely state-of-the-art. Christine had produced a USB drive and had the footage transferred to it.

Christine asked, "Can we see the footage from above the front door to see him arriving and both leaving?" Giovanni played the video recording and transferred the footage to the USB drive.

Christine said, "Thank you, Giovanni. Our tech people will be here tomorrow to take a copy of the various drives the footage is on." Seeing Giovanni about to protest, she added, "With an evidence warrant. Please ensure no one alters the drives before then."

As they drove back to the incident room, Christine called the DCI.

"Boss, we have video footage of Sebastian. Dave and I are heading back now. Ask Pete to get an evidence warrant for a copy of the CCTV hard drives at the restaurant."

"Fantastic work; the team's all here now, so you can brief us when you get back."

Chapter 45

Christine gave Pritch the USB drive, which he plugged into his computer. He swung the monitor around so the team could see and pressed play.

The first footage they had seen at the restaurant appeared on the screen. Lucy standing by herself. Christine looked around her colleagues, and to a man, they were all wiping their eyes.

As the video played, Sebastian and Lucy looked like they were having the most perfect time. They both laughed and touched hands across the table. No red flags at all.

They all noticed, and Ray said what they all must have been feeling, "Damn." when the video showed Sebastian paying for the meal with cash.

Christine said, "We checked the reservation details before we left, and they only had Sebastian's name and the mobile number we already have."

The video changed to outside the restaurant. They saw him hail a black cab, hug Lucy, and give her a kiss on the lips. Lucy climbed into the cab, and it drove away. They saw Sebastian walk in the other direction and out of shot. Pritch switched the video off.

There was silence in the room.

The DCI spoke first, and Christine detected a slight croak in his voice, "OK, we have a picture. Pritch, print off enough of the best pictures from the video for everyone. Pete, write actions for people to canvas the local shops in the Fulham area within the cell tower triangle. Have someone access any other CCTV footage from around the restaurant? Anyone think of anything else?"

"After what happened to Lucy," Christine said, "I feel I should say this. Something about Sebastian seems familiar. I can't put my finger on what it is, but it's there. Niggling in my brain."

Kumar said, "Someone you've seen on this investigation?"

"No, I don't think so. But something. Hopefully, it'll come to me soon."

The DCI cleared his throat and said, "I've heard from Sam Phillips. You know he attended the post-mortem this morning. As we expected, the killer had been busy with bleach again, and they'd be surprised if there's anything forensic-wise. Unfortunately, the long plastic tubes, which we haven't seen before, were used to an effect. Not only were Lucy's mouth and nostrils foamed, but the killer reached down with the tube and filled her lungs and the oesophagus. Everything. The second can with the long tube he put up her vagina and anus and filled her from the inside out."

Christine began to cry. Kumar handed her a tissue. She saw tears in his eyes and those of Pete and Dave. Pritch couldn't be seen because he was looking for something below his monitor. She saw the blood drain from Ray's face. He shook his head slowly and squeezed the arms of his chair.

The DCI said, "OK, I know that was difficult to hear. We all knew Lucy and want her killer caught. So, take as much time as you need, but we need to solve this case. For Lucy, the other women, and for ourselves. When you're ready, and I don't want any machismo here, when you're ready, take the actions from—"

Pritch let out a loud, "Oh fuck. Sorry, boss. There's a new update on the website."

He didn't have to tell any of them which website. They had all been expecting it, eventually. Christine could tell from the look on the rest of the team's faces they were not in a hurry to see what the update was.

The DCI was the first to react. "Listen up. I expect the killer, this Sebastian, has put on the website details of how he killed Lucy for the very reason you are feeling what you are feeling right now. He wants to mess with our heads and disrupt the team however he can. We can read it together, share the pain and move on, or look at it individually and then talk about it. What do you want to do? Show of hands for reading it together?"

Everyone raised their hands.

"OK, meet back here in ten minutes, and we'll take a look."

Christine was pleased she didn't have to share the women's toilet with anyone else as she washed her face. As soon as she thought it, she understood what it meant, and burst into tears again.

In less than ten minutes, the team was back together. Professional faces in place, stoic and resigned to what they would see.

The DCI said, "OK, Pritch, turn the monitor around and join us. We can view it together."

Pritch clicked his wireless mouse, and the website came up.

Good afternoon, one and all, or whenever the time is for you.

It became necessary to take a piece off the game board yesterday.

Meet Lucy.

Lucy was a police officer on the team hunting me.

We met in a coffee shop, by chance or not!

We were close, but she was getting too close, so she had to go. If you know what I mean?

We had fun. She was an excellent fuck!

Too soon?

Interspersed with the text were graphic pictures of Lucy on the bed.

As you can see, Lucy was a leaky sieve. She had to be shut up. And shut up, so nothing came out of her ever again. Shut up for ever.

Those of you who love your pets, look away now!

A picture of DeeJay flashed onto the screen, there for ten seconds and gone again.

How Lucy loved her cat. But it needed to be shut up, too. Whining and mewing all over the place.

Luckily, I had some extra foam (Smiley face emoji), so no problem. Now, back to work.

Christine, my dear, we will meet soon unless you catch me. But not much chance of that, is there? Please, don't think moving out of dear old mum's flat will stop me. Sorry, I forgot, you were the cuckoo in the nest, weren't you?

Still mourning little Samantha, are we? Bless.

When will you understand Christine? You can't save everyone?

We are almost done. The puzzle pieces are coming together nicely, but only I have the puzzle box with the picture on the front. You are scrabbling in the dark, deciding which puzzle piece goes where.

All my love 'till we meet,

Sebastian xxx

The DCI and Christine were the only members of the team who saw Lucy's body at the scene. The rest sat in stunned silence, processing what they had just witnessed.

Pritch said with tears unashamedly running down his cheeks, "It doesn't get any easier. Does it?"

Shaking his head, the DCI said, "No, it doesn't. Thoughts, anyone?"

Kumar said, "Damn, I never knew." He took a deep breath to settle himself before continuing, "He is taunting us with the 'Too soon?' remark, and he knows a lot about Christine and her family connections. As you said, boss, he's trying to mess with our heads. Put us on the back foot."

Dave said, "Christine appears to be Sebastian's next victim. He basically wrote it for all the world to see."

Pete spoke up, "Boss, we have to protect Christine. Keep her safe. Sorry, Christine, but I don't think you can be out and about until we catch this bastard."

"Pete, he knows I've moved out of my flat because he probably saw us finding the cameras, even though we didn't take them. He told us to exhume my mother, so he knew the family history wherever he got his information. We should have worked out sooner he had insider knowledge, but we didn't. Now, I'm his front and centre target. We can't let the killer dictate who does what on this case. I belong here, working the case. I owe it to Lucy, my half-siblings, and myself. Hell, even to you guys. We're in this mess because of something to do with me."

The DCI said, "Dave, are you still willing to work with Christine and have her stay at your house knowing what we now know?"

"Yes, boss."

"OK, Pritch, I want you to go home with Dave now and set up surveillance in the house and, if you can, on the front and back of the house. Do you have enough cameras, etc.?"

"More than enough, boss. I can set up triggers to let me know when there's movement on my mobile."

"OK, get on with it. Dave go with him. Everyone else, apart from Christine, go home but keep your mobiles charged and switched on. Christine, grab a couple of coffees and come into my office. Dave, swing by and pick up Christine when you're done at home."

Chapter 46

When Dave arrived home, he put the kettle on while Pritch set to work, setting up a camera that gave a view of the front door. He asked Dave for a stepladder and placed the camera in the branch of a tree on the pavement a few yards from Dave's front path. He checked the live feed and secured it in place. Satisfied, he moved through the house into the back garden and set up a camera on the garden shed.

"Pritch," Dave called, "Coffee's ready."

"I'll do another sweep before I put my cameras in."

Pritch returned to the kitchen ten minutes later and said, "Still clear. As I walked 'round, I think I'm going to put a camera in the hallway down here, the landing upstairs and some sensors on the downstairs and upstairs windows. I've covered the front and back, and I'll get an alert on my mobile and in the office."

Dave smiled and handed Pritch his coffee. "You know, for a computer nerd, you're quite a useful chap to have around."

After coffee, Pritch placed the cameras and sensors, and they headed back to the incident room.

Pritch said, "This case is messed up, eh?"

"Too right it is. Lucy was happier than I had ever seen her. No one, especially Lucy, deserves to die like that. You saw her, didn't you?"

"Nah, she was screened off. But it messed with my head. And the fucking cat. Its body was almost bursting with the pressure of the foam. I won't forget any of it anytime soon."

They drove on for a while.

Dave broke the silence. "What do you think the foam's all about?"

"The killer, Sebastian, seems to have a problem with women talking. Maybe he's a psychopathic misogynist, or maybe he's just fucked in the head."

Dave smiled, "Spoken like the caring and sharing person I know you to be."

Pritch said with a taut mouth, "Just let me have the opportunity to show how much I care."

Dave decided he needed to keep an eye on his drinking buddy. This case was definitely getting to him, and he didn't want Pritch to be another casualty.

———◆○◆———

Dave and Pritch walked into the incident room. The DCI was still in his office, but everyone else had left except for Christine.

Christine said, "Hi, guys."

Dave said, "You ready for the off?"

"Yeah. I'm grounded. Your house and the incident room."

Pritch said, "Because of what the bastard said on the website?"

"Yep. I'm lucky not to be in protective custody or witness protection or what have you."

Dave said, "Well, at least you'll be here when we bring him in. Ready?"

"Are you sure? Sure you want me at your place? I could stay in a hotel, protected round the clock by armed officers and hidden cameras."

"Pritch has already got the hidden cameras covered. I'm an officer, and I have arms."

Christine burst out laughing. It wasn't a brilliant joke, but it cut the atmosphere, which was what Dave intended. Christine grabbed her bag, waved to the boss and followed the other two out into the corridor, smiling as they play-acted close protection officers.

In the car park, Christine climbed into the pool car, and they drove to Dave's home.

Chapter 47

After changing out of her work clothes, Christine went downstairs to find Dave searching through the kitchen cupboards.

Dave sheepishly said, "I guess I didn't think this through. I normally either eat at work or live on takeaways and toast. I used up any reserves making those sandwiches."

"We can order in. My treat. What do you fancy? Do you like Indian?"

"I normally have a vindaloo or a madras. Hot or not?" He smiled, "Probably not, as there's company."

"Lamb Rogan, peshwari nann and bindi bhaji for me."

"Trouble is, the best Indian doesn't deliver. It's only down the road. We passed it as we came here. It's on the corner."

"I'll be fine. Phone the order in, and you'll be there and back in ten minutes."

"OK, if you're sure? Now I'm thinking about it; I could really do an Indian."

Dave had the restaurant on speed dial and called in the order.

"They said I can collect it in twenty minutes. Do you fancy a beer? I have beer or wine."

"Beer with curry. I'm an old-fashioned girl."

Dave fetched the beers, and they depressed themselves, watching the 24-hour news channel until Dave said, "Right, I'm off to get the curry. Won't be long."

Christine heard the front door shut and went into the kitchen. As she was searching for plates and cutlery. The doorbell rang.

Pritch had just arrived home when his mobile pinged. Looking at the phone, he saw the tree camera outside Dave's house had activated. As he looked, he saw Dave walk up his footpath and turn left. Pritch knew him well enough to know 'curry night'.

He shook his head; one toilet in the house and Dave having a curry. Christine will wish she took the witness protection.

He put the mobile in his back pocket and went to his kitchen to heat a pizza. His mobile pinged again. He looked at it. Someone was walking up Dave's path, and it wasn't Dave. In fact, it looked very much like Sebastian.

Pritch dialled 999. After it rang twice, he said, "Police. Urgently." The operator picked up in the control room. "I'm PC Dave Pritchard from the Major Incident Team. Officer needs urgent assistance. He gave his identification number and Dave's address. "There is a multiple killer at the front door now. DS Christine Woolfe is inside. Send armed officers if possible. DC Dave Wilde has just left the address and will be returning, so make sure the officers know there are two friendlies on scene."

He made sure they understood his message, gave Sebastian's description, and disconnected. He rang Dave's mobile.

"Pritch, my man, what can—"

"Dave, get the fuck home. Sebastian's at your door now. I've called it in. Expect armed response."

Pritch could hear Dave running for all he was worth. He hadn't disconnected the call. His mobile pinged a minute and a half later, and he switched to camera view. He saw Dave race up the path. The front door was open, and Dave charged in.

Switching cameras to the hallway, he saw Dave run towards the kitchen. He launched himself in a semi-rugby tackle, semi-stumble. He heard Christine scream and the sound of the Dave locomotive hitting something. Hard.

Dave shouted, "Christine, are you OK? Pritch, call an ambulance. It's bad, so bad. There's blood everywhere." Dave disconnected the call.

Pritch called the ambulance as instructed and then called the boss.

The DCI picked up, and before he could speak, Pritch said, "Boss, Sebastian turned up at Dave's house. I called it in, asked for armed response and alerted Dave, who left to get a curry. He ran back and went charging in. I heard Christine scream, and then Dave said 'It's bad, there's blood everywhere. Call an ambulance'. I'm going over there now.

"OK, I'll call it in to make sure the armed officers don't shoot the wrong person. I'll meet you there."

Pritch arrived at Dave's house as the ambulance pulled up outside. An armed response car and a local patrol car were already on scene. A uniformed constable who stood by the front gate stopped him from entering.

"I'm on the MIT. My colleagues are in there." He flashed his warrant card and strode towards the front door. "Dave? Christine?" he called.

Christine appeared in the hallway and walked towards him. She was pale and shaking, obviously in shock, and covered in blood. A lot of it. She held a large kitchen knife in her right hand. Blood covered it and extended over her hand and up her arm.

"Are you hurt?"

Before Christine could answer, two paramedics ran past them into the kitchen. As Christine moved to let them by, Pritch saw Dave kneeling beside a male, Sebastian?

Pritch went to Christine, wrapped his arm around her shoulders, and guided her into the living room. He sat her on the sofa, and she looked at him. He saw recognition dawn on her.

"Pritch. I thought it was Dave at the door." She stared at the knife still gripped in her hand.

"Let me take that," he said, pulling on disposable gloves. He took it gently from her hand and placed it on the coffee table.

She trembled, her body quivering as tears ran down her cheeks, carving trails in the drying blood. Pritch held her as she sobbed into his shoulder.

They both looked up towards the living room door when they heard the DCI's voice calling their names.

"In here, boss," Pritch said.

The DCI appeared and looked in from the doorway.

"Boss," said Dave, who appeared at his shoulder. The DCI turned to look at him. His face was ashen. There was blood on his hands and up the cuffs of his jacket, also soaked into the knees of his jeans.

"Come in and sit down. You look as if you might collapse at any minute."

"Thanks, boss."

"Are any of you injured?"

All three shook their heads.

"So the blood is from the male lying on the kitchen floor, I take it?"

Nods from Dave and Christine.

"I've sent the armed response away and called for the forensic team. When they get here, they'll want all your clothes. From the amount of blood I saw on the kitchen floor and on you two," he said, glancing at Dave and Christine, "I think we may have a police-related death."

Christine burst into tears. Physically shaking, rocking back and forth. Pritch held her tighter. She let out a wail as if he was squeezing the air out of her. Similar to the noise a set of bagpipes makes when tuning up.

The DCI said, "Did any of this happen upstairs?"

Dave shook his head.

"Ok, if I go up and grab some clothes for you and Christine."

"Yes, boss. Mine's the first door on the left, and Christine's at the end of the landing."

The DCI returned with trainers, jogging bottoms and sweatshirts a few minutes later.

"I'm going to see how the paramedics are getting on."

The DCI left and walked a few steps to the kitchen doorway. "How's he doing, guys?"

One paramedic looked up at him. "Not well. We've called a specialist trauma doctor. We need to stem the blood flow. If he makes it, he'll be going to King's College. They're the South London trauma centre."

"Thanks. I've got a forensic team arriving shortly. One of my team will go to King's with you. Is that ok?"

"Not a problem if he makes it. Here's the doctor."

The DCI turned and saw an Asian female about five feet tall carrying a large rectangular green rucksack down the hallway. He pressed himself into the wall to allow her by, and immediately, the paramedic relayed the patient's situation to her. It didn't sound good.

The DCI returned to the living room and said, "The forensic team should be here soon. I'm going outside to make a couple of calls. Once the team is finished with you and you've changed clothes, I'll see you back in the incident room. Ray and Kumar are on their way. One of them will go to the hospital with the suspect, and when Pete gets here, they can start talking to neighbours and any potential witnesses."

He turned to leave.

Christine called out to him, "Boss, I recognise Sebastian. I know her."

They all stared at the use of the female pronoun.

"I don't know how, but Sebastian is my sister, Samantha."

Chapter 48

The paramedics and the doctor worked on the suspect for over an hour before being transferred by ambulance to King's trauma centre.

By the time Christine, Dave and Pritch had made it back to the incident room, as expected, officers from the Professional Standards Department were there to meet them. The officers from PSD split them up. The senior officer interviewed Christine.

"I'm Detective Chief Inspector Rowland, and my colleague is Inspector Trammel. We're from the Professional Standards Department. Are you up to being interviewed about what happened this evening?"

Christine said, "I'd like to get it over with."

"You're entitled to legal representation or a Police Federation Union rep?"

"No, I'm happy to go ahead. Although I'm still trying to process what happened."

"Your DCI has given us the details of the case you've been investigating, how you became involved, and the lowdown on the family connections to the case. This interview is being recorded, and

I will caution you once the recording has started. If you're OK, we'll begin."

Christine shifted nervously in her chair across the table from the two senior officers. Her palms were sweating, and she rubbed them on her jogging bottoms to dry them. She had done nothing wrong, but she felt guilty. Did all the suspects she interviewed feel like this?

The buzz of the recording starting snapped her back to the room.

"This is a Professional Standards Department interview. I am Detective Chief Inspector Rowland, my colleague is—"

"Inspector Trammel."

"Please state your name for the recording."

Christine stammered, "Detective Sergeant Christine Woolfe."

"Thank you. I am required to caution you. You do not have to say anything. But it may harm your defence if you do not mention when questioned something which you later rely on in court. Anything you do say may be given in evidence. Do you understand?"

"I understand."

"You do not have to answer my questions, but you are required to give a duty statement. Failure to do so will result in disciplinary action being taken against you. Do you understand?"

Christine nodded.

"For the recording, please."

"I understand." A rookie mistake; she knew how it worked.

"Do you confirm you have consented to this interview without legal representation or support from a representative of the Police Federation?"

"I do."

"OK, please tell us what happened this evening?"

"A threat made against me on the 'I'm coming out' website raised concerns regarding my safety. My DCI sent DC David Wilde and PC David Pritchard to Dave's house to install surveillance cameras. I had moved out of my flat as we had found covert cameras, presumably planted by the serial killer we were hunting. I had moved in with Dave Wilde temporarily for my protection rather than a hotel or witness protection."

"Carry on."

"Dave and Pritch, that's what we call Dave Pritchard, so we don't have two Daves, returned to the incident room. Dave and I then drove to his house. When we got there, we decided we would like a curry. Dave said the best Indian was down the road, but they didn't deliver. I was OK with him popping out to collect it. About twenty minutes after ordering, he left. I was getting the plates ready in the kitchen. Around two or three minutes after he left, I heard the doorbell ring. I thought it must be Dave. Thought he had forgotten his wallet or something. I went down the hall to the front door and opened it."

Christine tried to swallow, but her mouth was dry. She gave a cough and worked her saliva glands to wet her mouth.

"It wasn't Dave. It was someone I had last seen on the video from the Italian restaurant. The man said, 'Hello Christine, I'm Sebastian'.

"I knew it was the serial killer we had been hunting, and I ran down the hall back into the kitchen, intending to leave by the back door. I could hear Sebastian walking after me, and I realised

I wouldn't have time, so I grabbed a kitchen knife off the worktop and held it in front of me.

"Sebastian said, 'Christine, you won't need that.' He smiled at me. I looked at him properly for the first time and recognised him. Something about the eyes. I heard a loud growl from behind him, and Sebastian cannoned into me, and we both fell to the floor. Me underneath and Sebastian on top. Dave must have charged down the hallway, and rugby tackled the suspect, forcing him into me. He couldn't have seen I was holding a knife."

Inspector Trammel said, "Do you want a minute?

"No, I'm OK. When Dave pulled Sebastian off me, I was still holding onto the knife. Shock, I suppose. Anyway, as Dave pulled, he rolled the suspect off me. The blade came out of his body, and that's when the blood flowed out of him."

Christine wiped her eyes with the sleeve of her sweatshirt, but the tears kept coming.

"Maybe this would be a moment to take a break?" DCI Rowland asked.

"I'm OK. I want to carry on."

She sniffed and wiped her eyes again. Inspector Trammel handed her a paper tissue, which she held in her hand, ready for the next flow of tears.

DCI Rowland said, "You mentioned you recognised Sebastian. Who was it you thought you recognised?"

"There was something about the smile and the eyes. I knew it was my sister Samantha."

"When had you last seen your sister? This was a man, after all."

"Someone abducted Samantha when we were both nine from Tooting Bec swings. I haven't seen her since until today. Do you know how she is?"

Inspector Trammel said, "The latest we heard before we began this interview was the suspect was in surgery at King's College hospital."

"Thank you."

DCI Rowland said, "We'll probably want to talk with you further, but that's it for now. I think DCI Balcombe has arranged a hotel for you and DC Wilde. Interview stopped at 23:07 hours."

All three stood, and as Christine opened the door, DCI Rowland put his hand on her shoulder.

"DS Woolfe, you've been through a lot. Getting shot last year, losing a colleague on this case, and now whatever this turns out to be. Take it easy. Don't rush back to work would be my advice."

"Thank you, Sir. I'll bear it in mind."

As she walked down the corridor towards the incident room, she thought, bugger that. I'm staying to see this through to the end.

Opening the incident room door, the boss was in his office talking with Dave and Pritch, who had already finished their interviews. He waved her to join them.

"Everything OK?" he asked.

"I think so. Any update on Samantha? Inspector Trammel said she was in surgery last they knew."

"How certain are you, Sebastian is your sister?"

"As certain as I can be. When I turned in the kitchen and saw him for the first time in the light, I just knew. I didn't feel threatened. He stood there and smiled."

Dave said, "I'm so sorry. I thought... I didn't want what happened to Lucy to happen to you. I just reacted."

"Dave, you have nothing to blame yourself for. I understand why you did what you did. However, he may look now. Sebastian is our suspect. He will have to answer for his crimes."

The DCI said, "To answer your question, before you came in, Ray called from the hospital. Sebastian is out of surgery and put into a medically induced coma. The doctors told Ray it may be days, could be weeks before they know what the damage is or if he'll survive. I'm sorry, Christine."

"Don't be. I thought she was dead at the scene. There's hope now. I want to ask him why?"

"If we interview him, I'm sorry, but you won't be anywhere near it. Talk about conflict of interest. No, me and Pete will interview. If I'm still on the case, that is. I'm summoned to Morning Prayers at the Yard. Can't say I'm looking forward to it."

Dave said, "They can't take us off the case now, boss."

"They can and they might, but I'll dig in for us to stay 'till the end. Now, you two, I've booked a hotel, not the Ritz, but decent. I don't want to see either of you until Monday. And if you don't feel up to it by then, no pressure, give me a ring. Same goes for you, Pritch, but you don't get the hotel."

"OK, off with you. Here's the address. There's a uniform car waiting downstairs to take you there. Dave, your place is out of bounds for now, so take this card and both of you buy some clothes and what you need. It's a corporate card for which I'm responsible for the spend. So, nothing too fancy. The hotel's already paid for."

"Thanks, boss," they both said and headed to the lift and the waiting car.

Chapter 49

Dave and Christine attended the briefing on Monday morning. The DCI brought everyone up to speed.

"OK, quieten down. So, not surprisingly, Kumar and Pete came up empty-handed on the house-to-house around Dave's home. No one saw anything until the armed response and the ambulance appeared. Then it was a free show, much better than the telly, as one elderly lady told them."

There were grim smiles at that.

"They did, however, find our suspect's car by a process of elimination. No one else claimed it, so it must be the suspects. And indeed it was. Paperwork from the Fulham address we've been searching for and, interestingly, a couple of takeout wrappers from the kebab shop close to this office. My current thinking is on a day before the incursion into Dave's home or on the day the suspect must have tailed Dave home. He probably found our location from conversations with Lucy. Sebastian has been using Sebastian Shaw."

"Sebastian Shaw is a villain in the Marvel X-Men comics."

"Thank you, Pritch."

Christine asked, "Boss, how's Sebastian doing? Any update on his condition?"

"Nothing further. He's still in a medically induced coma."

"The doctors have confirmed Sebastian underwent extensive gender reassignment surgery. Probably outside the UK, possibly in Thailand. Fits with Christine recalling Lucy saying he lived in Thailand for a while. We have contacted Border Force and the Thai embassy to find out if they can tell us about Sebastian's movements in and out of the UK and Thailand. But as most of you will know, no record is kept in the UK if Sebastian Shaw holds a UK passport. We may have more luck with the Thai authorities. But don't hold your breath.

"Ray and Kumar searched the Fulham address, which was basically a fancy squat. A bed and a few clothes. They found an excellent forged UK driving licence with Shaw's picture on it. So we can assume he was comfortable in the Sebastian Shaw persona."

Dave asked, "What ties him to the killings of the women?"

"We're awaiting DNA results, but I suspect we know the answer, given Christine's identification. Ray obtained pre-transfusion blood from the suspect, having got permission from the emergency department staff at King's. It's not that we were short of blood, but Ray did a good job getting the official sample. It will strengthen our case in court. Pritch, what can you tell us about your research into Samantha Woolfe?"

"Nothing at all, boss. I found the abduction case from back in the day, but nothing since. The person who took her must have either changed her name, taken her out of the Country soon after or kept her locked up." Pritch glanced at Christine. "Sorry, I didn't mean to say that."

"It's OK. I came up with the same conclusions over the years."

"How certain are we Shaw is our suspect?" asked Pete. "I know he dated Lucy and turned up at Jasmine's house. That was stupid, given we had found the surveillance cameras. And our suspect is anything but stupid. Deranged and working to his own unique psychopathy, but not stupid."

Christine, willing to clutch at any straw, said, "I understand it maybe nothing, but as I told the officers from Professional Standards, I didn't feel threatened by Sebastian. I know it's wishful thinking, and I can't think of any explanation for why he dated Lucy and followed Dave about and all the rest."

"Occam's razor," Pritch said, "The simplest explanation is usually the best."

Christine said, "My gut doesn't agree. Hopefully, we'll get to interview him soon. I think there's more to come.

The DCI's phone in his office rang. "OK, carry on detecting. I want to find out more about Shaw and where he's been. Pritch, get the driving licence picture blown up and sent to Edinburgh, Leeds and Hove. See if anyone recognises him. He can't have been staying at Fulham too long. It's a short-term kind of place. Also, canvas the graphic design firms in the West End to see if what he told Lucy is true. OK, that's it."

The DCI's phone started ringing again. "Bloody phone!"

He walked back into his office. "Yes! Sorry, it's been a long day, and it's only nine-thirty."

He listened to the caller. Thoughtful, he said goodbye and replaced the receiver. He went to his office door and beckoned Christine to join him.

When Christine had taken a seat, he said, "That was the John Tweed from the laboratory; he has the DNA results from Sebastian."

"I assume it's not good news?"

"Well, I'll leave you to decide. As expected, you share a paternal DNA link with Sebastian. But he was your mother's daughter. Surgery doesn't change DNA. So you were right, unless your mother had another daughter you knew nothing about, Sebastian Shaw is Samantha Woolfe."

Christine's heart raced, her emotions in chaos. The bloody worm in her stomach was doing somersaults. She wiped her clammy palms on her trousers. Confusion and disbelief filled her mind as she muttered, "What the fuck?"

"Are you OK, Christine?

"It explains a lot. After Samantha was taken, Mum blamed me and truly wished I had been the one to be abducted."

"I can't believe that."

"No, it's true. She said as much to me several times over the years. It got so bad I moved out at sixteen. She never forgave me. Didn't even make a will. Only inheritance law allowed me to get her flat, and it came at a price. When we discovered I wasn't my mother's daughter, I hoped Samantha and I would have that in common. Obviously not."

"I'm sorry, Christine."

"If it's OK with you, boss, I'll take the rest of the day off. I need to sort my head out."

"Of course. Is the hotel alright?"

"It's fine. When do you think I can go back to my flat or even back to Dave's?"

"Maybe in a couple of days for Dave's place. Not yet for your flat. I'd feel happier after we interview Sebastian, if that's possible."

"Have you heard anything from Professional Standards?" Christine asked.

"An email to say they're looking at all the interviews and handling of the case up to this point."

"So you're being put through the wringer as well as Dave and me?"

"The buck stops with me, I suppose. To be honest, I wouldn't have it any other way."

Christine rose from the chair. "I'm OK with you telling the team about the DNA results. See you tomorrow. I'll tell Dave I'm heading back to the hotel."

"Take care of yourself. Come back when you're ready."

"I'll be here tomorrow, boss."

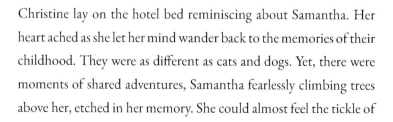

Christine lay on the hotel bed reminiscing about Samantha. Her heart ached as she let her mind wander back to the memories of their childhood. They were as different as cats and dogs. Yet, there were moments of shared adventures, Samantha fearlessly climbing trees above her, etched in her memory. She could almost feel the tickle of leaves falling against her face and Samantha's laughter echoing in the air. It was a stark contrast to her own nature, content with sitting in the shade, seeking solace in the pages of a book. The bittersweet emotions surged through her, caused a tightening in her chest. Tears welled up, blurring the image of her twin sister. Yet, despite their contrasting personalities, their bond remained unbreakable. Until it broke.

Chapter 50

Nothing had altered on the 'I'm coming out' website. The investigation was in a holding pattern, waiting for their suspect to recover enough to be interviewed.

Sebastian's consultant brought him out of his coma a few days later.

The DCI informed the team, "Depending on how Sebastian Shaw has recovered from his trauma. His doctor said we could interview him at the hospital next week."

Christine didn't know how to feel about the situation. She had her sister or her brother back. Either way, she could think of him as the same person she had grown up with. Just different. But that could change.

He could be a serial killer who had killed his siblings and tried to put his half-brother in the frame for the murders. Sebastian could have killed Lucy, who was in love with him. He could have threatened to murder her. Yet in her eyes, and probably only in her eyes, it didn't scan. What she had seen in his eyes that night before Dave had propelled Sebastian onto the knife she was holding wasn't anger. Wasn't murderous intent, but sadness and love.

At the Tuesday evening briefing the following week, when the team was all gathered, the DCI said, "OK, everyone. I've heard from the doctors at the hospital we can have a preliminary interview with Sebastian Shaw on Thursday. Pete and I will take the portable equipment and interview him. He's already in a side room, so we should have privacy.

"I arranged on Friday for a uniform guard 24/7 now he's out of his coma. I discussed with his doctors whether we needed any restraint, and they said although he was coming around, it would be a long while before he could attempt to get out of bed. In light of that, I have decided not to restrain him yet, but Pete and I can decide when we see him."

Pritch said, "Boss, I've been reviewing the language he used on his website. Now we know Sebastian is transgender; he may have made some slips, or at least unintentional word usage."

"Like what?"

"Well, when he talks about performing oral sex on Sarah Davies, and she says 'You have no idea how good it is', he thinks, 'Really, no idea.' We now know Sebastian used to be a woman and could have experienced such an act performed on herself. Also, when the pathologist said it's unusual for those with piquerism to also have penile penetration, maybe Sebastian doesn't see the use of his penis as actual sex. And in the Jasmine post, he says, 'I was pumped' He could be referring to a scrotum pump used to get erectile function for the created penis."

"That's good work. It could be a slip-up, but he hasn't made many. But now we know he is transgender; it gives some added impetus to what he wrote. OK, anyone got anything else to add?"

Kumar said, "The French on the website when Christine was told to exhume her mother's coffin. Christine said Lucy had said Sebastian spoke several languages. Just a thought."

"Thanks, Kumar."

Pete said, "I think we need admissions from him if we're going to charge him for the murders of the women fathered by the rapist. If the elderly lady who lives in Lucy's flats can pick him out in an ID parade, we can place him at the scene around the time of her death. The Charlotte Seymour murder, we have nothing on. We need to prove he was in Weston-Super-Mare at the time to kill her. He has been clever regarding the forensics.

"Now we know his name and have a photo. We can contact the murder team in Weston and task them to ask around the hotels and bars to see if anyone recognises him. Apart from that, even him turning up at Jasmine's place doesn't, in itself, mean we're any closer to nailing him for Jasmine's murder."

"All good and relevant points."

"Also, and this won't be popular," Pete added, "if Sebastian turns out to be innocent in some altered universe or timeline, we'll have Professional Standards on our case for assault. Given all the circumstances, I think Christine was more than justified in taking up the knife, and I don't think he would win in a court of law. After all, he entered without permission, but we should think about it."

"Thanks, Pete. Write up actions for Weston-Super-Mare. We found nothing techy at the Fulham address, not even a laptop. So, how did he create and update the 'I'm coming out' website? Where does he keep the surveillance equipment? Let's get our thinking caps on. We need answers to all, or at least some of those questions, before we interview at the end of the week."

As the meeting broke up and the officers drifted out of the room, Christine went over to Pete. "Thanks for saying what you did. I know he's our prime suspect; he dated Lucy and was at Jasmine's house, but I can't see it. I didn't want to say in front of everyone, but when I looked at his face for the first time in the kitchen, it was my sister, Samantha, looking at me. I didn't feel threatened." She slowly shook her head. "I have a gut feeling — but maybe that's his way, the charming serial killer."

"I know what you mean; something feels off here. But if it's not Sebastian, it's back to the drawing board."

Dave called out, "Christine, you ready?"

"Coming. Thanks again, Pete. See you tomorrow."

The DCI and Pete strode into the hospital on Thursday morning; Pete carried the portable interview recording equipment. They had discussed their interview strategy before leaving the incident room, and both were clear about their roles.

Arriving at the ward, they asked a passing nurse to direct them to Professor Farouk, the consultant responsible for Sebastian Shaw's care. The nurse showed them to a small office and knocked. A man called out, "Enter."

The DCI opened the door and saw a man aged about fifty, with a full head of dark hair, slim with a well-fitting white and yellow striped shirt with white collar and cuffs and blue suit trousers, rise out of the chair to greet them.

"The detectives, I presume?"

"DCI Steve Balcombe and DS Pete Rabbet," the DCI said, glanced at the pile of case files on the consultant's desk, similar to his own desk.

"Take a seat," the Professor said, gesturing towards two utilitarian chairs against the wall.

"DS Rabbet has drawn up the statement we'd like you to sign along the lines of yesterday's conversation with him. It states medically and mentally, you believe Sebastian Shaw is fit to be interviewed. He is not on any medication that will impair his cognitive thought process and can understand what is being asked of him."

"Nothing has changed since we spoke yesterday. I'd like to ask you to limit your interview to about twenty to thirty minutes this time. He is still very fatigued and finds it difficult to concentrate for long periods. Also, is the uniformed officer sitting in the room absolutely necessary?"

"I'm afraid the officer will stay until Shaw leaves the hospital. Do you know when that might be?"

"If he continues to make the progress we have seen so far, about a week, if he is to go home or maybe two if he is destined for a police cell?"

"It will probably be the latter," the DCI said, "he is suspected of multiple serious crimes."

"OK, let me read and sign the statement, and I'll walk you down to the sideward and introduce you."

"There's no need. I can see you're busy. We can find our way."

"I insist. My patient needs to understand I have sanctioned this. Also, if he feels fatigued, he can press the nursing bell. If he does, you will be asked to leave and return on another occasion."

He saw the look passed between the officers. "DCI Balcombe, you have your job, and I have mine. My job is to take care of my patient until discharge from this hospital. Despite what he may or may not have done."

The Professor opened the door to his office and ushered both officers out. After a short walk, he opened another door. The room contained a single hospital bed, a hospital table on castors, and a bedside cabinet. The room also contained a seated uniformed constable who shot to his feet as the senior officers entered.

Pete stared at the person lying in the bed. His first sight of their serial killer, who had murdered six women and one of their own.

"Sebastian," said Professor Farouk, "this is DCI Balcombe and DS Rabbet. They are here to ask you some questions. I told them to keep it short this time, no longer than half an hour. You can press the call bell if you feel tired. Right, I'll leave you to it."

Sebastian smiled and said, "Hello."

The DCI looked at him. The bastard actually smiled. He thought of Lucy and Sebastian together. What he had done to her, how he defiled her, taunted them on the fucking web for all the world to see. He realised he was clenching his fists; the knuckles turning white with the effort. He took a deep breath.

"Constable, go grab a coffee. Wait outside when you get back."

The officer left and closed the door behind him.

Sebastian said, "Would one of you mind putting a pillow behind me and helping me to sit further up the bed?"

Pete looked at the DCI and moved to help Sebastian. He knew the look. Intentional or not, the suspect had already got under the boss's skin.

Once Pete had made Sebastian comfortable, the DCI said, "We have brought a portable interview recorder. Before we start, I believe the Professor asked you yesterday if you wanted legal representation here this morning, and you declined. Is that still the case?"

Sebastian smiled again. "I don't think I need it. I hope to convince you all of this is a mistake. A very sad one because lots of women have died, and Lucy is gone too."

"DS Rabbet set the recorder up, and we'll begin."

Pete did so and pressed the recording button. Before the DCI could speak, there was a loud hiss from the bed.

Sebastian said, "Ignore that. It's the air mattress ensuring I don't get bedsores."

"I am Detective Chief Inspector Stephen Balcombe, my colleague is —"

"Detective Sergeant Peter Rabbet."

"Please state your name for the recording."

"Sebastian Shaw."

"Can you confirm you do not require legal representation at this time?"

"I can."

"If you feel you need it, we can stop the interview and call a solicitor to represent you."

"Thank you."

"As we suspect you of multiple crimes, I must caution you." The DCI gave the caution, and Sebastian said nothing in reply.

"You are calling yourself Sebastian Shaw. Has that always been your name?"

Sebastian smiled, "I think you know the answer to that already, Chief Inspector. I was born Samantha Woolfe. Daughter of Sandra Woolfe and Norman Etches, the rapist. How is Christine? Please tell her I don't blame her for stabbing me."

"How do you know your father was a rapist?"

"He told me after he took me from the swings at Tooting Bec when I was nine. Not at first. First, he locked me away in a basement, but over time, he became chatty."

"I am told you have had extensive gender reassignment surgery. Where was it carried out?"

"I prefer the term gender-affirming surgery. I knew I was in the wrong body from a very young age. But to answer your question, in Thailand, fifteen years ago. I came back to England for my mother's funeral."

"Do you know Gillian Michaels, Rachel Evans, Jennifer Simkins, Sarah Davies and Jasmine Cooper?"

"I know of them. Norman talked about them all the time. His children. He never stopped going on about them. So often, I blocked most of it out. His wife died during childbirth, so he only had one child. He wanted more."

Sebastian rested his head back on the pillows for a few seconds before continuing.

"He wasn't a good-looking man, not big on social graces. Honestly, I'm surprised he found someone to marry him in the first place."

"So, you know he was the father of all the women I named?"

"All I can tell you is he claimed to be. And Christine, don't forget my sister, Christine."

"Christine is actually your half-sister. Isn't she?"

"When you've had the childhood I had, family is family. Norman said Christine's mum was committed to a mental hospital and put into care when Christine was under a year old. Norman snatched her, paid Sandra a visit, and somehow persuaded her to take her in. Sisters from another mother, so to speak. Jasmine's mother committed suicide when Jasmine was sixteen. So I heard. As far as I know, the rest had their mothers, and some, like Sarah, had a mum and dad."

"You seem to know a lot about Norman's children?"

"As I said, he became chatty."

"Did you know where they were living?"

Sebastian shook his head. "Not until they started to be killed."

The DCI stared at him, "Sebastian, did you kill them?"

"No."

Pete looked at his watch, fifteen of the thirty minutes.

"Tell us about Lucy?" The DCI said.

Were those tears welling up? The bastard was crying.

Sebastian grasped for a box of tissues just out of reach.

"Please?" he said.

Pete passed him the box, and Sebastian took one and dabbed his eyes.

"Lucy was a lovely woman. The best. We met in a coffee shop, and we hit it off."

Pete said, "Did you target her?"

"I did."

"Why?"

"At first, to get inside information on who was killing my sisters. I know it wasn't Norman. I heard he died around the same time as my mother, Sandra. But as we got to know each other, we..." He dabbed his eyes again to stem the flow of tears. "We fell in love."

"Yet you killed her?"

"No!"

He said it with such force the constable opened the door and asked, "Is everything alright, sir?"

The DCI barked, "Shut the door and wait outside." Taking a calming breath, the DCI said, "We know you were at her flat on the night she died," the DCI said.

"I was there, but Lucy was alive when I left. Angry and upset. She wouldn't let me explain." The tears streamed down his cheeks, making damp patches on his hospital gown. "I had gone to Jasmine's house. So stupid. She confronted me. She said her colleague put up surveillance cameras, and she recognised me. I can still see the hurt in her eyes. I couldn't take it. She thought I was the murderer and only made love to her for information."

Sebastian was hyperventilating and getting agitated.

Pete said, "Charlotte Seymour. Another sister of yours?"

Taken aback by the sudden question pivot, Sebastian pressed his call bell. Both detectives noticed it, but a nurse appeared before they could say anything.

"Is everything alright, Mr Shaw?" she said.

"I'd like the officers to go now. I'm tired and upset."

The nurse saw he was crying, looked at the two officers, and held the door open, indicating they were to go. They both stood.

Sebastian said, "Chief Inspector. I'm sorry Lucy and all the others died, but I didn't do it. Come back and see me tomorrow if you like. Please tell Christine to take care. If I can find her, the killer can, too."

Pete realised the recorder was still active and said, "Interview ended at 11.20."

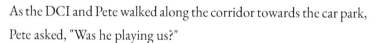

As the DCI and Pete walked along the corridor towards the car park, Pete asked, "Was he playing us?"

"Too soon to tell, but he was rankling me. A couple of the times he smiled, I wanted to punch his lights out. Not very professional of me, but you didn't see Lucy's body."

"I saw it on the website. If for no other reason, I want to lock the bastard who did that to Lucy away for the rest of his life."

"Are you still not convinced Sebastian Shaw is our guy?"

Pete shook his head, "There's something—something doesn't sit well with me. Why did he turn up at Jasmine's house if he knew we had found the surveillance equipment? And he admitted he targeted Lucy. What's that about?"

"You're right, there is something. Let's get back. I'm sure the others will be waiting to hear about the interview."

As the DCI and Pete walked into the incident room, it was no surprise to find the entire team there, and they all turned towards them in anticipation.

The DCI said, "OK, grab a drink and come back here. I think it's best to play the interview so you can all hear it. Christine, a quick word, please."

The DCI entered his office and closed the door after Christine joined him.

"I need to prepare you for something you'll hear in the interview. On the recording, Shaw discloses when you were a year old you were put into care after your mother went into a mental hospital. Your biological father, Norman Etches, snatched you and persuaded Sandra Woolfe to take you in."

Christine took a deep breath and let it out slowly, "Norman Etches? Is that the rapist's name?"

"According to Sebastian."

"In my head, after you told me Sandra wasn't my biological mother, I wondered how I came to be there. Now, there's a chance I might find her. I'll see you outside, boss."

With all the shocking revelations of the last few weeks, Christine was elated her birth mother might still be alive. A chance to know her genuine family. Family. This entire case was all about family.

Five minutes later, the team gathered around the table where Pete had set up the recorder.

The DCI said, "OK, the consultant wanted to introduce us to Shaw and told him if he felt tired or in any way pressured, he could press his call bell. He also told us only thirty minutes this time. OK, save questions until the end. It's not too long. Pete, do the honours."

Pete pressed play, and the team listened, with all except Christine, Pete and the DCI hearing the voice of their suspect for the first time. When the interview ended, Pete pressed stop on the recorder.

Pritch was the first with a question. "So, he's denying killing the women. Vehemently denied killing Lucy and ended the interview when Charlotte Seymour was mentioned."

Christine flexed her right hand to ease the build-up of tension as she squeezed her coffee mug and said, "I don't think he did it."

Seeing the looks of the others, she explained, "I don't believe Sebastian came to Dave's house to hurt me. He's obviously involved, as I am, but he admitted targeting Lucy and falling in love with her. I heard Lucy speak about him. She said he was kind and gentle, and in the short time I knew her, I thought Lucy was a fair judge of character. I know she blamed herself on the phone message, but I didn't think her radar was that far off."

"But he went to Jasmine's house," Kumar said.

Pete spoke, "I mentioned that earlier. I don't understand why he did it if he knew we had found the cameras. He may not have seen us, but someone as careful as our killer would surely have checked the feeds before setting foot in the place."

Christine said, "I hate to say it, but he may have learnt about Jasmine's house, at least its general location, from Lucy. A little research and, hey presto, he could have the address."

Ray said, "If not Sebastian, then who?"

That silenced the room.

The DCI said, "OK. Pete and I will interview Shaw again in the morning. One thing we didn't get to pick up on was when he said Etches's wife died in childbirth, so he only had one child. We need a name for that child. Pritch, search records of births, father Norman Etches, between thirty to forty years ago. Start in London and slowly work out. The rest of you finish what you were doing and head home. I want you fresh and clear-headed tomorrow, and you deserve a little chill time."

The team returned to their desks. Pete followed the DCI into his office.

An hour later, most of the team had left. Pritch tapped on the DCI's door, and he beckoned him in.

"Boss, so far, I've trawled the databases for London and the Home Counties; Surrey, Kent, etc. I can't find a record of any child being registered with a father called Norman Etches. I've checked the PNC and can't find anyone of that name either."

"OK, pack up now and head home. Tomorrow's another day. Maybe we'll be lucky tomorrow."

"OK, Boss."

Chapter 51

Professor Farouk fixed them with a stare that would have frozen a penguin.

"If you had told me you were returning this morning, I could have told you Mr Shaw was due an MRI scan. But you didn't. You turned up and barged into his room, expecting my patient to be there, ready and willing to answer your questions. It's bad enough I have to put up with one of your uniformed colleagues trailing after Mr Shaw everywhere he goes."

The DCI held himself in check, frightened he would say something he would later regret. In fact, he probably wouldn't regret it too much. It could be worth putting this jumped-up pompous quack in an expensive suit in his place.

"We are investigating the murders of seven women, including a police officer. One of our own. Right now, Mr Shaw is our prime suspect. As long as it doesn't cause him additional harm, we need to interview him to ascertain his involvement in those crimes. Mr Shaw agreed to be interviewed again this morning. Seven families are waiting for closure. So, while I respect your Hippocratic oath and the fact he is your patient, he is my suspect, and I need to interview him."

"That may be the case, Chief Inspector, but as you say, he is my patient, and in this hospital, my word, like I suspect it is for you at the police station, is law. I have agreed for you to interview Mr Shaw as I understand the time factor. But I insist you tell me when you intend to conduct your interviews. Mr Shaw is still not fully stable, and his health could deteriorate at any time. I understand one of your officers stabbed him?"

Before the DCI could react, Pete said, "Thank you, Professor. Can you tell us when Mr Shaw is expected back in his room?"

"You probably have another hour to wait. He only went down five minutes before you arrived. I'll need to confirm he is still willing to be interrogated when he returns. I'll call the restaurant to let you know. If you intend to stay and wait."

"Thank you," Pete said. "I could do with a coffee."

Pete headed to the door, and the DCI followed him out.

"Steve, this case is really getting to you, isn't it?"

The DCI stopped in the corridor and turned to Pete. "It really is, and the worst thing is, I'm coming around to believe we're barking up the wrong tree with Mister Sebastian Shaw. No matter how much I want it to be him. And the thing that really gets to me, as Ray said yesterday, is if it's not him, who is it? They'll take this case away from us soon if we don't develop a viable suspect. No one else will give it the same as our team would."

Pete said, "Come on, let's grab a coffee and wait for his highness to call us into Mr Shaw's presence."

That brought a smile to the DCI's lips. But it never reached his eyes.

Pete turned the recorder on. After reminding Sebastian Shaw he was still under caution and checking he still didn't want legal representation, the DCI said, "You told us yesterday you knew the names of the murdered women but didn't know where they lived until they were killed. Did that include Charlotte Seymour?"

"No, I learnt her name from Lucy. She went to Weston-Super-Mare with Christine to check up on some guy and found they had a murder done the same way."

"She wasn't one of Norman's children?"

"He never mentioned her as far as I can remember. Sorry."

Pete said, "Have you seen the 'I'm coming out' website?"

"Of course I have. Millions of people have seen it."

"Whoever updated the site after Lucy's murder signed off last time with the name Sebastian," said Pete.

"And you think I did it? I threw up when I saw the last page. What that bastard did to Lucy was truly evil. I was trying to stop him."

The DCI said, "So you're saying you had nothing to do with the website or the murders of seven women?"

"Absolutely, one hundred percent not."

"So, if you were trying to stop him and you knew your sister Christine might be in the killer's sights. Why didn't you at least try to warn her?"

"It's complicated."

Pete said, "We have time."

Sebastian sighed. "After Norman snatched me from the swing park, he kept me in the basement for months. I imagined the police crashing through the front door to find me. But week after week, month after month, nothing happened. Norman told me little by little my mum was not my mum, but he was my dad, and he loved me."

Pete noticed Sebastian pulling at the bed sheets with his right hand as if trying to tear off strips.

"He told me my mum had died, so he took me away from fake mum to come to live with him. It sort of made sense because, over the years, I found out he had left his other children with their mothers. So, I believed him. But I resented Christine because she was never my sister and didn't try hard enough to look for me. I didn't want to live with fake mum, but I hated Christine could. You have to understand I was nine years old. I had Norman telling me things and that weird son of his backing him up."

The DCI said, "What was the son's name?"

"Mostly, we called him John, but I think his name was Jonathan. A couple of times when Norman was mad at him, he would call him Jonathan."

"So, Jonathan Etches?"

"I think so."

Pete said, "Have you ever heard the name Simon Jessop?"

"No."

The DCI said, "Take a look at this picture. Do you recognise him?"

Pete placed a photograph of Jessop on the bed. Sebastian studied it briefly before saying, "No, who is he?"

The DCI said, "His name is Simon Jessop. The killer tried to set him up for the murder of Jasmine Cooper. And he's your half-brother."

"Another secret my dear old dad kept from me. He kept tabs on all his children over the years. He got emphysema when I was fifteen. John, who was a few years older than the rest of us, was told by Norman to spy on his girls for him. Take pictures when he could. Norman would like to look at his children. It gave him some kind of sick pleasure."

"So, you're saying Jonathan, Norman's son, would know where all his siblings lived?"

Sebastian nodded. "At the time. A year later, I left Norman's house and went up north. I started to get feelings. Feelings like I was in the wrong body. I had always been a tomboy, and wearing the girl clothes Norman insisted I wear felt fake. So, I left, snuck out one night, and never looked back. I caught a coach to Newcastle. Found someone to provide a false passport and driving licence and got some bar work.

"I was a late developer, but my fake body started to show. Baggy clothes can only hide so much. I went to the doctor and to the hospital. Still, without a support network and counselling, nothing would happen. By then, I had decided to go to Thailand."

The DCI said, "Thank you for sharing that. I'm more interested, though, in where Norman's house was and how we might locate Jonathan Etches?"

Sebastian laid back on the pillows. His story, his life, still didn't matter. Wasn't important.

Norman gave him his surname, and as Samantha Etches, she attended the local secondary school from the age of eleven. She had been home-schooled or held prisoner until Norman was confident she had bought into his bullshit. John walked her to their school each morning as he was a couple of years above her. Of course, both the boys and girls bullied her. She was between two genders, and non-binary wasn't a term back then, but it described her exactly.

She sought other pupils who were being bullied, feeling like there was strength in numbers. But for the bullied, that doesn't apply. It just means more people witness the humiliation. She started hanging out with the loners and delinquents. Drinking, popping pills and smoking weed. Norman had gone spare when he found out. John had grassed her up, as he was even too weird for the wrong crowd. The teachers didn't care. One of the older pupils was selling weed to two of them. But for Norman, looking back, he must have been terrified the school would call the police, and the house searched.

"Sebastian?" Pete said, "are you OK? You looked like you zoned out there for a bit."

"Sorry, I drifted thinking about days gone by."

"Do you want to tell us about them?"

"No, you're alright. You wouldn't be interested. More pressing matters."

The DCI said, "Norman's house?"

He gave them the address, adding, "I went there when I first heard about the murders. Neighbours said Jonathan sold the house after Norman died years before."

Sebastian laid back into his pillows before raising himself again.

"Where Jonathan Etches is now is anybody's guess, but I think he's your best bet for a suspect in these murders. As a young girl, I feared him. I woke up one night to find Jonathan sitting on the bed, staring at me. I screamed, and Norman came running. He cuffed Jonathan 'round the head, grabbed him by his neck, and marched him out of my room. Before Norman shoved him out of the door, Jonathan turned his head and smiled at me. It sent shivers right through me. After that, each night, I'd fix the back of a chair under the door handle."

The DCI said, "What makes you think Jonathan Etches might be the suspect?"

"Well, I know it isn't me. I don't recognise the Jessop guy, and I suppose you've ruled him out. And apart from Christine, everyone else I know about is dead. Look, I'm tired now. You probably have more questions, but can we do it tomorrow?"

"Yes, I think that's for the best."

Pete switched off the recorder.

As they packed up and prepared to leave, Sebastian said, "Norman wasn't a terrible father. The way he went about getting his children was violent and creepy, but by his standards, he cared about us. I know what I said probably sounds like Stockholm syndrome to you."

"It does a bit... We may be back tomorrow or the next day. I'll let Professor Farouk know so he can tell you. I'll be leaving the uniformed officer in place."

"For my protection or because I'm a suspect, Detective Chief Inspector?"

"A bit of both, if I'm honest."

Chapter 52

Back in the incident room, all but Ray were present. After everyone grabbed a drink, Pete played the recorded interview.

Once the interview ended, the DCI said, "OK, a lot of food for thought there. Pritch, I want you to research Jonathan Etches. I want him found and brought in for questioning. Look at the school records. Pete has the name of the school. Christine and Kumar can help with the research. Dave, I want you and Ray when he shows up—"

Dave said, "He had a flood at home. His washing machine leaked all over the kitchen floor. I heard from him before you walked in. He should be here soon."

"Thanks, Dave. As I was saying, I want you to go to the Etches address. Make sure Jonathan is not still living there in spite of what Sebastion Shaw says. Speak to neighbours and local shopkeepers to understand when they moved out. We know Norman died around ten years ago as we found his head in Sandra Woolfe's coffin, which was interred ten years ago."

Christine noted the DCI had stopped calling Sandra her mother. Did she think it, too? Sandra was the only mother she could remember, but she would try to find her birth mother once this case was over.

"OK, everyone, briefing at 5 pm."

The DCI approached his office but stopped and turned. "Pritch, just a thought. Sebastian said when he was fifteen, Norman had emphysema. He must have sought treatment for it. Check local GP surgeries close to the house and local hospitals."

"Will do Boss."

That evening, the team assembled for the briefing and waited for the DCI to finish his phone call. He walked out into the incident room. Christine saw he looked beaten down. Not the same DCI she had encountered all those weeks ago at Sarah's home.

"OK, the call was from AC Ops, my boss's, boss's, boss. We have a week starting today. If we don't solve this case, they will give it to another team. We were lucky to keep it after what happened to Lucy, but we're going to lose it in six days. I don't want that to happen. None of you do either. I'm coming around to the thought maybe Sebastian isn't our killer. Maybe Jonathan Etches is. Either way, we need to find him, charge him, or rule him out."

He looked at the gathered team and knew they all felt the same as he did.

"OK, what have you found out?"

Dave said, "Ray and I went to the Etches' house. Spoke to the people living there, Mr and Mrs Benson. They bought the place four years ago from a family called Winters. The Winters were selling to move to Northumberland to be close to the wife's elderly mother.

"Mr Benson was a copper's dream. He had all the house documents in a filing cabinet. We looked at the records, and the Winters bought the house six years before from Jonathan Etches after his father, Norman, died. They didn't have a forwarding address for Jonathan. In fact, they never met him. The estate agents and a conveyancing solicitor handled the sale. We checked, and the house has a basement, which backs up Sebastian's story."

Ray said, "I spoke to a few neighbours. One lived next door for over forty years, Mrs Armstrong. She really didn't like Etches and his son. She said his wife was lovely, but she died during childbirth. Jonathan, according to her, was a little git. He had a catapult, which he used to fire stones at birds landing on the back fence. She also said there was a stage where neighbours' cats would go missing. One time, she had a go at Jonathan about the catapult and the birds. The next day, she found a decapitated pigeon with its legs pulled off on her front step.

"She remembered Samantha, first saw her when she was eleven or twelve. Mrs Armstrong believed she was from a liaison Norman had, and her mother died. So, Norman took her in."

"Thanks, Ray. Pritch, Kumar and Christine, what have you got?"

Christine said, "Pritch did most of the work, but we confirmed Jonathan and Samantha attended the school. Samantha started at eleven and left at sixteen. Jonathan also started at eleven and left at eighteen. Jonathan was two years older than Samantha, so they left in the same year. Kumar did the hospital research."

"Norman did have emphysema," Kumar said. "Doctors diagnosed it when Sebastian was fifteen, as he said. Jonathan would have been seventeen. It made life difficult for Norman but, according to medical records, not necessarily life-threatening. Dave and I have compared notes, and Norman stopped attending his appointments just before Jonathan sold the house. Maybe he died, or something more sinister happened. His head turned up in another person's coffin after all."

Christine winced. In her mind, she saw everything. Her mother's body, Norman's head, with his dick in his mouth. There was a buzz in the room, or maybe it was her little worm, but she knew what Pritch would say. Things were falling into place.

The DCI said, "Pritch, what have you got?"

"Well, boss, something pretty interesting. I've been taking a bit of a dig into Jonathan Etches' life. The census shows Sally Bertram living at the address at the time Jonathan was born. There was a birth certificate for a Jonathan Bertram with no father listed. No marriage certificate for Sally and Norman. Jonathan attended the local infant school as Jonathan Etches and attended the secondary school with Samantha. I assume Norman got a friend to run up a birth certificate for Jonathan with his surname, or maybe the school accepted Jonathan Bertram, but everyone called him Etches?

"But the interesting bit comes after he left school. He basically drops off the grid, and there's no trace apart from selling his father's house ten years ago. I've searched social media, NHS, and tax records. In fact, Jonathan Etches has never paid a penny in tax, never claimed the dole, and has never been sick in the last eighteen years. He's done a Casper."

From the quizzical look the DCI gave him, Pritch added, "Casper the ghost. Jonathan Etches just vanished."

"OK, Dave and Ray, first thing in the morning, I want you to go to the estate agents and see who handled the sale. They must have records and transferred the sale money to Norman, so maybe a bank account? Something."

"Well done, everyone. I think we're getting somewhere at last. Go home and get some rest. See you in the morning."

Christine said, "Boss, can I have a quick word? Dave, do you mind waiting?"

The DCI said, "Follow me."

He led her out of the incident room and down the corridor to one of the interview rooms. He closed the door behind them.

"I think I know what you're going to ask, but the answer is not yet."

Christine's face fell. "I just want to talk with him."

"I understand, really, I do. I'm not sure he is our killer. It took me longer than you and Pete, but I'm getting there. But, and it's a big but, you and Dave are still being investigated over the stabbing. He is still our most likely suspect, although Jonathan is rapidly gaining ground. I can't allow you two to play catch-up at this moment. I'm sorry, but that's my final word on the matter. As soon as I think it won't compromise the case, I'll let you and Sebastian see each other."

Christine turned towards the door and grasped the door handle. "I understand, boss." She turned her head to look at him. "I thought my sister was dead all those years ago, then I thought I had killed Sebastian... It's a lot."

"You get off home with Dave. We're getting close. I feel it in my water."

Christine smiled, "Night boss."

Chapter 53

After dropping Christine off at the incident room the following morning, Dave collected Ray, and they drove to the estate agents listed in Mr Benson's records.

As they entered, Dave muttered to Ray, "I bloody hate estate agents."

All the agents were on their desk phones or their mobiles. No one looked like they were going to offer any help. Dave strode purposefully towards the back office, where he saw a balding man in a cheap suit pecking at his keyboard.

Before they reached the office door, a young woman, perhaps only twenty, stood in their path and said, "Can I help you?"

Dave said, "I hope so, DC Wilde and my colleague is DC Finn. We're from the Major Incident Team." They both brandished their warrant cards. "We need to speak with the manager. Is that him in the office?"

"Yes, Mr Jenkins. I'll see if he's free."

"No need." Dave knocked on the door.

Mr Jenkins looked up from his keyboard and saw the two men at his door. As he stood, they came in.

He looked flustered by the intrusion into his domain. "Can I help you?"

Dave made the introductions, and Mr Jenkins sat down anxiously.

"We want to look at the records for a house sale ten years ago." He gave the address.

"I'm sorry, but it may take some time. I wasn't here then, but we used a hybrid system, paper and computer records. Now it's all computer secure cloud storage."

Ray said, "But the files are here?"

"Yes, but I don't know if I can spare anyone today to sort through the boxes—"

Dave interrupted. "This is a murder investigation. The killer has slaughtered seven women. Find someone, or we can get a warrant and close the place down while we look."

In about ten seconds, Mr Jenkins went from too busy to ruffled to shocked to subservient. A joy to watch, thought Dave.

Mr Jenkins gave Mandy, who they met when they first entered, the task. Two hours later, they had the file, and seconds later, they discovered it contained nothing. Mr Jenkins exclaimed he couldn't understand it. In all his years, this had never happened before.

Dave asked, "Will the file be anywhere else?"

Mr Jenkins and Mandy both shook their heads. He said, "I can't understand it. I know it's out of our file storage protocol by now, but I've previously seen files from fifteen or twenty years ago. Also, the folder is there, but not the documents."

Dave said, "Is anyone working here now who was also working in the office ten years ago?"

Mr Jenkins put on his thoughtful face. To Dave, his face looked like he was straining to take a dump, but he didn't comment.

"There might be. David Baxter. I believe he was here then."

Unbelievably, he stopped talking, causing Dave to ask, "Is he here?"

"No, he's on holiday, back next Saturday. He's gone to the Seychelles. It's a fantastic place have you ever—"

"Give me his mobile number?"

"Oh, I don't know if he'll have it turned on. He is on holiday."

Dave and Ray stared at him until he folded and gave them the number.

"Thank you. If we need anything else, we'll come back."

In the car, Ray called the mobile number. "Straight to voicemail, I'll leave a message. This is a message for David Baxter. I am Detective Constable Ray Finn from the Major Incident Team in London. Please call me back as a matter of urgency. It has nothing to do with your family or home, but I need to speak with you. Thank you." He tapped his mobile to disconnect the call. "I added the last bit 'cos if I got that message, I'd be panicking. Something might have happened to someone I love."

"Good thought," said Dave.

They found the boss in his office when they entered the incident room.

Dave said, "Boss, the transaction file for the sale of Norman's house was empty. The only person still working there is on holiday in the Seychelles, back on Saturday. Ray left a message on his mobile asking him to call."

"Damn, can't we catch a break on this case? Sorry, we need action to stop the investigation being taken away from us. OK, see Pete for any outstanding actions. Back here at five for a briefing."

Dave and Ray wandered into the incident room at twenty to five. Time to grab a mug of coffee and a catch up with the team before the meeting. Ray's mobile rang. He showed Dave. It was a number he didn't recognise, and he crossed his fingers.

"Hello, DC Finn."

The line was crackly, and the voice disjointed, but he made out the name David.

"The line's bad. Is this David Baxter? OK, thanks for calling back. We are working on a murder case involving the Etches family. Jonathan Etches sold his father's house ten years ago." He gave the address. "Can you remember anything about the sale? No, I asked if you could recall anything about the property sale. What was that? You think the trainee agent handled it? What was his name? Sorry, can you repeat that? Thank you so much."

Ray disconnected the call. The boss had just walked into the main room for the briefing.

"Boss, you are not going to believe this. The trainee agent who Mr Baxter believes handled the sale of Norman Etches' house was a young lad called Simon Jessop."

"What? Jessop was working at the estate agents ten years ago. Christ, did we mess up big time? Pritch, research the hell into Jessop's life - birth to present day. This is too close to be a coincidence, and I won't make the same mistake again. Pete, call the area surveillance team. I want round-the-clock surveillance on Jessop, home, work, wherever he goes. I need to be able to grab him up at any time. But warn them he may be our killer. And I want surveillance in place yesterday. OK, the rest of you gather 'round. We've already had Jessop in custody for the murders, and the custody time has almost run out. If we bring him in on those murders by the time his brief gets here, we'll have to release him or charge him. So, if we arrest him, it will be for Lucy. I'm going to update my boss and eat some humble pie."

The DCI shuffled back into his office like his feet were clad in metal diving boots. He sat at his desk and held his head in his hands. "FUCK."

Five minutes later, Pete knocked on the door. He could see the boss still bent over his desk, staring at the keyboard. He knocked again; this time, the DCI raised his head and waved him in.

"Boss, we caught a lucky break. The area surveillance team can scramble on Jessop. I've given them the lowdown, and I'll send a package over to them, so they know the history. They think given he works in central London and can drive anything from the showroom, his home address is the best place to pick him up. Once on him, they can give us three days full 24-hour cover."

The DCI appeared to not hear his old friend. "Did I let Lucy down? We had him here in the interview room. We had the bastard. I let him go. I believed his bullshit."

"Steve, you weren't to know. None of us could've guessed. Jessop must have been planning this, or some version of it, all along."

"The bastard play acted out the door. We need to nail him good and proper this time around. Watertight. No escape. Get some of the surveillance team to draw weapons, and I'll speak to the yard about tasking India 99."

"Do you think they'll give you the helicopter?"

"I'll bloody well make them. We lost one of our own. I won't take no for an answer."

Pritch tapped on the glass. The DCI waved him in. "Sorry to interrupt, boss. Simon Jessop appeared out of nowhere two years before Norman Etches died. I can't find any trace of him being born, being sick, schooling; nothing until he was twenty. We know uniform arrested him at twenty-two for drunkenness, as we have his DNA on file. I messed up. I knew about the DNA match in the name of Simon Jessop, and I checked nothing further. He doesn't have a passport or a driving licence on file. Yet he must have at least a driving licence as he drives cars all the time. A Mercedes' main dealership is going to check."

The DCI said, "I think that confirms it. Jessop must be Jonathan Etches."

"Don't forget," Pete said, "Sebastian didn't recognise the photo of Jessop."

"I haven't forgotten, but I'm not a hundred per cent on Sebastian yet. He may not have recognised the photo for his own reasons. Thinking about it, we may have made a link for him if he is trying to find the killer. Is the team still outside?"

"All of them," Pritch said, checking over his shoulder.

The DCI stood, rolled his shoulders, straightened his back and strode purposefully to the incident room. "OK, gather 'round."

Ray, Dave, Christine and Kumar grouped around the boss. Pritch and Pete joined them.

"OK, the area surveillance team is scrambling to get contact with Simon Jessop. They will try to pick him up at his home. Failing that, they will attempt to find him at the car dealership, although they think it might be difficult as he could drive any vehicle.

"Pritch has discovered some things about Jessop. There's no trace of him before the age of twenty. He doesn't have a legal passport or driving licence. Given he works for a Mercedes dealership, he must have a driver's licence. Fake? I believe so. He may also have a fake passport. If so, we didn't pick that up when we had it. If we consider that, we should also consider he may have other identities he could slip into at a moment's notice.

"We know he shares paternal DNA with all our murder victims, except Lucy and Charlotte Seymour. Of course, Christine also shares the same DNA link. Sebastian says Jonathan Etches was Sally and Norman Etches's natural child and was two years older than the other women. His mother died in childbirth."

Christine said, "So what are you thinking, boss?"

"I think Simon Jessop is Jonathan Etches, and for whatever reason, hates his siblings and has been murdering them for the last five years. I think he killed Charlotte Seymour as part of an elaborate rouse to put us off the scent, and I believe he killed Lucy."

There was silence in the room as the team digested that.

"We have the surveillance team for three days, and in that time, we must prepare for Jessop's arrest. His solicitor will no doubt kick up a fuss over us arresting his client for Lucy's murder, but that's his problem. However, we must ensure we have all our ducks in a row. Pete, I want you to take Dave and interview Sebastian again. Get everything out of him you can.

"We need to know what Jonathan was like growing up in Norman's house. What was the true story behind Sebastian leaving the house and going north? Most importantly, what might Jonathan's motives be for the murders, and did he suspect Jessop to be Etches after we showed him the photo?

"Pritch, I know you've tried before, but take another look at where the website is from. We didn't find his computer the last time we searched his house. I suspect Jessop will keep it well hidden if he constructed the website on it."

Pritch said, "If we find a computer, I might find a link on the web. Jessop may have created the whole thing and added content via the dark web."

"Thanks, Pritch; if you need anything, let me know."

Christine said, "I've been thinking about the Charlotte Seymour murder in Weston-Super-Mare. I know we were all thinking it looked like a setup, and that's why we didn't inquire too deeply into his car when we checked if he could have made the journey to London and back to kill Jasmine Cooper."

"What's the significance of that?" asked Kumar.

"He works for a Mercedes dealership, and most salesmen were at the conference in Weston. I'm sure they all took their dealership cars, and it would have been simple for Jessop to take spare keys. We only checked for his Mercedes on the ANPR cameras."

The DCI said, "That's an excellent point. We will need to re-visit everything regarding the Weston killing and what we thought we knew about Jessop. Christine, I want you, Ray and Kumar, to get digging. We can't leave Jessop running around too long, but we have to have something to put to him before we arrest him. OK, everyone, get on with it."

Chapter 54

In the morning, Pete rang Professor Farouk and arranged for Dave and himself to interview Sebastian. Sebastian had moved to a different room when they arrived at the hospital, as he didn't need to be monitored as closely. Pete explained they would record the conversation once again, and introduced Dave Wilde.

Sebastian said, "We met already."

As Dave started to speak, Sebastian interrupted with a smile, "Don't worry, I'm not going to sue."

Dave switched the recorder on, and Pete reminded Sebastian he was still under caution. Sebastian agreed to the recording and was content to be interviewed without the benefit of legal advice.

Pete said, "The first thing I'd like to ask is, what was your relationship like between you and Jonathan?"

Sebastian gave a derisory laugh. "We didn't have a relationship. He was a little shit. When I first arrived and Norman kept me in the basement, Jonathan used to spill half of my food coming down the stairs on purpose. Sometimes, he would tip the plate, so all the food ended up on the floor. I could hear him chuckling to himself as walked up the stairs and locked the door."

"Did it get any better over the years?"

"No," Sebastian shook his head, "if anything, it got worse. He watched me like a hawk on the way to and from school. I complained to Dad—"

Seeing the looks on both their faces, he said, "It's what Norman wanted me to call him. To be honest, it was easier. It avoided awkward questions, especially at school. Anyway, I complained to Norman, who always took Jonathan's side. I don't recall a time when he didn't. Jonathan was the golden child, yet I believe he hated his father. My best guess is he resented the time and effort Norman put into his other kids and when he got sick, he forced Jonathan to do the same."

Pete said, "So we know about your half-siblings Gillian, Rachel, Jennifer, Sarah, Jasmine and, of course, Christine. Do you know of any other children Norman claimed as his?"

"No, I never heard him mention anyone else."

"So, what was going through your mind when we spoke about Simon Jessop the other day?"

There was a long silence, which Pete was happy not to fill. Detective School 101 let the suspect feel uncomfortable with the silence and make the first move.

Sebastian broke first. "I suspected Jonathan was Simon Jessop, which is why I presume you're asking these questions. But I didn't recognise him when you showed me the photo. But I'm unrecognisable from my former self. Jonathan could have had minor cosmetic surgery. It doesn't take much to pass as someone else. Norman knew a lot of shady people. If Jonathan had wanted false documents, Norman could have pointed him in the right direction."

"When you left school and went north, why didn't you seek out Christine and your mum?"

"I was changing, coming to terms with myself, my sexuality, my identity. It's hard to explain. Norman told me Sandra was not my real mum. My biological mum had died. I didn't want to hurt either Christine or Sandra, but I was angry with them both. It was in my head neither of them tried to look for me properly. I suspect Norman and my teenage angst worked together. I just wanted to get away. A new life, a new me."

Dave said, "OK, I get that. But now, when you're happy in your skin, with who you are, why didn't you reach out to Christine or any of the women? Especially when the murders happened?"

"I didn't know where any of them were living until I saw the reports of the murders online. I didn't know what names they may live under. Christine was the only one I knew. I saw the news of her shooting."

"But, Dave said, "before Sarah's killing, you targeted Lucy?"

"I suspected Sarah lived in the area and I did my research. I thought an MIT team would investigate and got lucky with Lucy. Her team caught the case, as she put it."

"You befriended Lucy, and she must have spoken to you about Christine. You could have prevented the death of Jasmine Cooper and Lucy?"

Sebastian started to tear up at Dave's question. He reached for a tissue from the box beside the bed and dabbed his eyes.

"I did nothing about it. You must understand that, Sebastian said, "but I wanted to. I wanted to hurt Jonathan. I wanted to find him and hurt him. Maybe even kill him. Even after all these years, the hatred was still there. He was, is, a sick bastard who enjoyed torturing animals, and humiliating and hurting girls and women. He couldn't stand women talking to him. Something must have messed with his head after his mother died.

"I was nine years old when I came to live at Norman's house. Jonathan made sexual advances to me. He never raped me, at least not physically, but with objects. Things I later knew were called dildos and vibrators. He forced me to touch him, play with his dick. He got so angry when, after no end of stroking him and him forcing his dick into my mouth, nothing happened. Jonathan would slap me and punch me in ways that didn't show. He never tried anything when Norman was in the house, but he often went out before he got ill. I lived in fear of him leaving the house for years."

Sebastian dabbed his eyes again and blew his nose into the tissue.

Pete said, "You know how he kills the women? You've seen it on the website; do you think the foam is to stop them talking?"

"I think that's spot on. When I began to feel I was in the wrong body. No, that's incorrect, I always knew, but when I started to understand those feelings and what they meant, Jonathan paid me even more attention. He enjoyed my rejection of him. The stuff on the website. His sexual exploits. It's bollocks. He couldn't get it up with scaffolding! I made a joke about it when I was fourteen. He broke my arm. I had to make up a story about falling over in the playground."

Dave said, "And you couldn't tell Norman? You mentioned earlier, Jonathan would wait until Norman was out before sexually assaulting you."

"Jonathan was Norman's pride and joy, his blue-eyed boy. His only son. I learnt very quickly not to go to Norman with anything against Jonathan. I think Jonathan didn't want to be disturbed by his dad walking in on us."

Sebastian made air quote marks with his fingers. "Norman was 'proud' of his offspring. Liked to boast to Jonathan how he had such a big family. Which only made Jonathan enraged. Rage, he took out on me."

Pete said, "Thanks, Sebastian. I think you've helped a lot. I can tell it's been emotional for you. Can we get you anything before we go?"

"No, thank you."

Pete and Dave stood and switched off the recorder.

As they turned towards the door, Sebastian said, "Actually, there is one thing I'd like to ask. I'm not proud of what I've done, and Lucy's death will be on my conscience forever, but does Christine have to hear this interview?"

Pete said, "That's not my call. I haven't known her long, but if you want to have anything with Christine, I should say start with a clean slate. Tell her how you felt and what you went through. She might surprise you. Christine was in your corner right from when you got stabbed."

As the two detectives walked out of the room, Sebastian smiled and mouthed, "Thank you."

Walking back into the incident room, Pete went straight into the DCI's office, knocking as he entered.

"Boss, the interview went well with Sebastian. It answered a lot of questions about the murders. As we pulled into the car park, I heard from the surveillance team. They sacrificed one of their officers, who is going on holiday tomorrow, to enter the dealership. As he looked at the cars, Jessop was in the showroom, and the officer overheard him talking. Jessop and another salesman have been selected to attend a two-day course in Germany the day after tomorrow."

"OK, send a message to the surveillance team. We'll embed Kumar and Ray with their team first thing tomorrow, and they can effect an arrest before he gets to the dealership. I want it done away from his home before he gets to work. It can't be helped, but this has moved the schedule up a notch. After you've spoken to the surveillance team, message our team to return here ASAP for an update briefing."

"Right, boss. Sebastian asked if Christine had to hear the latest interview? He said some things she may not want to hear."

"I'll speak to her. She's around somewhere. Send her into me."

As Pete walked out of the DCI's office to make the calls, he saw Christine returning with a mug of coffee. He called to her, "The boss wants to see you."

Christine knocked on the open door and the DCI waved her in.

"Christine, Pete says the interview with Sebastian went well and answered many questions about the murders, but Sebastian asked if you had to hear his interview. He said there were some things you may not want to hear."

"I'm in this 'till the end, boss. If I have a relationship with Sebastian after this, I need to know all about him and what motivates him."

The DCI smiled, "I knew you were going to say something like that. OK, Pete is calling the team back for an update. Jessop is heading to Germany the day after tomorrow, so we'll arrest him before he gets to work in the morning. Let me know when everyone's here."

About forty minutes later, the entire team had gathered, and Christine knocked on the DCI's door. He was on the phone, but raised his hand to acknowledge her. Hanging up the phone, he walked into the main room.

"OK, Pete and Dave interviewed Sebastian this morning, and he mentioned some things which Pete feels explains some details about the murders. Pete, can you play the recording?"

The team sat in silence, listening to the interview. Pete watched Christine to see if she would react to certain parts of the conversation. She didn't.

When the recording finished, the DCI said, "Thoughts?"

Christine spoke first. "It was fascinating when Sebastian spoke about Jonathan's sexuality. We never found where the women had spent the night, the clubs and the almost pornographic descriptions of the killer's exploits. How could one man be so attractive to so many women? Enough to get them to take him home on the first date. I think Sebastian is correct. I believe Jonathan learnt from Norman. Stalking and a blitz attack. Or maybe he was in the house already. We know for Jasmine and Lucy he had been there before because we found the cameras. He's also been in my place."

The team nodded in agreement.

Dave said, "And what he said about not liking women to speak fits with the foam."

"Also, thinking back to the Sarah Davies murder, what the Pathologist said about Paraphilia and Piquerism and what Sebastian says about Jonathan's impotence. It all fits." Christine said.

The DCI said, "Just before this meeting, I was on a call with the ACC Crime. I explained to her we would arrest Jonathan Etches, a.k.a. Simon Jessop, in the morning. For those who don't know, the surveillance team sent an officer into the dealership, and they overheard Jessop talking. He and another salesman are going to Mercedes HQ in Germany for two days.

"Ray and Kumar, I want you to liaise with the surveillance team and meet the team early doors. After Jessop leaves his house to go to work, let him get a distance from his house and arrange for a hard stop on his car so you can effect an arrest. He is to be arrested on suspicion of murder, specifically the murder of Lucy Worthington. Bring him to Wimbledon nick. We'll set up camp there. Pete will give you the surveillance team's contact details."

"Boss," Ray said, "Just thinking, the current owners of the Etches house said they never went down into the basement. They are thinking about doing it up, but not yet. They have bolted the door as they have kids. From what they described; the previous owners didn't use it either. We need to prove Jessop is Etches. We have Jessop's DNA, but we're no closer to proving he was Jonathan Etches. I'm thinking, what if we got a SOCO team 'round there, in the basement? Sebastian said Jonathan was always down there, and there might be stuff from when the Etches lived there. We think Jonathan is Jessop. Currently, it's a theory. If we could prove this by DNA or prints lifted from the Etches house basement, it would strengthen our case."

Dave slapped Ray on the back. "Well done, mate. Glad you went with my idea."

Ray looked at him askance and laughed, "The last time you had an idea, it was whether to poo in your nappy or suck the breast."

Dave smiled and said, "On that occasion, I did both."

The DCI said, "OK, settle down. It's a good idea, Ray. Call the scenes of crime team and tell the householders to expect them. The rest of you, go home. We have a busy day tomorrow."

Chapter 55

The next morning broke with dark clouds and the threat of torrential rain hanging over it. Ray and Kumar joined the early surveillance team as they swapped with the night duty team at 6 am. The primary team took their positions around Jessop's house to cover whichever way he left. They expected him to travel to work in his dealership car, but they could also handle a walk to the tube station. A short distance from Jessop's house, in the rear of a backup car, were Ray and Kumar. The team expected Jessop to leave his house as he had done yesterday, about 7.30 am. Their driver, John, told them the team leader was coming to see them.

"This is him in the blue Audi."

The team leader parked his car and jumped into the passenger seat next to John.

He turned to face Ray and Kumar. "I'm Sergeant Chris Olsen. Just wanted to go over the arrest plan with you. Pete said you wanted him away from his home address but arrested before he gets to the dealership."

Kumar said, "That's right."

"OK then, when he leaves his house, we expect him to take the car, a black Mercedes CLA. Jessop is Tango one, his car is Zulu one.

We'll communicate in plain speech instead of code today. If he does as expected, he could take a couple of routes to the West End. Once we're certain he's not going anywhere else other than to work, I'll notify John to move up. We will box Jessop in a rolling block. When you hear 'Execute, Execute' we'll stop his car, and John will bring his car up to where you can safely make the arrest.

"Pete told me he shouldn't be a problem, but we're ready if he is. Bring Jessop back to this car, and John will take you to Wimbledon. We'll meet you there for a debrief and breakfast. It's unlikely, but if he goes by tube, we'll have foot officers deployed to box him in, but you need to be ready to make the arrest before he gets to the tube. John will get you where you need to be. All good?"

Both detectives nodded.

"OK then, see you at Wimbledon."

The rest of the team, minus Christine and Pritch, was already at Wimbledon police station. Pritch elected to stay behind in the incident room in case the interview team needed anything checked out. He could have used a laptop, but he had what he thought was the perfect set-up on his desk. Two thirty-inch monitors, a custom tower system with ridiculous amounts of RAM and three terabytes of storage, linked into the Met's Crimint system and HOLMES2. He had the world at his fingertips. And, with the rest of the team out of the office, full access to the coffee machine.

Reaching into his rucksack beside his desk, he withdrew a six-box of doughnuts. He bought them on his way in from the local supermarket express. Smiling as he remembered why only four were in the box now. He stretched and arched his back. Something clicked. Enough exercise for one day, then. He was in heaven alone in the office with his computer, unlimited coffee, doughnuts, and backup supplies. Taking a bite out of another doughnut, followed by a large swig of coffee, he put his fingers on the keyboard and did his magic.

Christine sat in the London Heliport waiting room in Battersea, South London. She waited for India 99 to fly in from the National Police Air Service at Lippetts Hill in Essex. She had never been in a helicopter and waited with a sense of excitement tinged with anxiety. Her role was to liaise with the surveillance team from the sky and direct them to where Jessop or his car was if they had a loss.

There was a roar of a turbine engine and the whumph, whumph of the rotors as India 99 came into land on the helipad. One of the crew jumped down and, crouching, ran under the blades. Christine met him at the door.

He shouted, "DS Woolfe?"

She nodded.

"Follow me. Keep your head down as I do."

He hurried back to the waiting aircraft. It hadn't powered down, and the tail and main rotors were still spinning. He opened the rear door for her, closed it and took his place in the front. Another man in a flight jumpsuit in the rear handed her a set of headphones with an attached microphone. As she put them on, he secured her seatbelt. Christine heard the pilot talking to her.

"DS Woolfe, I'm Captain Liam Barclay. To my left is Constable Fisher, and to your right is Constable James. I'll hand you off to Doug Fisher, as I need to get this thing airborne."

Christine heard another voice in her headphones. It felt strange. She had no sense of who was speaking as all three men were facing forward.

"DS Woolfe, Doug Fisher, pleased to meet you. Geoff James is on your right and will be our map reader. I know you lot all call the helicopters India 99, but today you're flying in India 97."

Christine's stomach lurched as the pilot took off and the aircraft moved forward, nose down. As soon as they were clear of the pad, it rose quickly. Christine looked out of the window. Already the people, cars and buildings appeared like a model village. She could see a child's train set, but she knew it was Clapham Junction train station a little way off.

Another voice in her ears, "Geoff here, we'll circle around, not getting too close to the target house. We'll move in if they think they may get stuck. If you switch the frequency knob on the armrest from one to two, you can hear the surveillance team. If you stay on that frequency, Doug and the pilot will stay on one. I can easily switch between if required to instruct Captain Barclay."

Christine switched the frequency and heard the eyeball saying, 'No change'. She had no idea where she was now. Her perspective was different. Nothing looked familiar.

"Tango One, out, out, out. Stand by. To Zulu One. Reversing."

The helicopter banked right.

Geoff said, "We're about a mile away. If Doug moves his head out of the way, you might see the target's Mercedes."

Christine couldn't see anything. These guys must live for this stuff. She was excited, but knew the tension Ray and Kumar would be feeling.

She followed the surveillance chatter, and it appeared Jessop was heading towards Central London. The helicopter closed up, and she could see the Mercedes in the distance. Zulu One was being handed off as required to other cars as they took up the 'eyeball'. Without warning, the Mercedes stopped at the curb, and Jessop left his car and ran into a newsagent. She saw a figure exit a vehicle up ahead of the Mercedes and wander towards the shop. Just as quickly, Jessop came out of the door and got back into his car, and wheel spun away in the direction he was heading.

The surveillance team continued their follow, but now the chatter on the radio was where to effect the arrest. She heard the team leader ask John to start moving up. Christine didn't know who John was, but thinking it may be Ray and Kumar's driver, her adrenaline started pumping off the scale.

She watched as the surveillance vehicles boxed the Mercedes. Another car came up the outside, stopped short of the rear bumper, and Ray and Kumar got out. She saw Ray open the driver's door and

Kumar manhandle Jessop out of the car. He put Jessop against the Mercedes and handcuffed him. That was it, job done. It was all a bit of an anti-climax. As Kumar escorted him back to the waiting car, Jessop looked up at the hovering helicopter. Although he couldn't know or see her, Christine felt Jessop's eyes boring into her skull.

Christine arrived at Wimbledon police station as Robert Southgate, Jessop's solicitor, was being let into the custody area. She had grabbed a black cab when the crew of India 97 dropped her back to Battersea. She didn't want to miss out on anything. They were going to nail this bastard.

She found the DCI, Pete and Dave in the CID office. The boss and Pete were busy discussing interviewing strategy, but Dave noticed her and waved her to join them.

Dave said, "Well?"

Christine gave a broad grin. "Went like clockwork. He stopped suddenly and went into a newsagent's. The team scrambled to get into position. I don't know what he did in there, but a minute later, he came out. I don't think he's concerned about the old bill as he spun his wheels like a drag racer into the traffic. The team boxed him in about half-a-mile later and Ray and Kumar did the biz and cuffed him. I saw it all from my bird's-eye view."

"Jammy git," said Dave, "always wanted to go in a chopper."

Christine smiled and teased, "Helicopter flight is everything you imagined and more so."

She turned to the DCI, "Boss, I saw Robert Southgate being shown into the custody suite as I arrived. Any news from the scenes of crime at Norman's house?"

"Pete got a call about ten minutes ago. They found some old stuff last evening under a pile of other junk at the rear of the basement. They're checking it all now. Dave, if the call hasn't come through before we start the interview, I want you to interrupt at a suitable moment. Call me out and tell me."

"Right, boss," Dave replied.

The DCI stretched on his chair, "Let's give Mr Southgate another twenty minutes to wind Jessop up to boiling point. Another mug of what passes for coffee here, I think, then we'll go down."

"Is there an observation room, boss?" Christine asked.

"There is, and I'm sure you, Dave, Ray and Kumar, will watch with bated breath."

Chapter 56

It took another hour before Robert Southgate told them Jessop was ready to be interviewed. As the DCI and Pete entered the interview room, Southgate and Jessop sat in the same positions they had been in the last time, although in a different room. Before they could sit down, Robert Southgate protested on behalf of his client.

"Why has my client been arrested again? You told me yourself he had been ruled out as a suspect for the previous murders."

"And it was the truth. At the time." The DCI said.

"What does that mean?"

"It means we will not interview Mr Jessop regarding the murder of Gillian Michaels, Rachel Evans, Jennifer Simkins, Sarah Davies and Jasmine Cooper. But we'll accept his confession if he wishes to confess to those crimes."

"I have advised my client not to say anything."

"I wonder, is that the best advice?" The DCI saw Southgate redden. "In any case, we want to talk to him about the death of Detective Constable Lucy Worthington."

Instantly, Jessop was on his feet. "Who the hell is that? This is a stitch-up."

"Simon, sit down and remember what we spoke about," said his solicitor.

"We'll get into all of that, don't worry. DS Rabbet, start the recorder please."

Dave whispered in the crowded observation room, "Could the boss be any more patronising? But the plan seems to be working. The brief and Jessop are on edge before the interview has even begun."

In the interview room, they had all introduced themselves for the recording, and Pete had finished giving the caution again.

"Mr Jessop," the DCI began, "do you recall when DS Rabbet and I came to tell you we were not pressing charges for the previous murders you were suspected of?"

Jessop said, "No comment," with a smirk, like he took immense pleasure in saying it.

"I also told you as the result of us having your DNA from an arrest in your twenties for drunkenness, we were able to confirm you shared the same paternal DNA as the murdered women. We have now been able to identify the rapist..."

Christine could see Jessop's knee start to bounce. He lowered his left hand to stop it.

"... as Norman Etches. Does the name mean anything to you?"

His knee bounced again.

"No comment."

"Really? We'll get back to that. Have you ever worked as an Estate Agent, Mr Jessop?"

"No comment."

"Answering that isn't going to convict you of murder, is it? We could pull your tax records, and it would show it. We know you did anyway."

"Then why ask the bloody question?"

"Because they want to get you talking. Remember what we spoke about," said Southgate.

"It's true; we think you were instrumental in selling the house that belonged to Norman Etches after he died. One of your colleagues, Dave Baxter, remembered you handled the sale. He even recalled why you left. Getting arrested wasn't the done thing in the estate agency business, apparently."

"OK, I was an estate agent, and I think I sold the house belonging to Norman Etches. Happy now?"

Christine noticed Robert Southgate's mouth go tight.

Pete said, "Did you meet Lucy Worthington?"

"I don't know who that is."

"Oh, she was a detective constable on the Major Incident Team. In fact, on his very team. She was an intuitive detective, an asset to the team, and a thoroughly lovely woman. She lived not far from here." He gave the address. "Nice flat. Ever been there?"

"No."

"Her ground floor neighbour, lovely old lady, but nosey as all hell. She doesn't miss much. She hardly ever goes out. Are you sure you haven't been to the address? Perhaps visiting another flat in the same block?"

"No. You can keep asking me the same question, but the answer will always be the same. No."

"But you must know where the address is; you were an estate agent, after all?"

Pete was getting under Jessop's skin, his ears were turning red, and there was a vein on his temple. She could see it pulsating from the observation room.

Jessop let out a long breath; he placed both palms flat on the desk, leaned towards both detectives, looked into their eyes and said, "I was an estate agent, but not around here. I don't know where the address is and I've never met your female detective. I've never been to her flat or any other flat in that block or any flat in Wimbledon. If this is all you've got to ask me, can I go?"

Christine saw the look that crossed Robert Southgate's face. She read it as, 'You've just fucked yourself, lad.'

In the observation room, Dave reached into his pocket and withdrew Pete's vibrating mobile.

He pressed the answer key. "Pete's phone... no, he's interviewing. I'm DC Dave Wilde, I'm on his team... OK, is it confirmed? Fantastic. Thanks for the call."

Dave left the observation room and knocked on the interview room door.

The DCI said, "Interview suspended. Excuse me a moment."

The DCI returned three minutes later. He nodded at Pete, who restarted the recorder.

"Interview resumed. All those present at the start are still present," said Pete.

The DCI stared at Simon Jessop for what seemed like a long while.

It must have seemed like it too for Jessop, who said, "What do you want?"

"We had your passport. You surrendered it when you were on bail. Do you have a driving licence?"

"I work at a car dealership. I drive and deliver cars and have my own Mercedes to get about in. Of course, I do."

He was shaking his head in what appeared to be a pitying way. As if he thought the DCI had lost his marbles. Yet Christine noticed the knee bounce again.

The DCI changed tack, "When you sold the Etches house, did you ever meet the owner, Norman?"

"No, from what I remember, he was already dead. It was a probate sale. The new owners got a deal there."

"So, you must have met the son. Jonathan Etches?"

"I did, on a couple of occasions. Seemed a nice guy. Wanted a quick sale. I think he was going travelling. Or that's what he told me."

Christine observed Jessop was putting tremendous effort into being matter-of-fact and good-humoured now, but it was costing him. His ears were a deep red, yet his face was draining of colour. She saw the eyes didn't match the smile Jessop had set on his face.

"When you visited the Etches house..."

Christine saw each time Etches was mentioned Jessop gave an involuntary twitch of his left eye. Like he was winking at the DCI. She thought the boss had noticed it, too.

"... did you ever go down into the basement?"

"I looked down there from the top of the stairs. I thought it might make a good media room or a gym. It was messy down there, and Mr Etches said they used it for junk storage."

"Just to clarify, Jonathan Etches?"

"Yes."

"You will recall I mentioned about your passport and your driving licence? It's just we can't find a record of any such documents being issued to you."

The knee bounce, colour drain, and twitch all happened simultaneously.

"Well, they were. I applied for them, and they sent them to me from the passport office and the DVLA." He turned to his solicitor. "Should they be asking me about these things? They arrested me for murder, not driving matters?"

Before Robert Southgate could reply, the DCI stated, "It's just we don't believe you are who you claim to be."

From the observation room, Christine saw Jessop made a sterling attempt to appear shocked and outraged by the suggestion.

"What are you talking about? Can they ask me this stuff?"

Southgate was about to speak when the DCI cut across him again, "I think Simon Jessop is a fabrication. I think you are Jonathan Etches."

The shock on Jessop's face was real this time. If she had x-ray vision, Christine could have seen the cogs whirring in his brain, trying to figure this out. How much did they know? How to get out from under?

"That's ridiculous," was all he could come up with.

"Our tech guy couldn't find anything on Jonathan Etches after he left school at eighteen. Yet, two years later, Simon Jessop appears on the scene with no previous history. Simon Jessop, with your date of birth, does not have a legal driving licence or passport."

"I can't explain it. Really, I can't."

The DCI smiled, "I think I can. Yesterday we sent a scenes of crime team to your old home. They found your fingerprints."

"I told you I went to the house a couple of times. Why are you persecuting me?"

"I'm not persecuting you. I just want the truth. Which seems in short supply today."

"The fingerprints they found were in the basement. It's why I suspended the interview earlier. One of my officers gave me the update. They found your fingerprints underneath some old junk right at the rear of the basement. And you told us you didn't go down there."

The knee was bouncing again.

"It was a long time ago. I could have gone down there; must have done if you think about it. I probably forgot."

"The Simon Jessop's fingerprints they found were on Jonathan Etches' school exercise books. They were child size."

Robert Southgate interjected, "This would be a good time for me to talk with my client. I could also use a cup of coffee if that would be OK?"

The DCI stood, "We're only after the truth here, Mr Jessop. Interview suspended. I'll send some coffee in unless you prefer tea?"

Jessop shook his head, "Coffee's fine."

Chapter 57

The team met back in the CID office. They all grabbed a mug of something hot and gathered around the boss.

Dave was the first to speak. "I think we have him, boss. He was nervous as hell, knee bouncing, twitching."

The DCI said, "I think when we go back in, he'll admit to being Jonathan Etches. By inference, we have him for some fraud matters regarding the driver's licence and passport. But truthfully, we're no further forward to nailing him for Charlotte Seymour or Lucy's death."

Pete said, "He admitted he had never been to Lucy's flat or anywhere near the block, so if something comes up, we'll have him."

Kumar said, "I spoke to Pritch before the interview started, and the search team is at Jessop's house and the Mercedes dealership. Apparently, his colleagues are in shock. Pritch was waiting for the car list from the team at the dealership to know which cars to search for on the CCTV."

"For Jasmine's murder?" Ray said.

"Yes, we only searched for Jessop's car on the night of Jasmine's murder. He could have used any of them. He had access to the keys."

A telephone rang, and a local CID officer picked it up. "You the guys from MIT?"

The DCI nodded.

"The solicitor is ready to restart the interview."

"Thanks," the DCI stood, as did the others. "Round two. Let's hear what he has to say this time."

Pete and the DCI returned to the interview room, and the rest of the team crowded into the observation room. Christine noted Jessop was different. Calmer, almost detached. In control. *This will be interesting.*

Pete started the recorder. "Interview with Simon Jessop, Robert Southgate, DS Peter Rabbet and DCI Stephen Balcombe present as before. I remind you, Mr Jessop, you are still under caution."

Robert Southgate said, "My client would like to answer your previous question regarding his identity."

"I'm listening," the DCI said.

In a deadpan voice, Jessop said, "You are right. I was born Jonathan Etches. When I left school at eighteen, I knew I had to leave my father's house. My half-sister Samantha also left. I don't know where she is now or if she's even alive. I knew from a young age what my father, Norman, was. He raped women and tried to get them pregnant. The number of children he had was impressive. He must have picked on women who he thought would keep the child, no matter how it was conceived.

"I feared my father, scared for my life at times. Norman always moved on the fringes of society, and he knew lots of dodgy people. I knew them, too. Sex offenders, fraudsters, burglars, counterfeiters. Basically, any criminal other than paedophiles. He hated them. Couldn't understand how they could do that to kids. He loved kids. When he got sick, my job was to keep tabs on his children.

"Yet somehow, I was never good enough. I had to get out from under his influence, his control. I had saved up some money and stole some. After Samantha ran off, I skipped out, too.

"My dad was not the most good-looking guy, and I inherited his looks with a slight bit from my mother. I found a shady plastic surgeon to do some tweaking to my face. Just a little. Changed my hair colour and style and became Simon Jessop. I tapped up one of my father's contacts and got a driving licence and passport. He didn't recognise me. I can't blame him. As Jonathan, I was a bit of a non-entity. I had to make my own way in the world. So, there you have it. The truth."

The DCI leaned forward, "You're admitting to possessing a fake driving licence and passport, using them for identification?"

Jessop nodded.

"For the recording, please."

"Yes. But that's all I've done."

Pete said, "Simon Jessop, I'm arresting you for possessing a driving licence and UK passport, which you know to be false and producing a false instrument, the licence and passport." Pete cautioned Jessop again.

Jessop looked pleased with himself. Not the underdog at all.

The DCI said, "OK, let's take a break. I'll let Mr Southgate know when we're ready to start again. Probably late afternoon."

Kumar returned Jessop to the custody area, and Dave escorted his solicitor to the front reception.

The team relocated to a local cafe and spoke about anything as they ate, except how the interview was going and the case. Christine joined in with the banter and good-natured ribbing, but she couldn't help at least part of her mind being on the interview. She knew they needed to prove Jessop, or Etches, as she thought of him now, was responsible for Lucy's death. But as had been the case all along, they had some, but not all. Getting Etches to admit being Jonathan was a giant leap up the ladder. They needed something to push him out of his smugness. She could see he thought he was the smartest guy in the room. They just needed something.

As they wandered back to the police station, the DCI's mobile rang. He hung back to take the call.

"Pritch, any further news? We could use a leg up here."

"I found the car Jessop may have used. I finessed my way into the video feed at the Weston Hotel, where the conference was held. You can't see the driver leaving the hotel, but the car belongs to one of his colleagues."

"When you say 'finessed', do I want to know what that means?"

"Probably not, boss. I'll make an official request for the footage. I'm checking the route back to London. We may get lucky, but I doubt we'll acquire better footage of the driver. I've asked the scenes of crime to speak with Daniel Cook at the dealership. It was his car. I just want to check he didn't take it out that night or if he noticed anything about the car when he next used it."

"Good work, Pritch. Not too lonely there?"

"No, boss. I'm high on caffeine. But depressed, I've eaten all the doughnuts!"

"OK, thanks for the call. Keep me updated, or better yet, call Dave. I might be interviewing."

"Boss, there's something else. The scenes of crime techs found a key taped under one of Jessop's desk drawers. They almost missed it. Could be a front door key, but they say it looks more like a high-end padlock key. I'll keep you posted on that and anything else."

Back in the CID office, the DCI told the team about the call from Pritch. There were hopeful murmurings, but he interrupted them.

"I believe we'll have one more go at Jessop before Robert Southgate calls foul, and we're out of time. I'm loathe to go back in now. The leads Pritch spoke about might strengthen our hand at the next interview. So, I propose we regroup back at base. Pete let custody and Southgate know we intend to interview in the morning. I'll speak to the local Chief Super to get his authority to extend the PACE time to thirty-six hours. See you back at the incident room."

Chapter 58

As the team strolled into the incident room, Pritch was fit to burst with news.

"Where's the boss?"

"Should be back any minute," said Dave. "What've you got?"

"Just a storage locker," said Pritch.

The rest of the team gathered around, firing questions at him. The DCI and Pete walked in and the team parted like the Red Sea to allow the boss access to Pritch.

"What's going on?"

"I found a storage locker for Jessop."

The DCI clapped his hands together, "Fantastic. How did that happen?"

"After the team at the dealership found the key, which they thought was a padlock key. It got me thinking. I pulled up storage facilities around Jessop's house and rang each one and asked if they had a unit rented by Jessop or Etches. I came up blank. Then I thought about Norman's house. I pulled up the list around there. There are a lot of storage companies in London, you know. Anyway, I hit the bullseye on the fourth or fifth call. Norman Etches originally rented it twenty years ago. I guess Jessop kept paying the rental and saw no reason to change the name. Given what we suspect him of, the dead Norman Etches would provide an extra level of anonymity."

Dave said, "You don't know Pritch, but Jessop admitted to being Jonathan Etches—"

The DCI cut in, "Where's the key now?"

"The Scenes of Crime team have finished at the dealership and are heading back to base."

"Dave, head over to their base and get the key. Pritch will send you the address of the storage unit. Try to persuade at least one of the SOCOs to go with you and take an exhibits book. Ray and Kumar were up early, and I can't let Christine go with you because of her connection to the case..."

Ray said, "I don't mind going with Dave, boss. We all want to get this guy."

"OK, thanks, Ray. OK, get off and keep us posted."

Christine said as the two detectives left, "Boss, can I have a word with you and Pete? I may have an idea."

"Of course, Pete, join us in my office."

Christine said, "I've been reading a bit about serial killers. For instance, most of the time, they're very insecure people, and a surprising number were rejected or abandoned by their mothers. David Berkowitz and Ted Bundy, for example. They try to avoid painful relationships with others in adulthood. They will particularly avoid what they feel will be painful relationships with those they desire or covet. I'm quoting here. I rarely use words like covet. In turn, they will try to eliminate any objects of affection.

"Jonathan's mother died as he was born, the ultimate abandonment, and then his father, Norman, goes on a rape spree with the sole intent to father more children. He promotes them to his son throughout his life and forces him to keep tabs on them when he becomes too ill to do it himself. He makes sure all his children have mothers except Jonathan. We know that from my circumstance. Norman never takes a lover again. I'm not surprised Jonathan hates his siblings. He desires to be them and covets what they have. A mother."

The DCI said, "All interesting stuff, but you said you may have an idea?"

"Did you see the way he changed after Southgate spoke with him? You had him on the ropes; he was twitching his eye, his knee bouncing, and his ears were red. Yet when he came back, he was smug. That's when the psychopath kicked in.

"I'd like to take the interview tomorrow with Dave." As the DCI started to speak, she cut him off. "Hear me out. I'm one of the people he hates, apart from Sebastian. And Jonathan admitted he didn't know if Samantha was still alive. I'm the last one left, and I got to spend time with my mother while Sebastian didn't. Just me being there will put him on edge. I'm sure he'll try to lord it over me, belittle me, reject me. I hope the storage locker holds some secrets he wouldn't want to share with us, but I've had another thought. Given to me by my favourite author, Mark Twain."

Christine explained her thought process, and in the end, the DCI and Pete agreed with her strategy.

Chapter 59

When Christine arrived in the incident room the following morning, Dave and Ray had exhibit bags stacked on the floor and on two desks. Dave was recording them into the exhibit book, as Ray called them out. They both looked shagged out.

She said, "You two been here all night?"

Ray looked up with bleary eyes. "No, we got back here from the storage place about an hour ago. We called Pritch. He should be here soon. We found Jessop's laptop. What are we calling him now, Jessop or Etches?"

"I'll be calling him Etches. It's his name, after all."

Dave said, "At first, we thought the storage unit was empty apart from a battered wardrobe. But after we looked harder and moved the wardrobe, which swung out on castors and hinges, there was a metre of space behind a false wall. There was a desk, the laptop and some shelving."

"What else have you got apart from the laptop?"

Ray said, "Four small cans of plumbers foam, one large can with plastic straws, two ice picks, five paper coveralls like the scenes of crime techs wear but in black, and bottles and bottles of bleach with some filled spray bottles. Oh, and lots of plastic zip ties."

"OK then, a ready-made Aladdin's cave for a serial killer. Nice one, Pritch."

"Did I hear my name taken in vain?" Pritch said as he hurried into the room. "Can I have the laptop?"

Dave said, "It's all yours. Dusted for prints and hard drive copied."

Pritch's face fell when he heard that. "I hope they did it properly. There might have been anti-copying software on it, all sorts."

"Ray said, "I hate to break it to you, but you're not the only computer nerd employed by the Met."

Smiling, Pritch said, "Maybe not, but I am the best."

The DCI, Pete and Kumar drifted in over the next ten minutes.

Pete sidled up to Christine. "Heard anything yet?"

Christine shook her head.

Pete said, "OK then, we have eleven and a half hours before we have to go to a magistrate for an extension to continue to hold Jonathan Etches. What have we got?"

Ray and Dave explained what they had found in the storage locker. Pritch said he had made a copy of the hard drive, which now sat on his computer, and he was interrogating it.

"So far," he told them, "I have found protected files which contain drafts of the various posts for the 'I'm coming out' website. He's done some clever stuff here, so we couldn't track the computer. Give me time, though."

The DCI said, "Thanks. So, the plan for today. Christine will interview Etches as soon as some further information comes through." He looked at Christine, who shook her head.

"Considering Dave has been up all night, who do you want to take in with you?"

"Boss, I'm up for it. A couple of strong coffees, and I'll be good."

"You sure?"

Dave nodded.

"OK then. I'll ring Robert Southgate and tell him we'll be ready for the interview at eleven. In the meantime, I need to bring my boss up to speed. Regroup at Wimbledon nick at ten-thirty."

Christine beckoned Dave over to her desk. "Let me know when you've finished, and we'll go for those coffees and a big boy's breakfast. My treat."

"Great, I'll be about ten minutes."

Christine laid out her thoughts and plans for the interview in the cafe.

"I'm going to try and rile him up. So, he's not thinking straight. I'm hoping I have a plan to nail him for Lucy's murder. If it happens, I think he'll cough to the others. If I read him right, he'll go into full psychopath mode and boast about how successful he's been, how clever, and then I'll just let him talk himself into prison for the rest of his life. Don't react to anything I say. I may have to tell some white lies."

"Lie your head off as far as I'm concerned."

Christine's mobile rang, "Hello, it is... That's confirmed? You have made my day." Christine smiled widely and said, "I may not have to lie after all."

The DCI and the rest of the team, except for Pritch, were watching and listening as Christine and Dave walked into the interview room. They couldn't miss the surprise on Jonathan's face.

"Good morning, I'm Detective Sergeant Christine Woolfe, and this is Detective Constable David Wilde. The DCI, my boss, apologises for not being here in person, but he was called away on more urgent business."

Jonathan bristled at that.

"We're hoping to get this over with fairly quickly, so Dave, if you want to start the recorder, we can get underway."

Dave did as instructed, and Christine stated her name; Dave did likewise. "Please state your name for the recording."

"Simon Jessop."

"Robert Southgate from Paterson's solicitors."

"Jonathan, please state your full and proper name for the recording." Christine said.

The DCI saw the look on Jonathan's face then, he smiled, "If looks could kill, Christine would be dead right now."

"Jonathan Etches, but I prefer to be known as Simon Jessop."

"This is a legal interview. I think we should use our given names, not ones made-up name." Christine said, "I have to caution you—"

"I already know the caution. I've heard it countless times."

Ignoring him completely, Christine slowly read out the caution from a card taped to the desk.

"Do you have anything to say?"

"Yes, when can I leave here?"

"Dave here was busy overnight. You know Dave, don't you? He was at your first interview when you made up stories about having sex with a woman."

Jonathan turned to his solicitor. "She can't say that! Can she say that?"

"Anyway, moving on. As I was saying, Dave was busy overnight. Can you guess where he spent most of the night? No? Want to have a stab at it?"

She saw Jonathan fighting to control himself.

"Give up? He was in your storage locker." Christine smiled. "What a lot of weird stuff you keep in there behind the false wall. Plumber's foam, bottles of bleach and spray bottles, plastic cable ties and a couple of ice picks. And, of course, your laptop. We wondered where that was."

"Anyway, when I attended the post-mortem for Sarah Davies. You remember Sarah, don't you?"

Jonathan said nothing, just stared at Christine with malevolence in his eyes.

"Cat got your tongue? Oh, sorry, I forgot you don't like cats, do you, or pigeons? Or so your old neighbour said. Where was I? The Sarah Davies post-mortem. The pathologist, who was from Australia, by the way, said the strangest thing. Have you heard of

Paraphilia? I hadn't. Anyway, he said it was a strange case because the killer had a form of paraphilia called Piquerism. Again, I didn't know what the hell that was. He could have made it up. I wouldn't have been any the wiser. But he explained it like this: the killer got his rocks off by sticking objects into people, in this case, an ice pick, rather than his penis. He hadn't made it up. I checked, and it's true. Did I mention we found a couple of ice picks in your storage locker?"

Robert Southgate said, "Is there a question coming sometime soon?"

Christine smiled, "Quite soon. Where was I now? Oh, yes. Sticking objects into people rather than a penis. My boss spoke with Sebastian or Samantha, as you knew her, the other day. He told him a story about when you and she were together. She was nine or ten at the time. When you tried to get hard by having her rub your penis, and you forced it into her mouth. It was a long time, but nothing happened, did it?"

She saw Jonathan gripping the table's edge; his fingers were as white as his face.

"In the end, you gave up. Well, not forever, because he said you kept on trying. He said you seemed to try harder when she had realised she was a boy in a girl's body. Did that excite you? Are you gay? There's nothing wrong—"

Jonathan exploded out of the chair and lunged across the table, grabbing for Christine, who had deftly stepped away.

"Shut your fucking mouth. You whore. You'll get yours."

Dave, who had been ready for such an outburst, pinned him to the desk as Jonathan continued to rant. Robert Southgate looked shocked and backed away to be closer to the door. This was obviously a side of Jonathan he hadn't seen or expected.

Christine said, "OK, let's all take a breath and calm down. Dave, I think you can release Jonathan now. Mr Southgate, would you like to re-take your seat?"

Looking like it was the last thing he wanted to do, manners got the better of him, and he sat.

"Our computer nerd, sorry, I shouldn't call him that. Don't you find people using derogatory terms more often these days, our computer expert? Yes, that's better. Says he has found the original pages and photos for the 'I'm Coming Out' website."

"What's that?" Said Jonathan.

"What it is, but you must know? You put it up on the web. Were you listening when I said our computer expert said he found the original pages and photos on your laptop?"

Christine could see that Jonathan was barely in control. Like waiting for a banger to go off. You know it's going to blow soon.

"Did you know I was a big fan of Mark Twain? Of course you did; you must have seen my Mark Twain book collection when you were at my flat planting all those surveillance cameras."

Jonathan stared at a spot on the wall as if he was somewhere else. Not in a police interview room being accused of multiple murders by his half-sister.

"Have you read any of his books? They're excellent. I particularly like Huckleberry Finn. In my dark days, after your dad stole my sister, I read and re-read the exploits of Huck Finn on a raft going down the river. But I digress. I also like his sayings. He may be the most quoted person ever, except for Jesus. Do you believe in Jesus, Jonathan?"

He continued to stare at the wall. He was visibly trembling now.

"If you believe in Jesus, then you must believe in the Devil. Satan, Lucifer. Do you know Lucifer means the light bearer or the brilliant one? I think Hell is a real place. Do you?"

Jonathan turned to look at her then. He was in control; the trembling had stopped, and he was relaxed. He sat back in the chair and surveyed her as if she was an interesting exhibit at a museum or, more likely, a bug crawling along the desk.

"Anyway, back to Mark Twain. I hold one special saying of his that is dear to my heart. I have it as my screen saver. Shall I tell it to you?"

"If you like."

"I know it by rote, 'The two most important days in your life are the day you are born and the day you find out why.' I think that is so true. And do you know what I think? My day, the day you find out why, was yesterday. That is when I recalled another saying of Mark Twain's, which has always made me laugh. 'A man who carries a cat by the tail learns something he can learn in no other way.' Again, so true, but of course you know that, don't you?"

Christine saw a flicker of fear before he regained control.

"When you killed Lucy's cat. Squirted enough foam into him to almost make him explode. He must have struggled so. Poor DeeJay. That was cruel and completely unnecessary. Anyway, as I said, I thought of that saying from Mark Twain last night, and do you know what I did? I'll tell you. I telephoned the forensic lab, and they took Lucy's cat DeeJay out of storage and examined his little claws. And do you know what they found? Blood. To be precise, your blood. We, of course, have your DNA on file, so they were able to make a match. I got the call whilst I was having breakfast with Dave here."

Jonathan looked at his solicitor like he was a piece of shit sitting on the chair next to him, then started to clap. "Well done, Christine. You and your band of merry men have solved the mystery. Southgate, you're fired. Please leave."

His solicitor started to protest, but Jonathan shut him down with a look. Dave stood to open the door. Robert Southgate picked up his notebook and briefcase and left.

"OK," Jonathan said, "let's get into this."

The interview lasted another thirty-five minutes after Robert Southgate left. Jonathan told them everything in a conversational, casual style, as if he were discussing a game of football at the local pub.

"My father, Norman, wasn't the best father on the planet. I was useful to him, keeping Samantha in check, making sure she towed the family lie. He never told me he loved me or gave any sign he cared. As Mrs Armstrong must have told you, I took my frustration out on the local animal population. I found I could hurt them, but nothing made it through to here." He thumped his chest to emphasise his point. "It was easy. I felt nothing. My father took such pains to make sure his girls had mother's yet until Samantha came to live with us

I knew nothing about it. You know, he actually told me Samantha was his first girl child. Later, I realised what he was doing and how he was fathering his children. He said he had to have her living with him. I'm skipping ahead, but when Samantha ran away, it almost killed him. But it didn't. He snatched her from Tooting Bec swings. But you were there, weren't you? Jonathan smiled a genuine smile, like he was relishing the anguish Norman caused.

"It seems Samantha, or is it Sebastian, has been talking to you? She's a liar, you know. I wouldn't trust anything that comes out of her whiny, screechy mouth. When she lived in our basement, I had to take her food down to her. I also had to empty the camping toilet. Did she tell you she got sick a lot? If I didn't spill the food on the floor, I mixed some of her shit into it."

Christine grimaced. "Why did you do that?"

"Because I could. I wanted her to suffer as I did. Also, I wanted my father to explain to the doctor or a hospital why he had a kidnapped child living with him."

Dave asked, "Did it work?"

Jonathan shook his head. "I had to be careful not to mix too much in as she would've tasted it. Surprising how much of your own excrement you can eat without being hospitalised."

Christine stared at Jonathan. She saw him as if from a sideways view. Not seeing the physical Jonathan but the shadow Jonathan. She realised his psychopathy, whether he was born with it or it manifested itself, was who he was. There wasn't a nice Jonathan under the surface. With his mother dying while giving birth to him and his personality traits, Norman, his rapist dominant father, nurtured his son to become the psychopath he truly was.

"I wanted a mother, my mother. But I think she wanted to die to get away from Norman. To get away from me. Hearing about Norman's girls' day in day out, month after month, year after year. How they were living happy lives with their mothers. That's where the hatred started. I tracked them down. Knew all their names. It took a while, as most had moved away from London."

"Why not kill Sarah, Jasmine, and me first?"

"Because I wanted to save you for last and to perfect my killing regime. I figured if the cops ever put it together, they would be looking for a serial killer of random women. It would give me time to complete the set."

Christine said, "Complete the set?"

"All of Norman's girls."

"But you didn't know where Samantha was or who he was?"

"That transgender fuck. I knew she was sniffing around. It's why I started the website. Sprinkled little hints and ended up naming her after I did Lucy. Trouble was, I'm guessing she got herself arrested and spilled her guts about the basement at daddy's house."

Dave said, "So, were the stories on the website just that? Stories?"

"Yep, I improved on Norman's technique by using surveillance cameras and lock picks."

Christine said, "So why did you murder Lucy?"

"Simple. She gave your sister what she always wanted. A loving relationship that was going somewhere. I couldn't have that. It just wasn't fair. Samantha had found her soulmate."

"You coveted what Sebastian had. Your mother abandoned you at birth. Women, although you desired them, just didn't do it for you—"

Jonathan flushed. "Look who's taken psych 101! You know nothing about me. I was watching when the idiot came to this one's house." Pointing at Dave. "I still thought I might have a chance, but when half the old bill in London turned up, I gave it up for the night. Then I couldn't find you. It was you in the helicopter, wasn't it?"

Iced water pumped through her veins. Transported back, strapped in the rear of India 97, looking down on Jonathan's arrest. Him staring up at the helicopter. She knew, somehow, he was looking directly at her.

Dave said, "Tell us about Charlotte Seymour?"

Dave's question jolted her back to the interview room. She saw Jonathan smirking at her. He knew where she had gone.

"Charlotte was simple. We had planned it together. She thought I wanted to make a girlfriend jealous. As soon as we left the wine bar, we went to the alley, and I killed her. She was a means to an end. Nothing personal."

Christine said, "Why the foam and the ice pick?"

Jonathan chuckled. "That pathologist had shit for brains, if you don't mind me saying. Nothing to do with sticking things in bodies. Women's voices sound like metal nails scrapped on a blackboard. It hurts my ears. So I repaid the favour and shut them up."

Dave said, "And Jasmine?"

Jonathan shook his head and smirked. "Nah, I don't think so. I'll let you do some work to figure out how I did that. I will tell you I've been planning this almost my whole life. When Norman got ill, he made me report on his girls. I hated them then and I hate them now. I will throw you a bone, though. When I heard Sandra had died, I decided Norman's time was up too."

"What did you do with Sandra's head?"

"I forget. I'm sure it's kicking around somewhere. You never know, it might turn up when you're least expecting it."

Christine thought all that was missing from his last statement was some Hammer horror film music and a maniacal laugh. Christine looked at Dave, who nodded.

Dave said, "Interview recording stopped," and pressed the button to end the recording.

As the interview finished, the DCI sent two constables to take Jonathan to the custody suite for charging and processing. The entire team walked into the interview room.

The DCI said, "You would have made Lucy proud. You've certainly got her justice. The interview was masterful. You played to his weaknesses and your strengths. Beers on me at the Dragon's Head when we get back to the office."

That caused a loud cheer from the team, not something usually heard in interview rooms.

Christine pulled her boss to one side as they left the room. "Boss—"

"I know what you're going to say. Of course, Sebastian should hear it from you. See you in the morning."

Chapter 60

As Christine walked down the hospital corridor, she wasn't at all sure how this would play out. She had thought Sebastian killed all those women and then stabbed him with a big knife. He almost died. She stopped a passing nurse.

"Can you tell me which room Sebastian Shaw is in?"

The nurse, whose name tag proclaimed 'I am Susan', said, "I'm not sure. I don't recognise the name, but I've just started my shift after a two-week holiday. Walk with me to the nurses' station, and I can check. Are you a relative, because visiting hours ended twenty minutes ago?"

Christine flashed her police warrant card, or as she called it, her access all areas pass.

"Oh, I see. Let me check. How are you spelling his last name?"

"S-H-A-W, first name Sebastian."

The nurse tapped a few keys, frowned and said, "Sorry, he discharged himself about an hour ago. Was he the one with a police constable minding him?"

"Yes."

"I heard about that; the officer went to use the toilet, and when he returned, Mr Shaw had gone. The officer was told by the police station it was all right. He's left now, too."

"Thank you, Susan."

As Christine stepped out of the sterile hospital and into the cool night air, a mix of emotions washed over her. They had caught the person who had murdered all those women. Yet the single most important person she needed to talk with had run away. Tears of frustration and anger welled up, and as her phone buzzed, she wiped them away. She looked at the screen with blurry eyes. The DCI.

"Yes, boss."

"I hear Sebastian's discharged himself."

"I just found out from a nurse. I can't believe he skipped before we had a chance to talk."

"For what it's worth, as you heard in the interviews, he felt bad about how he treated you."

Christine broke down, sobbing into her mobile. She heard the boss calling her name.

"Christine, where are you?"

She looked around. "I'm outside A and E, where the ambulances park; why?"

"I'm coming to get you."

"There's no need. I'll be alright."

"There's every need you're in no fit state to drive, and I have something for you. Sebastian left you a letter. The PC found it on the bed when he came back from the toilet. I'll be there in ten minutes."

True to his word, the boss arrived and took her home. She got out of his car and climbed the stairs to her flat. After the interview went so well, she should feel elated. But she didn't. Sebastian had left. The letter had better be good. She opened her front door, closed it, and leaned against it for a while, reliving the day in her mind. Letting the tension drain out of her. She shrugged herself off the door and went into the bathroom to splash water on her face to rinse the tear lines away.

She was so tired. She shuffled into the living room and switched on the light. Sitting on her sofa was Sebastian.

He stood, "I know I wrote you a letter, but in the end I couldn't leave without saying goodbye."

Christine ran to him, all thoughts of tiredness gone. She hugged him for the longest time, tears of joy this time streaming down her face.

Christine raised her face to look into his and mumbled through the tears, "Now I've got you back; I'm..."

Reality kicked in then. How did he know where she lived and how did he get in? She hadn't got the Banham locks yet, but still.

Sebastian held her shoulders at arm's length and gazed into her face. "About that?"

Confusion and doubt ran through Christine's mind. It's all over now. Does he resent me that much?

"What do you mean? I know we were apart for years, but I have never stopped thinking about you, looking for you." She shook her head and wiped her eyes. "I didn't mean to stab you. I knew it was you just before my colleague rugby tackled you and forced you onto the knife I was holding."

Sebastian looked deep into her eyes. "I couldn't have killed Lucy, not in the way Jonathan did. He was stupid to kill DeeJay. He knew he got scratched but hoped no one would think of it. Who was it? It was you, wasn't it?"

Christine's mouth had gone dry, and she was finding it difficult to swallow. She was feeling fuzzy as the blood drained to her core, ready for fight or flight. Now, when she looked into Sebastian's eyes, she didn't see her sister Samantha. Instead, she saw the dark malevolence she had witnessed in Jonathan's eyes. She had to move away from him, get some distance. She tried to step back to free herself from Sebastian's grip, but as she did so, pain shot through her shoulder muscles as his grip tightened.

He spun her around and pinned her arms in a bear hug. She attempted to fling her head back into his nose, but forgot he was taller, and just impacted his upper chest.

He squeezed tighter, and she felt the air leaving her lungs. He was squeezing the life out of her. Bucking and kicking backwards into his shins. Writhing frantically, she struggled for breath... She went limp in his arms.

Everyone had left for the night, but Pritch was still in his spot. Ray had brought him a kebab when they arrived back from Wimbledon. Pritch wasn't in the mood to join the others at the Dragon. He felt deflated somehow. The team had been on the treadmill for weeks, and they were all tired. He had been told Jonathan had admitted to the killings after Christine had nailed him for Lucy's murder. But something still didn't feel right. The boss was happy; the team was happy, and they were all detectives. He was just a computer geek. But he wasn't happy.

His mobile rang. He didn't recognise the number. "Hello?"

A male voice said, "I was asked to call this number by someone from the police. Sorry I couldn't call before now, but my mother was taken to hospital. Who am I talking to?"

"You're talking to PC Dave Pritchard. Who is this?"

"My name's Daniel Cook. I work for a Mercedes dealership."

"OK, thanks for calling back. We appreciate it. I have a question about the Mercedes dealership car you took to Weston-Super-Mare for the conference. I believe your car is a grey CLA?" He gave the registration number. "Is that right?"

"Yes, that's my car. What's this about?"

Pritch said, "You probably heard Simon Jessop was arrested this morning, and the scenes of crime team were searching the dealership?"

"Yes, I returned from a test drive with a client and found the place in turmoil. What's going on?"

"Sorry I can't tell you, but what I wanted to ask you is we saw your car on CCTV leave the hotel car park on Wednesday night when you were at the conference."

"I don't understand. Did I do something wrong?"

"No, are you saying you were driving your car that night?"

"Yes, my wife's family lives just outside Bristol. I visited them."

With an increasing sense of dread, Pritch said, "But this was quite late at night?"

"Yes, the team from the dealership had an evening meal, and we all went to the bar. I only had water as I knew I was driving and going to stay the night at my in-laws."

"Thank you for the call, Mr Cook. A detective will contact you in a day or two to get what you have said in a statement."

Pritch cancelled the call and sat in thought for a minute, reviewing everything in his mind. Then he picked up his mobile. He rang Christine, but after ringing a few times, it went to voicemail. With increasing concern, he rang the DCI.

"Hi, Pritch, we're still here. Have you changed your mind?"

"Boss, I just spoke with Daniel Cook from the dealership. It was his car we thought Jessop may have used. He said he was driving, going to his in-laws to stay the night."

"It's noisy in here. Let me take you outside." There was a delay of around thirty seconds before the DCI came back on the line. "OK, Pritch, I can hear you now. What were you saying?"

"Boss, I don't think Jonathan Etches/Jessop could have killed Jasmine. I always thought the camera showing Jessop returning to his room was problematic, but we may have got around that. But if he didn't do it, maybe we were wrong about Sebastian. And if that's the case, where is he now? I called Christine but got no reply."

"Christine went to the hospital to speak with Sebastian before we knew he had discharged himself. I picked her up. She was pretty upset to find him gone, so I gave her the letter he had left for her. I dropped her off at her flat before I came on here."

"Boss. I've checked as you were talking, and the camera I put up in Christine's hallway has moved."

There was silence between them for a few seconds before the DCI said, "Pritch, grab a pool car, swing by the pub and pick Dave and me up. I think we need to get to Christine's. Just in case."

"Right, boss. On my way."

Sebastian picked Christine off the floor where she had collapsed and carried her into the bedroom, where he threw her on the bed. He reached under the bed and pulled out a small black bag. He took out an ice pick with a black wooden handle, two large cans of plumber's foam, and two clear plastic tubes.

He told the unconscious Christine, "I promised Jonathan, if he did Lucy for me, I'd do you. This will be fun. Your team thinks I'm on my way who knows where? And I will be before they find you."

Sebastian climbed onto the bed, knees on either side of her rib cage. He grabbed her blouse with both hands and ripped it open, revealing her white bra. Smiling, he stared at her for a few seconds. He bent his head towards hers.

Christine's head exploded forward, and her forehead connected with his nose. She heard a satisfying crunch and felt warm blood splashing on her face. She had faked passing out, but only just. In his shock, Christine was able to land a punch on his knife wound. She saw it hurt, and she pushed him off the bed onto the floor. Almost instantly, Sebastian was on his feet but leaning to the left side. He shook his head to clear the blood streaming from his broken nose.

Christine saw the pain on his face, and the ice pick in his right hand.

"You sick bastard. Lucy loved you, and you let Jonathan do that to her."

Sebastian smiled that smile of his with blood on his teeth and lunged at her with the ice pick. It caught in the seam of her jeans, and she felt it nip her thigh. Immediately, Sebastian pulled his arm back and thrust the ice pick into her stomach. She doubled forward and stepped back, trying to put space between them. He was coming again, going for another stomach shot. Christine knocked his arm away and landed another hefty punch on the knife wound. Sebastian doubled up and stumbled towards her, still hanging onto the ice pick.

"Not smiling now, are you, eh? Was it Stockholm syndrome? Was it? Or did you find you enjoyed killing things?"

"I came back to the UK and killed dear old dad. Jonathan started to kill the kids, as we called them, but we always had the plan to leave you 'till last."

He moved towards her, and Christine saw he stepped wide to the left to steady himself. Sebastian had put himself between her and the door and was still holding the ice pick. He kept wiping his left sleeve across his face to clear the blood, and he winced each time.

Christine's mobile rang in the hallway. He turned to look towards the sound and she darted forward, but he blocked her way and struck out at her with the ice pick. "You'll be my third. Jonathan did the whore, while I did Jasmine. She heard him gurgle the last, and he spat out a mouthful of blood."

To distract him and because she wanted to know the answer, she said, "Why'd you go back to Jasmine's house?"

"I wanted to get close to you." He spat out more blood. "Did the police all have the day off?"

Christine shook her head. She was feeling a little woozy. She couldn't feel any pain from the ice pick wound to her stomach, which worried her.

"To think I was pleased to recognise you at the house. My sister Samantha, back after all those years. Why'd you stitch up Jonathan?"

"Don't call me that. My name is Sebastian Shaw," he bellowed. "Samantha Woolfe is dead and good riddance."

Christine tried to circle him, trying to get to the door, but he moved to counter.

"As I told Lucy, I'm a great believer in karma. I couldn't forgive the things Jonathan did to me."

He wiped his face again. Seeing he was distracted, Christine launched herself towards the bedroom door with the last of her strength. Sebastian was too quick. He stabbed her again with the ice pick. This time, he held her, and before she could do anything about it, he stabbed her in the stomach twice more. She fell to the floor.

Sebastian dropped on top of her. By instinct, as he did so, she raised her right knee, intending to roll out of his way. His stomach landed on the point of her knee. It expelled all the air out of him. Yet he still tried to thrust the ice pick into her ear.

She grabbed his wrist and pushed it away from her head. She shot her head forward and connected again with what was left of Sebastian's nose.

Christine felt herself getting cold and guessed she was bleeding internally. She didn't have long. She was losing focus, and Sebastian came at her head again with the ice pick.

Suddenly, his eyes opened wide, his mouth gaped, a torrent of blood from his maw gushing over her face and into her mouth. She coughed up Sebastian's blood and some of her own. Sebastian was heavy on her, all his weight. His head lolled over her right shoulder.

Christine couldn't move and had lost feeling in her legs. Her left arm was trapped under Sebastian, and she was losing feeling in her right. It flopped down to the floor as her eyes closed.

Chapter 61

She couldn't breathe. Something was in her throat. Something sticky on her lips. Oh God, had Sebastian squirted the foam into her mouth? She thrashed about, panic replacing reality. Opening her eyes, she saw a bright white light. She had heard about this. She hoped there was an afterlife but had never believed in one. A hand on her shoulder. She tried to shrug it off but didn't have the strength. Oxygen was becoming an issue now as panic closed her airway.

The hand on her shoulder again, this time someone spoke, "Christine, you're in hospital. Welcome back. You've been intubated. Don't try to speak. Calm down. I'll call the nurse."

She recognised the voice. Pritch? She opened her eyes, still the bright light, but swivelling her eyes to the right, she recognised Pritch. He was smiling down at her. She had never been so pleased to see anyone in her life.

The nurse arrived, followed by a man in a suit who introduced himself as Mr Simpson, her consultant.

"Christine, now you're awake, I'll ask the nurse to remove the airway and I'll come back in about thirty minutes. I'll let you recover from being intubated and explain what we had to do and how long you'll be here."

Christine couldn't quite make out what he said. The consultant left as if he had never been there.

The nurse was speaking to her now. Something about relaxing and ripping tape off.

The tape ripped off, her neck extended. She coughed, and she could breathe.

The nurse said, "Take a little sip of water, but don't take too much. Your throat will feel sore for a couple of days."

Then there was just Pritch.

"I've texted the boss. He'll be here shortly."

Christine tried to speak, but what came out was a rasping noise, and it hurt. She tried to ask with facial expressions, but obviously failed.

Pritch said, "I don't know what you're asking, but I can guess. Sebastian didn't make it. He bled out at the scene. I'm sorry."

She shook her head. She mouthed, "He killed Jasmine. He was going to kill me."

Nothing came out, but Pritch nodded and said, "I understand. Rest up; the boss will be here soon, and he'll fill you in."

Christine mouthed, "Water."

Pritch filled a cup and brought it to her lips. "Take a little."

"Thank you," she managed to say. "They were talking to each other."

"We know. We found Sebastian's phone. His actual phone. They had been communicating since he came back from overseas."

The door opened, and the DCI said, "I hear you're awake. How are you feeling?"

She raised her left hand and made a rocking motion.

"I'm not at all surprised. I think he stabbed you with that bloody ice pick four times in the stomach and once in the thigh. Sebastian bled out. We think you raising your knee as he fell on top of you forced his internal stitches apart. You also bled internally, but thankfully, not as much as him. To be honest, we thought we had two bodies when Pritch and Dave kicked your front door off its hinges."

Christine looked at Pritch, who mouthed, "Sorry."

She smiled and slowly shook her head.

The DCI said, "I'll leave you with Pritch. I'll fill you in on the other stuff tomorrow."

Christine shook her head, "Now, boss."

"If you're sure?"

She nodded.

"After he knew Sebastian was dead, Jonathan retracted his confession. He let it be known he will plead not guilty. He said he got scratched by DeeJay while planting the cameras. Says he only confessed because he was caught and Sebastian wasn't suspected. But now he's dead. It's all down to Sebastian."

"There will be a wash-up and a meeting with the CPS to discuss the way forward to trial once you're up and about. I'll be off now. See you in a day or two."

Chapter 62

The cemetery was quiet, the crunch of gravel beneath Christine's feet the only sound. She walked down the familiar path, a bouquet of lilies clutched in her hand. The autumn mist clung to the ground, ethereal and still.

It had been six months since Sebastian's death, half a year since her world had shattered and reformed, the pieces not entirely fitting the way they used to.

She reached the grave, the headstone still shiny and new. Sebastian Shaw carved into the granite. The dates beneath a testament to a life cut short. Christine laid the flowers at the base, her fingers tracing the cold stone.

"I miss you," she whispered, her voice catching in her throat. "And hate you. Every day."

She thought back to their final gladiatorial battle, the moment when everything changed. The sting of the ice pick as it found its mark time and time again. Sebastian's blood spewing from his mouth over her as she fought not to lose consciousness.

Ultimately, the damage had been too significant, the ruptured wound too deep. Sebastian had slipped away, taking any chance of redemption with him, of the reunion Christine had hardly dared hope for. Yet, the killing of her sister, who she needed to save, diminished her.

The sound of approaching steps pulled her from her thoughts. She turned to see Pritch, hands jammed into his pockets. He nodded in greeting, coming to stand beside her at the grave.

"Thought I might find you here," he said.

Christine managed a small smile. "Am I that predictable?"

"Nah. Just know you, is all."

They stood silently, the weight of shared grief hanging between them.

Pritch cleared his throat. "Jury's back on the Etches' case."

Christine tensed. The trial had been a media circus. Jonathan's crimes splashed across every newspaper, television and internet news outlet. She had testified, of course, reliving each horrific detail for a rapt courtroom. It had taken every ounce of strength not to crumble under the weight of it all.

"And?"

"Guilty. Life, no parole."

Christine took a shuddering breath; tears rolled down her cheeks for Lucy, her half-sisters and, yes, for Sebastian.

It was justice, or as close as they were likely to get. Jonathan would spend the rest of his days behind bars, never again able to hurt the people she cared for. But the victory felt hollow, a cold comfort in the face of all she had lost. Lucy, bright and brave, her life snuffed out in an act of unthinkable cruelty. Her own birth mother in a mental institution.

Pritch said nothing, but placed his arm around her shoulders.

They stayed like that for a long while; the light fading as the sun ebbed into evening. She took one last look at the grave, the finality of it settling into her bones.

"Dave is waiting for us in the pub," Pritch said.

They walked back through the cemetery, shoulders brushing with each step. The world felt different now, sharper and more brittle. But Christine knew she wasn't alone. She had her team. Her friends. The family she had built from the ashes of another life. She had found something. Something the darkness couldn't take from her, and she would treasure it.

A message from Christian Barnes

Thank you for reading Caterpillar Days. I hope you enjoyed the story. As an author, your support means the world to me. If you have a moment, I'd be incredibly grateful if you could leave a review on Amazon. Scan the QR code below with your smartphone camera and click the link to share your thoughts. Your feedback helps other readers discover the book and supports independent authors like myself. Thank you again.

And finally, if you'd like to find out more about the author and why I write what I write, scan and click the QR code below. It will take you to a sign up page for my Very Important Readers (VIR) newsletter.

Printed in Great Britain
by Amazon